LAST BREATH

mariah stewart LAST BREATH

a novel of suspense

BALLANTINE BOOKS NEW YORK

Published in the United States by Ballantine Books, an imprint of The Random House Publishing Group, a division of Random House, Inc., New York.

BALLANTINE and colophon are registered trademarks of Random House, Inc.

Library of Congress Cataloging-in-Publication Data
Stewart, Mariah.
Last breath : a novel of suspense / Mariah Stewart.
p.   cm.
ISBN 978-0-345-49224-1 (alk. paper)
1. Archaeological thefts—Fiction. I. Title.
PS3569.T4653L37 2007
813'.54—dc22   2007021142

Printed in the United States of America on acid-free paper

www.ballantinebooks.com

1 2 3 4 5 6 7 8 9

First Edition

Book design by Susan Turner

For Kathryn Campbell Robb, M.A., with much love

ACKNOWLEDGMENTS

Over the past several years, I've offered the opportunity to name a character after the winner of several charitable auctions. The winner gets to choose if they'd like their name to be used for a vixen, villain, or good guy. (Interesting enough, so far, all but one has chosen villain—not sure what that means!)

Sabina Bokhari, D.M.D., was the winning bidder at the Gladwyne Montessori School's fundraising auction. Libby Herron, Montessori teacher and dear friend, hosted Sabina and I for an unforgettable lunch at her lovely home. I should note that the real Dr. Bokhari is every bit as charming and beautiful as her namesake.

Tonia Burnette's winning bid at the fundraiser for Union Hospital in Elkton, Maryland, resulted in a most unusual Christmas gift for her mother, Louise, who, as I recall, had only two requests: she didn't want to be a bad guy, and she didn't want her character killed off.

Her daughter and I agreed that *C. Louise Burnette* was an exceptionally fine name for a university president.

I'd also like to thank FBI Special Agent Pam Stratton for sharing her insights and her expertise. Her suggestions and her guidance were much appreciated.

Of course, as always, any errors are mine.

I've had the unique and incredibly fortunate experience to have worked with the same amazing group of women since my first book was published: my agent, Loretta Barrett, editors Kate Collins and Linda Marrow, and publisher Gina Centrello, whose signature has been on every contract I've ever signed. I can't imagine anyone being luckier than I have been.

Heartfelt thanks to the wonderful, hardworking crew at Ballantine Books who work so hard to get my books out there: Nancy Delia, Kim Hovey, Libby McGuire, Kate Blum, Brian McLendon, Scott Shannon, Carl Galian, and Penelope Haynes.

And very special thanks to Daniel Mallory.

PROLOGUE

OCTOBER 1908
On a hill in Asia Minor

T he sun had not yet risen, but the man climbing the hill was already dressed and warming his hands around a cup of strong Turkish coffee. Under his arm he held a leather folder, which he opened once he reached the top of the hill and sat upon a rock that overlooked the camp. He removed a sheet of pale ivory paper and began to read over the letter he'd written only moments before.

My most darling Iliana,

I am praying this letter finds you feeling well, and in good spirits, and that our sons are helping to fill the hours until my return. You will be happy to know that I will be home soon, and that over the past few weeks, we have prepared to take our leave of this wondrous place. As much as I long for the warmth and comfort of you and our home, I cannot deny the pangs of sadness I feel at having to leave behind this city where the dreams of my lifetime have been realized. If only I could describe to you the feeling that grows inside me when I stand and gaze down upon the ruins of this once grand city, this city where potters and weavers, engineers and farmers, glassblowers and jewelers once plied their trade. There is the temple where they worshipped their goddess, Ereshkigal, and the marketplace where the ancient merchants offered their wares to the caravans passing through. There is where the homes of the wealthy once stood, and here are their tombs, the contents of which I cannot recount to you. Soon, however, you will see with your own eyes, what your husband has spent his life in search of . . .

"Dr. McGowan," a voice called up from below.

"Yes, John?" Alistair McGowan turned to the sound.

"We are ready to begin loading the camels. Will you come?"

"Give me just a moment." He finished reading the letter, then placed it in an envelope. Once back in his tent, he would seal it with wax, then hand it to the member of his team who'd leave the camp before the others to arrange for passage from Constantinople to England, and from England to America. It would be a long and costly journey, but the expense would be more than worth it. He closed his eyes and tried to imagine the look on the face of his benefactor when he saw what Alistair had found buried in the desert sands, and a thrill of anticipation surged through him, head to toe.

Alistair McGowan had been a young and promising archaeologist when he'd first petitioned his university to fund an expedition in search of the fabled city, but had been denied time and again. Then fate, in the guise of a newly chartered university led by the forward-thinking and very wealthy Benjamin Howe, lured him with the promise of sufficient backing to send his expedition to Turkey to follow his dream. Alistair promptly set out to meet with Howe, who had been true to his word. Everything Alistair wanted or needed was supplied, not only that year, but the next, and the next, and the one following that. If Howe was becoming discouraged, he never let on, which had only fueled Alistair's determination to find the city and bring its treasures home.

And this time, he would.

Frustrating though it had been at times, in his heart he'd loved the game. He closed his eyes and recalled the day he'd uncovered the tombs where the treasures of the goddess had all but spilled into his hands. His heart had been pounding, his eyes clouded with a murky mix of dust and tears, the pick shaking in his hand. He'd fought the urge to plow through, choosing instead to painstakingly remove each block of the outer wall, one by one, until there was room enough to pass through.

Once inside, he'd stood by patiently while all was carefully photographed. It had taken forever, but he knew that what he'd found was a treasure for the ages. Here was a find as great as that of Troy, but no one in the archaeological community would be accusing Alistair McGowan of carelessness as they had Heinrich Schliemann. The excavation of Shandihar would be strictly by the book.

Yes, Alistair McGowan had loved the game, but the game was now over. It was time to gather the spoils.

From deep in the shadows, a figure watched the foreigner enter the sacred places that the descendants of the Holy Scribes had guarded for over two thousand years. Below him, the camp was coming alive. Helplessly he watched as sacred artifacts were packed into wooden crates for the journey that would steal his heritage forever.

"Forgive me, Goddess. I have failed you," he murmured into the wind.

"We have all failed." A second figure stepped out from behind the rock. "But what can we do? Their strength is in their numbers, and we few are all that remain."

"Then we must increase our numbers until the strength is ours. However long that takes."

He turned to his brother and rested a hand on his shoulder. "It's time to join the others."

"We will be struck down for helping them to commit this sacrilege."

"The desecration has been done. By accompanying them, we will know for certain their destination. And when the time comes, we will reclaim the sacred icons and return the goddess to her home. If it takes a millennium." His face hardened in the dawn light. "The faithful will remember."

The first man drew his cloak around him against the cool morning breeze and started down the mountain. His brother hesitated before following, whispering softly, "The faithful will remember. . . ."

LAST
BREATH

ONE

JULY 2007
Northwestern Iran

In the bottom of the earthen pit, two skulls lay side by side, their foreheads touching, eyeless sockets gazing eternally into eyeless sockets. A hand of bone lay across a forearm, and bony fingers rested on what had once been the cheek of a beloved. From above, faces stared down at the unique find, most definitely unexpected in this part of the world. Here one was more likely to discover swords and knives, perhaps the bronze or silver sidepiece of a horse's bridle. In some graves, a beloved horse had been buried with its rider. But lovers buried together, still locked in an embrace, *that* was a find.

"Have you ever seen anything like this, Dr. McGowan?" Sayyed Kasraian, the excavation director on the dig high in Iran's Zagros Mountains, crouched at the side of the opening.

"Never." Daria McGowan carefully knelt beside the top of the pit, shining a flashlight on the skeletal remains four feet below. "Not just the positioning of the two figures, but the artifacts that were buried with them . . . it takes my breath away."

She moved the light as a pointer.

"Look there, one is wearing some type of diadem, from here it looks like gold and lapis, see how blue? And the breastplates, also gold . . . rings on the fingers of all four hands, so we're looking at the remains of some very prominent lovers." She looked up at the Kurdish laborers who'd accompanied them, and said, "Gentlemen, we may even be in the presence of royalty."

Two of the men smiled; the third shifted uneasily and looked away, afraid, no doubt, of attracting the notice of any spirits that might still be lurking within the grave.

"And over here, see, glass bottles, dozens of them. They must have held water or wine or some type of oil that the dead would have wanted to take with them on their journey into the next world. And there, at the feet, see the bones?" She hopped into the pit, careful to land on the excavated area around the remains. "These appear to be canine."

She directed the light onto the skull, and her companion studied it from above for several minutes.

"It does look like a dog, doesn't it?" He smiled. "Well, that would be something new. I haven't seen that before. Not in this area, at any rate."

She knelt as carefully as she could to more closely examine the human remains.

"These two must have had a long and happy life together," she murmured. "The teeth are quite worn. They were elderly—for their time—when they died. Definitely a man and a woman, judging from the pelvic bones." She glanced up at the man whose face loomed above hers. "We're so accustomed to finding the bones of battle-scarred warriors, that when something like this is uncovered, well, it just melts your heart, doesn't it?"

The sound of a car engine drew her attention to the road behind the dig, and she climbed out of the grave as the vehicle pulled up and stopped.

She brushed off her hands on her pants and called to the man who had just arrived by Jeep.

"Dr. Parishan, come look! See what was found while you were back in Tehran at the museum having tea with your friends!" she teased the longtime friend of her father's.

"I heard there was a find and got here as soon as I could. Daria, thank you for coming." Under other circumstances the elderly man, the project director, would have offered a more gracious greeting to the American whom he had personally requested join them on the dig, but he was eager to examine the contents of the grave. He reached the edge and stared down. "Oh, look at them . . . look at them . . ." he murmured reverentially. "Perfect . . . they are perfect . . ."

"So, Dr. McGowan, what is your feeling?" An obviously pleased Korush Parishan stood and brushed the sand from his knees. "On the site, overall?"

"I concur completely with Dr. Karaian's assessment," Daria said without hesitation. "The artifacts he's already unearthed show such a vast mix of cultures, I can't imagine that these people were anything but nomadic. We've seen the Indian river goddesses on the vases, golden goblets in the style of Bactria. The pottery bowls with the horned dragon, the god Marduk—definitely Babylonian. So here we have clear influences from India, Afghanistan, Mesopotamia. They all came together here in the mountains." She pointed off to the east, then drew a line across the horizon with her index finger. "The Silk Road passed through this region. You'd have had travelers from China, India, Anatolia, Greece. Their cultures all intermingled through the centuries, which would account for the fact that some of the artifacts are of a different age from the others."

She turned to the others and smiled. "This could be an amazing find. The rise off to your left looks as if it might be a likely spot to start. I cannot wait to see what else you might discover here."

"Unfortunately, Dr. McGowan, you may have to postpone your

participation," Dr. Parishan told her. "As I was leaving the museum, I was handed an urgent fax to deliver to you, as well as a phone message from a Dr. Burnette. Forgive me, but I could not help but note that the message says it is imperative that you contact her as soon as possible."

He removed a folded sheet of paper from his shirt pocket and handed it to her.

Frowning, she opened it and began to read.

"Dr. Burnette is the president of Howe University back in the States." Daria continued to read, then looked up and asked, "Dr. Kasraian, may I use your computer?"

"Of course. It's on the table in the main tent. Please, whatever you need. . . ." He gestured toward the area where the shelters had been erected.

"Thank you."

Daria went directly to the tent, her mind on the fax and its request that she return to the States immediately. Having to leave so soon was not what she'd had in mind when she arrived in Iran late last week. That the Iranians had invited a well-regarded foreign authority—and a woman, at that—to this newly discovered site was evidence of their desire to participate in the international archaeological society. It was of particular importance to Dr. Parishan that the rest of the world understood how seriously the Iranian archaeological community was taking its obligation to not only protect but to share and showcase their distinct cultural heritage. Like those of its neighbors Afghanistan and Iraq, Iran's cultural treasures had been finding their way out of the country for years, legally and illegally. They were now determined to locate and safeguard whatever remained, and do whatever was necessary to recover those items that had, over the years, been lost due to an active black market in stolen antiquities.

Dr. Parishan had handpicked the team to work on this new find. He'd been unable to secure the services of Daria McGowan, a well-known expert in Middle Eastern archaeology, to participate in the initial excavation, but she had offered to come on board as a consultant as soon as her work in the Gobi Desert had been completed. To Parishan, that she was internationally recognized was the cake; that she was the daughter of an old and esteemed friend and colleague, Samuel McGowan, was the icing.

Daria returned to the others an hour later.

"I'm so terribly sorry," she explained, "but I'm going to have to leave right away. Dr. Kasraian, could I impose upon you for a car?"

"No imposition at all," he assured her. "I'll have a driver take you wherever you need to go. But your family . . . there is bad news?"

"No, no. Nothing like that." She dropped her duffel bag on the ground and slid a hijab around her shoulders. Once they neared the airport, she would use the scarf to cover her head to conform to Iranian law.

"Dr. Parishan, I feel awful about this."

"As long as everyone is well. When I heard 'doctor,' I feared perhaps . . ."

She smiled to reassure him. "Everything is fine with my family. Apparently Dr. Burnette has been trying to track me down for several weeks. Dr. Parishan, did my father ever speak to you of his grandfather who was also an archaeologist?"

"Alistair McGowan, of course." He nodded. "The man who found the city of Shandihar when no one believed it had ever existed. Your father told me his grandfather's journal inspired him to follow in his footsteps to become the great archaeologist that he is."

"Then perhaps he also mentioned that the backing for Alistair's expeditions had come from Howe University?"

"Yes, I believe so. Your father has lectured there, correct?"

"Yes, Dad lectured often at Howe before he retired. When my great-grandfather returned to the States following his discovery at Shandihar, he went directly to Howe and brought all the artifacts he'd found with him. The university had supplied the funding, so the spoils belonged to them. At least, that's how it worked at the turn of the century. My great-grandfather spent years cataloging the artifacts to display in the museum that Howe was building. Unfortunately, he died before construction was completed."

"Yes, yes, this I have heard." Parishan nodded. "But what does this have to do with you?"

"Apparently the university wants to commemorate the hundredth anniversary of Alistair's discovery. They want to put his findings on display, after all these years. Dr. Burnette has asked me to take charge of the entire project."

Parishan's eyes lit up.

"You would be designing the exhibits?"

"Everything, Dr. Parishan." She smiled with dazed pleasure. "They want me to do everything. . . ."

"Everything?" Samuel McGowan asked incredulously.

"Everything, Dad," Daria replied. "I can hardly believe it myself. I'm still pinching and pinching but I don't seem to be waking up."

"Well, that's wonderful, sweetheart. Just wonderful! Wait till I tell your mother." He put his hand over the phone. "Margarite! Pick up the phone! It's Daria! She has the most amazing news!"

"Oh, for heaven's sake, Samuel, you don't have to shout. I'm not deaf." Margarite McGowan lifted the extension. "Daria? Is that you?"

"I'm here, Mom."

"Where is here?"

"Morocco."

"I thought you were in the Zagros Mountains with Korush Parishan." Her mother paused. "How is he? He's well?"

"Yes." Daria opened the French doors that led out to the balcony off her hotel room. She pulled a chair close to the railing and sat.

"You've left Korush's dig? We were so pleased when he invited you."

"Yes, I was very honored." Daria raised her legs, rested them on the rail, and crossed her ankles.

"So why did you leave so soon?"

"For heaven's sake, Margarite, will you let her tell her story?" Daria's father sighed. "Go ahead, sweetheart. Tell her."

"Right now, I'm in Essaouira. At the Villa, just for an overnight. I'll be flying out tomorrow and I'll be—"

"You're coming home tomorrow?" Her mother's delight was apparent.

"I'm flying to London, then to New York, then to Myrtle Beach. I expect I'll be there at the island by the weekend, but only for a few days."

"So where are you going?" her mother asked. "And what was so important that you had to leave Korush's dig?"

"I have an appointment on Tuesday morning at Howe University," Daria told her. "With Dr. Burnette, the president."

"Louise Burnette?" her mother asked.

"Yes. Do you know her?"

"I know of her. She has a fine reputation. Has she offered you a position?" Daria could all but hear the frown in her mother's voice. "Are you thinking about going into teaching? Because if you are, you know, any of the major universities would be more than happy to have you. You don't have to settle for such a small school."

"I'm not going to be teaching, Mom." Daria took a deep breath and explained to her mother what the trustees of Howe University had in mind.

"That's . . . amazing. And I'm so envious I could weep."

"Mom, you're an anthropologist, not an archaeologist," Daria reminded her gently.

"I know, darling, but I've always wanted to do something fun and exciting like that."

"You've had your fun, Mom. Didn't you have a bestselling book last year?"

"Well, yes, but that was—"

"And another the year before that?"

"Yes, but—"

"Wasn't that fun?"

"Oh, of course it was. Part of the fun in living as long as I have, and traveling and studying cultures in all parts of the world, is getting to relive it all by writing books about it when you retire. But this, this is huge. You'll get to open all those dusty old crates and take out those artifacts that haven't seen the light of day in a hundred years. You'll be the first person to handle them since your great-grandfather packed them away while he completed his inventory. Isn't that what happened, Samuel?"

"What? Oh, yes, yes. My grandfather supervised the packing of every piece in the field, then unpacked each piece himself when he returned to Howe—of course, it was Benjamin Howe College, back then. Named for your great-great-grandfather. And my grandmother, Iliana Howe, was actually Benjamin Howe's only daughter."

"Where did the money come from?" Daria asked.

"Old Ben was quite the tycoon," Samuel said. "Owned a bunch of munitions factories, around the time of the Civil War. Later, he invested in railroads and several other highly profitable ventures. Then, while some of his contemporaries were building mansions in Newport and New York City, he built a college on land he owned in Pennsylvania, named it after himself, then waited for the school to catch on. Well, when it didn't, he knew he had to do something spectacular to draw attention to it. So he sent out two archaeological teams—archaeology was quite popular back in the day. Alistair went to Asia Minor—Turkey, now. The other fellow, Oliver Jacobs, went to Mesopotamia, now Iraq. It took Alistair four years to find and excavate his site. Took Jacobs slightly more. Alistair spent another eighteen months cataloging the artifacts, but the museum still wasn't ready. He died from a lung infection in 1910, I think it was. Jacobs's findings were placed in the opening exhibit, and my grandfather's were left in the crates where he'd kept them while he completed his inventory. Years later Benjamin Howe, my great-grandfather, died, then in the 1930s, my grandmother. By that time, her children were grown and had set out on their own paths."

"I don't understand how a treasure like the one he reportedly found could have been forgotten like that," Daria said.

"Oh, not so mysterious," Samuel responded.

Daria heard the sound of a match being struck softly.

"Samuel, I heard that!" her mother snapped. "Put the damned pipe away."

Ignoring his wife, Samuel continued. "Trustees change. Faculty come and go. Crates get pushed farther and farther back into the recesses of the basement as other items are obtained. Having served my time in academia, I understand completely how such things occur." He puffed softly on his pipe. "Out of sight, out of mind. Over the years, the story is forgotten; the items, unseen for all these years, lose their allure. And there's the tide of popularity. In one year, out the next. Back in the early twenties, Egypt became all the rage after Tutankhamen's tomb was discovered. Every museum was after mummies for quite some time."

"Well, something's brought Shandihar back into the foreground," Daria said.

"The anniversary, I suppose," Margarite suggested. "Did Dr. Burnette say when that would be? When they were planning to open the exhibit?"

"I'm sure I'll find out on Tuesday."

"You'll call us when you arrive in the States?" her father asked.

"Of course, Dad. But right now I'm going to have a long hot bath and a fabulous dinner, and my first night's sleep on a real mattress, on a real bed, in almost nine weeks." Daria stood and shielded her eyes from the sun, which had begun its afternoon shift lower in the sky. She said good-bye to her parents and hung up the phone.

She went into her room and found her sunglasses and put them on. Returning to the balcony, she leaned on the railing and stared out at the boats in the blue Atlantic. Blue skies, blue water. It was all very restful. She regretted she wouldn't be staying longer. But there would be time for that bath, and there would be the wonderful dinner promised by Magda, who with her husband Cyrus owned the Villa. And later, maybe, when the sun went down and the evening stole in, there'd be music in the courtyard.

Daria went into her bathroom and turned on the water in the tub, adding some of the sweetly scented bath crystals Magda had left for her. She stripped off her travel clothes and sank into the deliciously luxuriant bath and closed her eyes. It would take more than one bath to wash the desert sand from her pores, but for now, she was as content as she could be.

She idly wondered what Magda's chef was preparing for dinner, and thought back to her last stay at the Villa and smiled. For more than a year, Magda had been trying to set her up with a man Magda had assured her was "perfect for you." They'd finally met, months ago, and had shared a lovely evening in Magda's courtyard.

He'd been everything her hostess had promised, tall and lean with dark hair cropped very short and dark blue eyes. And very handsome. Not the kind of man who generally noticed women like her, but he was gracious about dining with her at Magda's insistence. He'd been very attentive throughout the meal and had seemed more interested in her and her work than in talking about himself, but, that was the polite thing to do. Magda had said he was well mannered for an American— which, as an American herself, had made Daria smile—and that he was one of her favorite guests.

Daria remembered that night as one of the best nights of her life.

"Hi," he'd said when he approached the table.

"Hello." She turned her face up to his, and her heart all but stopped beating.

"Mind if I join you?"

"Please." She'd gestured to the chair opposite hers. "Magda said I might have a compatriot at my table tonight. Daria McGowan."

She'd been acutely aware of how she must have looked to him, in her plain white shirt and khaki pants. No makeup, and her hair chopped short by her own hand.

"Connor Shields," the beautiful man had introduced himself.

"I know. Magda brings up your name every time I'm here."

"Nothing bad, I trust," he said as he pulled out the chair.

"No, no. Just, 'Daria, you really must meet Connor Shields. He's American, like you.' "

He laughed. "I admit she's used the same line on me."

"So where are you from?" She nervously sipped her drink, bottled water and lemon juice.

"I was brought up in Virginia."

"Ah, another Southerner. I'm from South Carolina. At least, that's where my family home is now."

"Where did you grow up?"

"Oh, let's see." She tilted her head to one side and pretended to think, then began to count on her fingers. "The Gobi Desert. Greece. Syria. Turkey. Afghanistan . . ."

"You have to be kidding."

"Not so much. My parents both worked in the field a lot, so we traveled a lot. Stateside, we lived in Texas, Georgia, New Jersey—we stayed there the longest, actually had a house there. I went to school there. For a while, anyway. My parents both taught at Princeton. Mom, anthropology; Dad, archaeology. We never knew where we'd be, come summer."

"Did you like that, traveling around so much?" He signaled for the waiter, then ordered a drink when one appeared.

"Are you kidding? We had adventures that other kids couldn't even begin to dream about. We saw places most people have never even heard of. We loved it."

The waiter appeared with Connor's drink—bottled water with lime and mint, the local Muslim laws regarding alcohol being strictly enforced this time of the evening—and went over the evening's dinner offerings. They both ordered baked sea bass, the chef's special.

"You were telling me what it was like to have been a kid on the go," he said, urging her to continue.

"It was tons of fun. There were four of us. My brothers, Sam and Jack, and my sister, Iona. We were a really tight band of four. How about you? Siblings?"

"I have . . . had . . . two brothers," he told her.

"Had?"

"One of them died."

"I'm so sorry." She paused to study his face, and recognized the sadness in his eyes. "It's very difficult, isn't it, to lose a brother. He's always there in the past, in your memories, but the present is just a big blank, as far as he's concerned."

"One of your brothers . . . ?" he asked cautiously.

"Jack. Disappeared. He was on an expedition into the Amazon and just, poof! Vanished. My parents have sent trackers in to search for him at least a half-dozen times, but it's as if he didn't exist. As if he hadn't been there at all."

"How long ago?"

"Ten years. He's been gone since 1997. I miss him every day. Think about him every day. Wonder if he's dead or alive. My parents never give up. Every other year or so, they hire someone to go down there to look for him."

"I have some connections in South America," Connor said thoughtfully. "Maybe I can have someone look into it."

"That's really very nice of you, but I don't want to waste anyone's time."

"You think he's dead?"

"You send teams of professional trackers into the jungle where he supposedly had gone, and they come out with no more information than they went in with, you have to suspect that—"

"That he may well have gone somewhere else."

She'd stared at him. When the waiter arrived to serve their dinners, she leaned back from the table silently.

"You're not going to tell me that no one considered that possibility, are you?" Connor asked.

"Yes. I mean, no, no one did. He'd been with a group, and all the investigators followed the trail the members of the group had given them. To the camp, then to the ruins . . ."

"So maybe for some reason your brother—Jack, was it? Maybe he took off on his own, or joined another group, or got lost and is out there somewhere."

"I'd like to think that. That somehow he's out there and that someday we'll see him again."

"I'd be happy to make some inquiries. Really. It's no trouble. I have some contacts in the area."

"That would be very kind of you. Thank you. I'll get you all of the information—when and where and with whom."

She tasted the fish, and smiled. "This is so good. Is there a better chef in all North Africa than Claude?"

"Not for my money, no." He appeared thoughtful for a moment before asking, "Have you ever taken an evening horseback ride on the beach?"

"Several times. You?"

"Yes, but the camel rides are more fun."

"Ugh." She wrinkled her nose. "I spend enough of my time on camels."

"Don't knock it until you've tried it. There's nothing like watching the sun set on the Atlantic from the back of one of those large, swaying—"

"Mr. Shields?" A man had appeared at his elbow. "You are Mr. Shields?"

"Yes." Connor nodded.

"The Madame asked me to give this to you. It was dropped off at the front desk."

He handed Connor an envelope bearing his name.

"Thank you," Connor told him. To Daria, he said, "Excuse me, I just need to . . ."

"Go right ahead."

Connor opened the envelope and read the note that had been tucked inside. When he was finished, he folded it, returned it to the envelope, and slid it into the inside pocket of his jacket.

"Daria, I really hate to cut this short," he said. "I've been enjoying this evening more than I can say, but I'm going to have to make my apologies."

"I hope it's nothing serious?"

"No, no. This is business." He stood. "I'm really sorry. Maybe tomorrow?"

"I'm leaving in the morning." She smiled to hide her disappointment. "It's all right, if you have to go. I understand. We all have those emergencies to deal with from time to time."

"Look, let me give you my card. When you're back in the States, maybe you'll give me a call and we can get together." He took a card from his wallet and wrote something on the back before he handed it to her. "Assuming I'm there at the same time. Or maybe, before you come back here next time, you'll get in touch. I can get all the info about your brother . . ."

Daria glanced at the card.

"That's the number for my office, back in the States."

"There's no company name on it." She looked at both sides of the card.

He lowered his voice. "I'm with the FBI. I don't advertise that around here, though of course Magda and Cyrus know. Call that number and leave a message, it will get to me. Anytime. Day or night. I'll get the message."

"Thanks." She half turned in her chair and offered her hand to him. "I'm happy to have finally met you. I hope we meet again."

"So do I, Daria." Then he leaned down and kissed her cheek. "As a matter of fact, I'm counting on it."

And with that, he'd disappeared, and her perfect evening ended.

She yawned and sank lower into the hot water, her eyes still closed. Certainly if Connor were here at the Villa tonight, Magda would have wasted no time letting her know. Maybe it was just as well, Daria thought. If he'd been there, she'd have been tempted to dress for dinner, to sit at the table for two in the corner of the courtyard, hoping he'd join her, hoping he'd invite her for a horseback ride on the beach later that night. She smiled wryly. She'd even be happy with a camel-back ride.

As it was, she'd call for dinner in her room, dine alone, and get the first good night's sleep she'd had in months.

TWO

Daria drove through the Pennsylvania countryside, trying to remember the last time she'd visited Howe. The only recollection she had at all was of one time when she was around eight, and the entire family had gathered for some type of memorial in honor of the first Benjamin Augustus Howe, the university's founder and her great-great-grandfather. She had a vague memory of a gathering in a fancy Victorian parlor where lemonade and petits fours were served. She'd been mesmerized by the tiny pastries, exquisitely decorated with flowers in shades of pink and yellow, and served on silver platters lined with lacy white doilies. The family had just returned from several months in the Jordanian desert, and such sweets were as foreign to her and her siblings as television. She smiled, recalling how she and her sister Iona had stuffed themselves with the delicious treats, and how sick they'd both been by nightfall.

Any subsequent visits they may have made to the university, however, were lost to the years.

The street sign on her left announced that Howeville was a half mile ahead. That, too, brought a smile to her face. She'd always thought Howeville sounded so Dr. Seuss, and she couldn't help but think of all those Howes down in Howeville whenever she saw the name of the town.

But Howeville it was. And it was straight up the road. She slowed to the speed limit, then slowed yet again when an Amish buggy pulled out from a side road up ahead. She had no recollection of Amish living in the area, but wasn't all that surprised to find they were. She'd passed several sizable farms since she'd left I-95, and Lancaster County was only a short drive away.

The town itself definitely had a split personality, an old country town with a modern attitude. Daria passed Howeville Feed and Grain, located across the road from a large field with a sign that promised Amish produce every Tuesday from eleven in the morning until four in the afternoon. There were two car dealers, a pizza place, a Mexican bakery with a hand-lettered sign, and a café. The brick hotel on a corner of the main intersection in town was now condominiums, and the old train station had been turned into an ice cream and sandwich shop. She drove through the green light at the center of town, past the library and a small old-fashioned diner that advertised the best burgers in town.

Main Street dead-ended at the entrance to the university. A wide brick arch bore the original name of the school—Benjamin Howe College—and its founding date, 1879. The arch covered a paved lane that wound slightly to the left and ended in a wide parking lot. A courtyard of sorts was formed by the three imposing buildings that framed the lot. All three were constructed of brick and appeared to have seen better days. While far from derelict, Daria noticed that the black shutters were all in need of paint, and the brick clearly needed pointing. She parked in a spot designated for visitors and got out of the car she'd rented at the airport.

She folded her arms across her chest, and took in the campus that sprawled out around her. Disappointed to find that nothing looked familiar, she hunted in her purse for the index card on which she'd written the directions Dr. Burnette had given her on the phone.

The building she wanted was directly in front of her. She swung her bag over her shoulder and headed up the front steps to a covered porch. Double doors—also needing a refresher—opened into a wide lobby. Steps to the third floor rose up in the center, and halls led off to either side. The carpets were just this side of threadbare and the paneled walls needed a good cleaning. Rectangular shapes on the walls above the dark paneling hinted of paintings that had once hung there, and the chandelier in the center of the lobby was unlit. The overall impression was one of past grandeur.

Daria took the hall to the left as she'd been instructed, and stood outside the door bearing a wooden plaque with C. LOUISE BURNETTE, PHD PRESIDENT painted in black script. She hesitated, not sure whether to knock or just walk in.

"May I help you?" a voice from down the hall called to her.

"I have an appointment with Dr. Burnette," Daria replied.

"Dr. McGowan?" The woman walking toward Daria was short and squat and had dark hair that just grazed her shoulders. She appeared to be in her mid-forties and walked with a spring in her step. "I'm Vita Landis, Dr. Burnette's assistant. You're right on time."

She shifted the stack of papers from her right arm to her left and opened the door, holding it for Daria to pass into the reception area. This room, too, had seen better days.

"How was your trip?" Vita asked as she walked around Daria and placed the papers in the middle of her desk.

"Fine, thank you. It was a good day for a drive. Last night's rain cooled things off a bit."

"Bound to get humid, though. Worst thing about this time of the year in this part of the country. Humidity. Means two things to me. Bad hair and mosquitoes." She hit the intercom button on her phone. "Dr. McGowan is here, Dr. B."

Vita hung up and opened her mouth to speak, but before she could get a word out, the office door opened and a tall, slender woman dressed in a lightweight pale green pantsuit with a short-sleeved jacket stepped out, hand extended. She appeared to be in her mid-sixties, with light brown hair cut in a short no-nonsense style.

"Dr. McGowan, I'm so pleased to meet you." She gave Daria's hand a hearty shake. "I cannot begin to tell you how happy we all are that you agreed to come."

"I'm delighted to be here," Daria said truthfully.

"Come in," the woman invited, "so we can chat. Vita, if there's any iced tea left, I'm sure Dr. McGowan would appreciate a cold drink after her drive. You did say you were driving from Baltimore, didn't you?"

"I did. I spent a few days with my parents in South Carolina, then flew into BWI and rented a car." Daria took one of the two armchairs that faced each other at the far side of the room. The chairs overlooked a garden where dozens of roses were in bloom, and paths led to a pergola where stone benches sat. "This is lovely. The garden is beautiful."

"One of our history professors found a description of the original garden in a journal that Iliana McGowan kept through the 1920s. After her husband died—your great-grandfather—she devoted herself to raising their children and tending to her father, serving as his official hostess. At the time, he was still president of the university. I'm sure you've heard the story before. This was his office." Louise Burnette had remained standing. "That's him, over the fireplace. It's one of the few paintings we kept out of storage when we removed the others."

Daria got out of her chair and walked to the portrait for a better look.

"He looks quite dashing, don't you think?" Louise Burnette asked.

"He certainly does," Daria agreed. "I've heard he was quite the rake. Loved the ladies, loved adventure, though supposedly after he founded the college, his adventures came to an end. He took his responsibility here quite seriously." Daria turned and smiled. "Or so the story goes."

"He did a wonderful job putting the college together, and his generous endowment has kept Howe going through the years." Dr. Burnette frowned. "At least, until now."

Daria looked at her quizzically.

Vita knocked once on the half-opened door, then came in bearing a silver tray with a cut-glass decanter and two goblets. Daria noticed that the silver appeared to be freshly polished and the glasses gleamed as if recently washed.

"I'll just set this here for you," Vita said as she placed the tray on a table between the two chairs. "Let me know if you need anything else, Dr. B."

"Thank you, Vita." Dr. Burnette poured the cold tea. Handing one to Daria, she said, "I suppose I should get right to the point. Howe is in desperate need of funds. Our athletic teams have never been strong enough to pull in student athletes, and our campus is, as you may have noticed, a bit run-down. Each year it gets more difficult to attract good students. This year, our enrollment hit an all-time low. We're not conveniently located, we don't have an all-star faculty, and we lack the funds to attract the type of professors that could help our reputation."

"I thought you said Benjamin Howe left a generous endowment."

"He did, but with the drop in the number of tuition-paying students, we're running through it more quickly than we'd like. The trustees met last month to discuss alternatives—selling off land, selling some paintings, perhaps a few of the buildings on the opposite side of the road—none of those options were particularly desirable, but the consensus was that we'd do what we had to do to buy a little more time. Later that night, after the meeting, I was walking back to my house—I live on campus—and I passed by the museum. It's been closed for a number of years."

"I wasn't aware of that."

"The funds weren't there for a curator, and the building isn't properly ventilated. It was closed 'temporarily' by my predecessor. It was pretty much forgotten. Well, we'd been talking about finding money for the school, and here we had our own museum with who knew what stored away down there. The next morning I started looking around, taking stock, and you'll never guess what I found."

"The crates my great-grandfather brought back from Shandihar." Daria found herself tapping her foot impatiently.

"No. Well, yes, eventually, I was led to them. They're buried somewhere deep in the basement behind a locked door, as I've since learned. But what I found that day was dinosaur bones, still on display from the last time the building was open, and some signs relating to another dig funded by the university around the same time as your grandfather's."

"Oliver Jacobs's dig." Daria smiled. "Howe sent them both off with the promise that whoever returned first would be the first to exhibit their find. My great-grandfather was the first back but the building hadn't been completed yet."

"And by the time the building was finally ready, he'd passed away. Jacobs's findings were put on exhibit and written up in all the newspapers and magazines, and your great-grandfather's discovery was pretty much forgotten over the years."

"And the Jacobs artifacts?" Daria asked.

"Remain in the basement of the museum. In the 1950s, the museum was turned over to a man named Casper Fenn, who decided the emphasis here should be on American natural history, so he proceeded to purchase or trade for all manner of things. Dinosaurs—small ones, of course—and animal skeletons, a collection of stuffed birds and monkeys." She rolled her eyes.

"He sold or traded some of the artifacts from the Jacobs dig for—"

"Bones and stuffed animals, yes. Oh, and some Indian relics. Buffalo skins and a tepee," she said drily. "They were a big hit with the school kids but really brought in nothing in terms of revenue."

"So what exactly remains of the Jacobs find?" Daria frowned.

"There are still several crates of objects in the basement clearly marked as his. We do have the inventory, and for all his faults, Fenn kept impeccable records. Every sale, to whom, how much, when and where, it's all written down. And in his defense, he did attract some positive attention to the school."

"Dr. Burnette, when we spoke, you said you wanted to talk to me about reopening the museum. That you wanted me to work on a display of my great-grandfather's find. I thought that was what you called me here to discuss. Please understand, I left an important dig thinking that—"

"Yes, yes, I'm getting to all that." Louise Burnette leaned forward and patted Daria's arm reassuringly. "I do intend to reopen the museum. I have every intention of displaying the Shandihar collection."

"And that would bring in the funds you need to keep the school going . . . how?" Daria wasn't following the logic. "Are you aware of how expensive it is to exhibit such a find? You're going to need to design special display areas. The building will certainly need upgrades of the mechanical systems. There's publicity, there will be staff needed, insurance, security once you start reminding people what you have here. And then there's my fee . . ."

"I understand. But here's what I'm thinking." She took a sip of her tea. "If you could appraise the collection—set a value on it—we would have collateral for a bank loan. Once the display is ready and we can reopen the museum, we'll be able to attract other experts like you from all over the world to view it. We can have symposiums here, host guest lecturers . . ."

"Which would bring in little more than a drop in the bucket, compared to the costs."

"Yes, but we'll be able to loan out the collection, won't we? For a fee?"

"Possibly," Daria responded cautiously.

"Until your great-grandfather's find, Shandihar was thought to be a place that existed only in the epic poems written by ancient scribes." Dr. Burnette's eyes narrowed. "Between the time he found his lost city and now, there have been two world wars and any number of political changes in Turkey, where he made his discovery. The treasures of Shandihar have been forgotten, essentially, for over two thousand years." She smiled. "There will be television specials, there will be books. And—God forgive me—if we're lucky, coffee mugs and coasters."

"You're looking at this as a strictly commercial venture." Daria's voice held a touch of disapproval.

"With all due respect, Dr. McGowan, I have no other choice. The revenue this collection will generate will not only save this college, it will offer an opportunity for countless scholars to study up close the treasures of a lost civilization that have never before been exhibited. We'll attract not only the most promising students in the field, but the best professors, just as we did a hundred years ago. Just as Benjamin Howe dreamed of when he financed not one, but two, expeditions."

She leaned closer to Daria and said, "Don't you at least want to open those crates and see what your great-grandfather spent his life searching for?"

"Dr. Burnette . . ."

"Please. Call me Louise."

"Louise, I need to think this over. This project would take, minimum, a year, a year when I would not be in the field, and I—"

"You've spent how many years 'in the field'?"

"What difference does it make?"

"Twelve years, I think I read, but I had a hard time believing that," Louise said. "That's a long time to be living out of a suitcase."

"Dr. Burnette . . . Louise . . . I'm an archaeologist," Daria said patiently, as one might explain to a child. "I'm the child of an archaeologist *and* an anthropologist. Until I was ten, I rarely stayed in the same place for more than six months."

"When you were ten, your parents both accepted positions at Princeton. They lived there for years. That's hardly an outpost." Louise had done her homework.

"Yes. But even then, as soon as school was out, we'd be off for several months."

"Are you afraid you can't remain in one place for a whole year?"

"Could be a challenge." Daria smiled in spite of herself. "I've been living in a tent for most of the past five."

"Might be a nice change, after all those years of living like a nomad."

Daria laughed. "Actually, I'm quite at home in a tent. I don't own much, and I have no one to answer to. The nomadic life suits me quite well."

"Interesting." Louise seemed to study Daria for a moment. "How about we walk over to the museum and take a look around?"

When Daria hesitated, Louise leaned forward and said, "Aren't you even curious? Don't you even want to take a look?"

"Of course, yes, I'd love to take a look." Daria finished her tea and placed the glass on the tray. "Lead the way."

On the way across campus, Louise pointed out each of the buildings and their functions.

"That's the arts building," she told Daria as they passed a building that appeared to have its roots in the 1920s. "Fine arts, mostly. Our art history and conservation departments have their offices on the second floor, and there are a few studios on the third. I've been told the light there is exceptional. There's an addition on the back of the building—you can't see it from here—where there are classrooms. Photography labs are in the basement."

"And the building next to it?" Daria asked.

"Mathematics and the sciences. They have labs in both wings. The next building houses liberal arts; that brick building in front of us with the white pillars is the library." She paused as they passed by. "Some of the archaeology professors have their offices in the basement." Before Daria could comment, Louise hastened to add, "Their choice, I assure you. The department is officially housed over here on our right, on the second floor of that back wing. The Victorian-style mansion was once Howe's personal residence."

"I'm pretty sure I was there once, when I was little, for some sort of reception."

"Oh, quite likely. Unfortunately, in the mid-nineties, the roof began to leak. It's paid for its own repairs, though." Louise smiled and added, "Wedding receptions. It's quite the hot business. We've been renting it out for weddings and other special events for the past five years, and I must say, the old girl is definitely paying her own way these days."

She pointed to a building straight ahead. One story high and built in a semicircle, it had a brick courtyard at its center. "There's the museum."

"It looks surprisingly contemporary," Daria remarked.

"It was designed by one of the architectural students here at Howe right around the turn of the last century," Louise said as she dug for keys in her purse. "There was a competition and Benjamin Howe chose the design from the entries."

"I would have expected him to opt for something that blended in with the other buildings on campus." Daria turned back to the building that had a different feel. "Except for the arts building and the mansion, all of the others look Georgian."

"Yes, very classical." Louise nodded. "Your great-great-grandfather was going for a look that mimicked the older, great colleges and universities. The University of Virginia, for example, has that classical look, as so many other campuses do. He had high hopes for Howe."

She shrugged. "Unfortunately, we've never attained the level of prominence he'd wanted."

She found the keys and jingled them as they crossed the brick courtyard. Grass and weeds grew up between the bricks, and the landscaping that followed the curve of the building was badly overgrown.

"It's been completely boarded up for years, but I had all that removed anticipating your visit," Louise told her as she pushed open the door. "It's going to be a bit stuffy and dusty."

"Dust doesn't bother me." Daria followed her inside. "I'm used to dust."

They stepped into a large round room that had elevated glassed areas off to each side.

"This is the reception room," Louise explained. "Howe planned it to work as a gallery, as an exhibition hall, and a reception room. He called it the Great Room. There are photos from the opening back in 1912 which I'd be happy to share with you. Of course, Alistair was gone by then—he died in 1910—but Iliana and her father were there. His death actually put the opening off by a year while they scrambled to get the Jacobs collection ready to be displayed."

"I'd love to see the photos."

Daria walked slowly through the room, studying the few exhibits that remained. Small dinosaurs roamed in a procession over a sandy floor against a backdrop of enlarged photos of a generic desert. She tried to imagine a throng of people crowding around the glassed display areas. The room was comfortable and functional, and she couldn't help but think how, if properly designed, the exhibits could be nicely arranged in the showcases. The natural light from not only the front and back, but overhead, enlarged the space and gave it an importance that artificial light would not have.

"Very nice. Whoever designed this space did a good job of utilizing the natural light and the flow of the room."

Louise smiled, pleased that Daria approved of the room's design.

The corridors off to each side offered more space for exhibits. At the end of the hall to the right there was a short flight of four steps leading to a lower level where several offices were locked and forgotten. Another longer set of steps led down to the basement, which had no windows and was in total darkness.

"Let me see if I can remember where the light switches are," Louise said. A few moments later, an overhead light went on. "There. That should do it. Now, this way to the storage rooms."

Daria followed her down the wide hall to a series of locked doors.

"The remains of the natural history museum are in here, if you're interested," Louise pointed to the first three doors on the right. "I'm thinking maybe we could hire someone to deal with that. I think, if nothing else, we should be able to sell the dinosaurs. I read somewhere that recently several were sold for hundreds of thousands of dollars."

"You might not want to get rid of everything," Daria told her, "at least, not all at once."

"This is not my field, Daria. I don't know what's valuable and rare, and what isn't."

"It isn't mine, either, but I don't think it's a good idea to dump an entire collection at once." She walked on down the hall. "What's over here?"

Louise unlocked the first door to Daria's right.

"The Oliver Jacobs collection." Louise pushed open the door to reveal a long room with shelves that reached almost to the ceiling on every side. Wooden crates were stacked almost haphazardly around the room, some opened, some sealed. Daria walked around them, occasionally touching one or another.

"Jacobs dug in southern Mesopotamia, if I recall," Daria said.

"So I've been told."

"Was his exhibit cataloged?"

"Yes. There are several copies around. In the office upstairs, in the library."

"I'd like to see the catalog, if I may."

"I'll get one for you."

Daria continued to survey the contents of the room for another ten minutes in silence. Finally, she said, "Where are the artifacts from my great-grandfather's expedition?"

Louise pointed to a door at the end of the room.

"Behind that door."

"Would you . . . ?" Daria pointed to it.

"Of course."

Louise made her way around the crates and boxes to the back of the room.

"I might need a hand with this," she told Daria.

Several large boxes were stacked near the door, partially blocking it.

The two women pushed the boxes to one side so that Louise could unlock the heavy metal door. Once it was opened, she turned on the overhead light and stepped back.

"Take as much time as you need," she told Daria. "Feel free to look around. I'm going to go back up to the next level and see what shape the offices are in."

Daria entered the room, and her first thought was how like a tomb it was, with its stale, lifeless air and dark corners. To one side was a small desk, and Daria knew immediately that this was where her ancestor sat while he inventoried his remarkable find. She crossed the room and sat on the chair, then opened the desk drawer. She found it empty save for some papers which she removed and studied for a moment. The writing was small and elaborate, the ink faded and almost illegible. They appeared to be worksheets of some kind. She set them aside atop the desk, then began to inspect the cartons.

Her mouth was dry and her hands shook with an anticipation she hadn't expected. She ran her hands along the crates, wondering what lay within each of the wooden boxes that had been packed on a Turkish plain almost one hundred years earlier. If Louise was correct, the contents had only been seen one time since then, when Alistair prepared his inventory. Daria began to count the crates. There were fifty-seven in the room. If the stories were true, a fortune in rare antiquities was just within her reach. Artifacts that had been hidden for centuries, never seen by the modern world, lay at arm's length. The thought made her mind go numb.

She noted the seals on the crates and wondered who would have placed them there. Would Alistair have done so, if he was planning on exhibiting the contents? Iliana, perhaps, after her husband's death? She toyed with the edges of one of the wax seals, sorely tempted to break it and look inside, but she hadn't been hired yet and really didn't have the right.

This was the chance of a lifetime, and she knew it. She gathered the papers from the desk before leaving the room, securing the door with the key that Louise had left in the lock, and went out through what she already thought of as the Jacobs room.

"I found some worksheets in the desk downstairs," Daria said when she found the office where Louise waited for her. "I took the liberty of bringing them up so I could look them over. I hope that's all right."

"Of course."

"How soon do you need an answer from me?"

"As soon as possible. I don't need to tell you how involved this project will be. I can't even begin to imagine." Louise stood. "But we'll need to open by November of next year if we're to going to do it for the anniversary."

"That's hardly enough time to do this correctly."

"That's all the time we have, unfortunately." Ignoring the layer of dust, Louise leaned back against the desk. "Here's what we can offer you. Besides the opportunity to be totally in charge of an archaeological event that will have everyone in your field talking for years, we'll pay you a salary." She mentioned a sum that was less than Daria made for consulting on a single dig. "The guesthouse will be yours for as long as you're here, and you'll have a car at your disposal."

Louise smiled. "Not a very new one, or a very sporty one, but it's a car, all the same."

Daria smiled back. If Louise could see what passed as working vehicles in the part of the world where she'd just come from she'd laugh out loud. Even the very basic rental she'd picked up at the airport seemed luxurious.

"And you'd have meals at the dining hall, whenever you chose." Seeing the look of horror that crossed Daria's face, Louise laughed. "I eat there myself, really. The food is actually very good. We have a wonderful cook. She's been here for over thirty years. Buys as much fresh in season from the local farmers as she can."

"I'll take your word for it."

"So what do you think?" Louise asked.

"I'd like to think about it. And while I'm here, I'd like to read over Alistair's journals."

"I'll get them for you. I can make accommodations available for you to spend the night here on campus."

"That would be fine, thank you."

"We can stop at my office and pick up the journals, and I'll turn over the key to the guesthouse." Louise started for the door and Daria followed her. "I had my housekeeper air out and freshen McGowan House over the past few days, in hopes that you'd accept our offer."

"McGowan House?" Daria asked as they walked from the dimly lit basement to the bright lobby.

"The guesthouse." Louise opened the front door and turned to lock it behind them. "Benjamin Howe had it built for Alistair and Iliana as a wedding present. I don't know if a McGowan has slept under the roof since she died in 1939. Though some claim to have seen her now and then," Louise said with a perfectly straight face. "And who knows, Daria, she might even like the company enough to stick around for the reopening of the museum . . ."

THREE

Having declined Louisa's offer to show her through the house, Daria unlocked the front door. The recent rain and humidity had caused the jamb to swell, and as a result, it opened only reluctantly after a good shove.

The front entry was long and narrow, with stairs that came down along the left wall. There were parlors to the left and right of the foyer, both with fireplaces, and sheets covering all the furniture. Behind the second parlor was a library straight out of an English novel, with shelves that ran floor to ceiling, an ancient oriental carpet, and a mahogany desk that any antiques dealer would love to take to auction. Chairs flanking the fireplace were, like those in the parlors, covered with sheets. Daria peeked and found both were of well-worn dark brown leather. A spacious dining room just down the hall opened into a butler's pantry and the kitchen. A small sitting room was off the kitchen, and a glass-enclosed conservatory lay beyond.

Daria was dazzled by all the space, the high ceilings and tall windows. She hadn't been exaggerating when she'd told Louise she'd spent the last twelve years living in tents. She dropped her bag in the front hall next to the steps, and went into the kitchen carrying the canvas satchel that held the journals Louise had given her. There was a swinging door between the butler's pantry and the kitchen, and it closed behind her with a slight *whoosh*.

The appliances were far from new, but Louise had assured her they worked. The cabinets were old but had been painted fairly recently. She opened one after another, pausing to examine the contents of each. A set of Fiestaware in colors popular in the 1930s, some pottery bowls, some glasses, but not surprisingly, no food.

She opened the refrigerator and noted that it had been turned on but stood empty. Behind the freezer door, ice trays had been filled. She popped a few cubes from a tray and slid them into a glass she took from the cabinet, then filled it with water from the tap. In the field, there were times when ice was more precious than gold. The first time she'd seen a refrigerator that dispensed not only ice water but ice cubes and crushed ice as well, she'd been fascinated.

Now, of course, such appliances were commonplace, and it seemed that every time she came home, there was more technology to be learned. For someone who owned so little, who spent more time in the past than in the present, the accoutrements of modern life were mind-boggling.

Daria had no such problems with computers, however, and used them in almost every aspect of her work. Remembering that she needed to charge her battery, she went back to the front hall, took her laptop from her shoulder bag, and plugged it into an outlet. She wandered upstairs, going from room to room, wondering which of her relatives had spent a night in this bed or that. It gave her an odd feeling, knowing that three generations of her ancestors had slept under this roof.

At the front of the house she found the master bedroom, complete with four-poster bed, bath, sitting room, and a balcony that overlooked the back of the campus. She thought of poor Iliana, who had spent many a night here alone after Alistair died.

Then again, maybe not, Daria mused. No one seemed to know much about Iliana. Maybe through her diaries and her husband's journals, Daria would get a glimpse of the woman who had been her great-grandmother.

Daria went back to the kitchen, opened the canvas bag and took out all the journals. She sat at the kitchen table in the corner of the room and leafed through them, hoping to put them in chronological order. When she felt she had it right, she took the top leather-bound book from the stack and began to read.

The year was 1864, and fourteen-year-old Alistair had just read the epic in which life in the city of Shandihar was described, written in the sixth century.

> There were houses several floors high, wherein dwelled the merchants and their families. There were slaves from the four corners of the world, and comforts such as cannot be described. There were foods such as we had not tasted, from cities far beyond the mountains, beyond the desert. And in the temple of the goddess, treasures unknown to any man . . .

The journal told how Alistair had been drawn in by the tale of the city of riches in the desert of Asia Minor, how he memorized every word ever written on the subject, and how, by the time he was twenty, he was convinced that not only had the city been real, but that he knew where to find it.

It took years, but in Benjamin Howe, he had finally found someone who believed him.

Daria closed the journal and rubbed her eyes, then glanced at the clock on the kitchen wall. It was almost seven-thirty. She'd been reading since one. In her eagerness to get to Alistair's journals, she'd declined Louise's offer to join her for lunch. Now she needed dinner, and couldn't remember where the dining hall was. She locked up the house and drove directly to the diner in Howeville, where she read over the notes she'd taken from Alistair's desk while she absently picked at crab cakes and a salad. On her way back through Howeville, she stopped at the renovated train station and picked up a cup of rum raisin ice cream—large, since she hadn't had this favorite in longer than she could remember—and returned with it to McGowan House. She took the last of the journals into the library where she removed a dusty sheet from an overstuffed chair and sat, reading and eating ice cream, long into the night.

> *For what had seemed to be hours, I dug through the dirt, where once bricks made of baked mud had formed walls. Upon the stone floor, beneath the sand, the mosaic outline of a woman was clear. With my hands, I brushed away the debris until the whole of her form was clear. She stood upon a lion, eagle talons where her toes should be and wings upon her back. In each hand she held an arrow, and upon her head was a tall crown. Around her, a ring of lapis lazuli formed a circle, and I knew immediately who she was, and what I'd found.*
>
> *The Queen of the Night. Ereshkigal, the goddess brought from Mesopotamia by the earliest settlers of the city. The Queen of the Underworld.*
>
> *I felt the breath leave my lungs as I stared upon the face of the goddess, a face that had not been seen since the great earthquake buried Shandihar beneath the desert sands . . .*

Daria blew out the breath she'd been holding. The goddess Ereshkigal was well known to her, indeed, to anyone who'd studied the early cultures of the Near East. In Mesopotamia, she'd been the sister of Inana, one of three great goddesses. Once transported to Shandihar, however, she had become supreme, the only deity, one who demanded total fealty and expected nothing less than total devotion. Her priestesses had ruled the city in her name, and for several centuries, all passing through Shandihar had been required to pay a toll. It was said that by the time the desert had reclaimed the city, its treasure had rivaled that of Solomon.

Daria closed the journal and took another long look at the work notes Alistair had left behind, but the ink was far too faded to make much sense of them in this light. She finished the ice cream and took the cup and the journals into the kitchen. She closed up the house and took her belongings along with the canvas sack to the second floor. On the landing, she debated which room to sleep in.

"Oh, why not?" she said aloud, then went into Iliana's room and switched on the light.

She took a long hot bath in the claw-foot tub, every word she'd read that day and night etched in her brain. Her great-grandfather had found an uncommon treasure. Much like Heinrich Schliemann had done in Troy, Alistair McGowan had used the tale of an ancient story-teller to find an ancient city. That he'd never doubted himself was clear in his writings, from the time he'd made his first journal entry as a teenager, until he was a man in his forties standing at the brink of an immense treasure. He'd never stopped believing that the city existed, and that he would be the one to find it. It had taken him four expeditions, but he'd been proven correct. Finding Shandihar had been his destiny.

Was bringing it to the eyes of the modern world hers?

"You understand how very costly this is going to be, Louise? It's something the trustees have to consider." First thing in the morning, Daria went to Louise's office, and over coffee laid out her plan.

"I do. I'd be relying on you to appraise the collection so that we'd have a number to take to the bank for the loan."

"I'm going to need staff. At the very least, to start, I'm going to need an assistant, preferably a fellow archaeologist who specializes in the region."

"We have Dr. Bokhari on staff," Louise said thoughtfully. "She's out of the country right now supervising a group of graduate students on a dig, but I expect her back well before the start of the fall term. I'm sure she'll want to be involved."

"Sabina Bokhari?" Daria asked.

"Yes. Do you know her?"

"I know of her. We have mutual friends. I think she worked on a dig in Afghanistan several years ago."

"She was on sabbatical then." Louise nodded.

"And she's on staff here?"

"She's head of the archaeology department."

"You're very lucky to have her," Daria said. "She has a fine reputation."

"And you're wondering why she's here." It was a statement, not a question. "I've asked myself that. Every time she makes an appointment to come to see me, I hold my breath, hoping that she isn't coming in to resign."

"Why didn't you ask her to work on this project?" Daria asked.

"It did cross my mind. She's certainly qualified," Louise told her, "but once the trustees decided to go ahead, they felt it necessary to start immediately. Sabina had already committed to being out of the country for part of the summer. They also felt—as I do—it was fitting that a descendant of the man who found the treasures be the one to supervise the exhibition. And frankly, they wanted a bigger 'name' in the field. Your name alone will make this of interest in the academic community."

"And if I'd been unavailable, or said no?"

"You still haven't said yes," Louise reminded her.

"I'm going to ask that you permit me to take an inventory first. If in fact the collection has been overstated, or if the artifacts aren't in condition to be displayed, it may not be worth it for the university to invest so much—to mortgage itself, in effect—if the return won't compensate."

"You've read the journals?"

"Yes."

"Then you know what Alistair described having found."

"Yes. But what I don't know is how much of it made its way back to Howe, and what condition it's in. Let me take a look, and we'll go from there."

"All right." Louise opened her top desk drawer. "Here's the key to the building; this one is for the room you were in yesterday."

"Thank you." Daria reached out a hand for the keys. "If you don't mind, I'd like to start."

"Absolutely. Go. Good luck." Louise stood and crossed her arms over her chest. "We'll send you some lunch around noon. I expect you'll forget."

Daria had forgotten. It was Vita who'd brought her the covered dish with a chicken salad sandwich, an apple, some grapes, and two brownies—"Because one is never enough. I made these, and they're amazing, if I do say so myself"—and a thermos of iced tea.

"How can you stand it in here? It must be a hundred degrees. And the dust!" Vita coughed for emphasis. "The air is just thick with it."

"Is it?" Daria looked up from the desk where she'd been poring over the inventory Alistair had written. "I suppose I might have kicked up a bit, opening the crates."

"So, is it as wonderful as you thought it would be?" Vita's eyes gleamed in the overhead light.

"What? Yes. I suppose." Daria stood and stretched. "I've only gotten through a few crates, but judging from what I've seen so far, it was a spectacular find."

"How can you be so calm?" Vita frowned and peeked inside an open crate.

"If I let my emotions take over right now, I won't be able to do my job." Daria smiled and uncovered the platter. "Thanks a million for bringing this, by the way."

"Dr. B. was afraid you'd get caught up in your work and forget to eat."

"Dr. B. was right about that."

"So is there anything you can show me?" Vita touched the paper wrappings in the crate hopefully.

"Sure." Daria took a bite of sandwich, then got up and walked to the crate. She took out the object Vita had been poking. "This was a ceremonial goblet. See the figures here? The woman with the wings and the eagle talons for feet? This is Ereshkigal. She was the goddess around whom the culture in Shandihar was built. There were no minor goddesses, or—heaven forbid—gods. This was strictly a matriarchal society. Women ruled. And the most powerful women in Shandihar were the high priestesses of Ereshkigal."

"What's that in her hand?" Vita took a closer look.

"That's a human head," Daria told her. "With its tongue cut out. See how the mouth is empty?"

"Oh, Good Lord! That's just gross." Vita backed away from it. "Why did they put that on the cup?"

"Ereshkigal ruled the afterworld. Her followers believed that when you died, you came before the gates that separated heaven from hell. In each hand, you brought an offering to the goddess. And you would stand at the gate and tell of all the good deeds you had performed while you were alive." Daria set the goblet on the desk and picked up her sandwich and took another bite. "The punishment for any transgression was to cut off the hands of the offender. Because if he showed up at the gate without an offering, he would not be admitted. Likewise, if he failed to tell of his good deeds, he would not get past the gate. So people who broke the law, or displeased the goddess or her priestesses, were punished by having their hands cut off, or their tongue cut out. Or both, if they'd been really bad."

"No thirty to sixty days plus probation?"

Daria shook her head. "Not in Ereshkigal's world."

"Guess the rate of recidivism was pretty low."

"Good point."

"Okay, then. Guess I'll head on back to the office." Vita paused in the doorway. "Doesn't this place give you the creeps?"

"No, why?" Daria frowned.

"No reason, I guess," Vita muttered as she left the room. She stuck her head back in and said, "Dr. B. said to let us know if you need anything."

"Will do. Thanks."

Daria rewrapped the goblet and placed it back in the crate, upon which she'd drawn a large number one. On the inventory sheets, she'd located each object she'd found in the crate, and marked it with a number one to designate where it could be found. She moved through crates two, three, and four, and by the end of the evening, her heart was beating so fast she was afraid it would beat out of her chest. Not because of what she'd found, but because of what she hadn't found.

She worked through most of the night, and into the morning. Louise had stopped by with a box holding some dinner, but Daria had not uncovered it. By ten the following morning, Daria was exhausted and shaking with dread. Telling herself she needed to open every crate before panicking, and admitting that fatigue might be getting the best of her, she relocked the room, then the front door, and asked Louise to assign someone from campus security to guard the building through the night. She returned to McGowan house and slept for six hours. She got up, showered, changed her clothes, and returned to the basement, this time asking Louise to join her.

"I realize you're busy, but if you could spare me a few hours," Daria had asked.

"Of course. What would you like me to do?"

"I need a hand with the inventory," Daria told her without voicing her suspicions. "But you might want to change your clothes. And bring some bottled water. You might get thirsty."

Louise did just that, and for the next ten hours, crossed off the artifacts as Daria unwrapped them. At the end of the day, Daria sat at the desk and covered her face with her hands.

"Daria?" Thinking the archaeologist was overcome at having handled so many priceless objects in one day—as she certainly was— Louise patted Daria on the back and said, "I know this is overwhelming, but imagine what Alistair must have felt when he first found these objects. It's like a fantasy, gold and jewels and treasure like you dream about when you're a child and read of such things. Remember the story about Ali Baba and the forty thieves, and their cave of treasure? I feel as if I've walked into it. So I don't blame you for being blown away. God knows I certainly am."

"Louise, is there anywhere else on campus we might find other pieces from the collection?"

"No, why?" Louise frowned. "No. Nothing was ever taken out of this room."

"I'm afraid that's not true."

"What do you mean?" Louise put down the golden mask she'd been admiring and turned to Daria.

"Some of the objects that should be here, according to Alistair's notes, are missing." Daria ran an anxious hand over her face. "I went through everything last night, but there are items that are not accounted for. They're on the inventory, but not in the crates. That's why I asked you to help me go through it all again today. I needed to make sure."

"What are you saying?"

"I'm saying that between the time Alistair inventoried his find and today, someone's made off with some very important artifacts." Daria's face was white.

"Are you certain?" Louise looked stunned. "Daria, you counted the crates. There should be fifty-seven. There were fifty-seven, correct?"

Daria nodded her head.

"And you yourself removed the seals from those crates," Louise continued. "The inventories prepared by Alistair show check marks next to every item. And every item was checked. So why would you think something was missing?"

"Several items checked off on Alistair's list are not checked off on mine. So unless some of the objects were removed and placed elsewhere in the university, or sold . . ."

"There is no record of that," Louise insisted.

"Then I'd have to say they were stolen."

"Stolen!"

"I can't think of any other explanation. As you pointed out, the crates were sealed and Alistair's inventories show that every item was checked off by him—found, examined, then rewrapped and repacked in its shipping crate. But see here . . ."

Daria pointed to an entry and read aloud. "Two large solid-gold griffins clutching arrows, lapis lazuli eyes and rubies at the mouth." She looked up at Louise and said, "There should be two. There are none. Not in this crate, not in any of the others."

"Maybe we missed them somehow."

"I've looked through every crate twice. When I asked you to give me a hand, it was to help verify my findings. I thought perhaps I was tired; maybe I'd overlooked a crate or two. Which is why I started marking the crates with an X on the corner after you and I went through the contents and checked off every item."

"Maybe we should go through it all again. Maybe something was misplaced, returned to the wrong crate and you only think we missed it."

"We've spent an entire day going through every single piece that's here," Daria said wearily. "I'm convinced."

"Then convince me," Louise told her. "We'll take one more day."

The two women worked until nine that night, then locked the room when they went for dinner. The dining hall had long since closed, so they cleaned themselves up as best they could and drove into Howeville for pizza, which did nothing to revive either of them. They agreed to leave guards posted overnight, and to resume working at eight the next morning.

By three the following afternoon, Louise had to accept what Daria had been telling her for the past twenty-four hours. None of the missing items had been found.

"I'll call the police." Louise patted her pockets for her cell phone.

"No, not for something like this." Daria shook her head and starting searching her purse for her wallet. "You're going to need the FBI, not the local police. I met someone who works for them. I have his card in here somewhere, and if it's all right with you, I'd like to call him . . ."

FOUR

Connor dove into the pool and made barely a ripple. He emerged at the opposite end, then began a methodical series of laps. He'd been here at his home in Maryland, surrounded by woods and little else, for the past week. He hadn't spoken to anyone since last Thursday—which was, for the most part, fine with him—but this morning he'd gone into the nearest town and spent nearly an hour in the supermarket. The variety of foods never failed to amaze him. He'd spent nearly thirty minutes in the produce section alone, marveling at all the offerings from all over the world. His last few trips to the Middle East had taken him to places where you had to buy your food every day, since there was no refrigeration where he stayed, and where the selection was limited to what the merchants had for sale that day.

He wandered through the store and was pleased to discover an entire aisle dedicated to organic food where he stocked up on cereals and other goods. At the meat counter, he picked up a few steaks, some chicken, ground beef, pork chops. *What a luxury to have such choices,* he was thinking as he went through the checkout line. *Not to mention a refrigerator with a freezer.*

He'd stopped on the way home at the local fish market and treated himself to some blue claws, then stopped again at a local produce stand for tomatoes, corn, zucchini, and hot peppers. When he got home, he put everything away, made himself some salsa, and put it in the refrigerator to chill. Then he stripped down, grabbed a towel from the laundry room, and headed out to the pool.

Unaccustomed to being in one place for any length of time, he'd grown restless. He ran every morning—eight to ten miles, regardless of the heat and humidity—and swam for at least thirty minutes after his run, and again later in the afternoon. Bored, he'd called his boss the previous morning and asked when he'd be getting a new assignment.

"I don't have anything that's quite right for you," John Mancini had told him. "But it wouldn't hurt for you to have a little down time."

"I've had over a week of down time. I'm ready to go back to work. I'm bored."

"So find a hobby. Take up knitting."

Connor wasn't looking for a hobby. He'd already caught up on his reading and taken care of things around the house that needed to be done. He'd had all the time off he felt he could take. Too much time off meant too much time to think about things he didn't want to think about. Like his dead brother, Dylan, and how he got that way.

He swam his last lap, then drifted on his back to the side of the pool where he hoisted himself up. As he rose from the water, he realized he was not alone. He hesitated for less than a second, then held out a hand and asked, "Would you toss me that towel?"

"And me without my camera phone."

"Very funny."

Connor caught the towel in one hand and wrapped it around his waist as he walked toward the lounge where his boss sat. Connor asked, "So, to what do I owe the visit?"

"I was in the neighborhood and just thought I'd stop by."

"Buddy, there's no one in my neighborhood." Connor dropped onto the chair next to John.

"True enough. Tough place to find." John sat upright, one leg on either side of the lounge. "How did you find it?"

"Realtor. I told him I wanted something secluded and quiet. I think he had me pegged for a serial killer, but he found it for me anyway."

"Well, secluded you got. I'll have to stop back with Genna one of these days."

"You and your wife are welcome any time." Connor studied John's face, looking for clues to the reason for his unannounced visit. Finally, he asked, "So what's up, John?"

"You got a phone call last night at the office. Woman asked for you, wouldn't speak with anyone but you. She finally left a message for you on my voice mail."

"And?"

"And I called her back this morning." John paused. "You know a woman named Daria McGowan?"

Connor nodded. "Yeah. She called?" He frowned. "And you couldn't have just called me with her number because . . . ?"

"Because she has a problem, one that doesn't fall into your normal field of expertise. But she insisted that she only wanted to talk to you."

"Something happen to her?" Connor sat upright, aware that John would not be oblivious to his interest. "Is she all right? Did she say where she was?"

"She's fine, it's nothing like that. But she's in a place called Howeville, Pennsylvania, and she—"

"Shit. She's in the States?"

"Where is she usually?"

"Iran, Turkey, Syria . . . but go on. Why is she in Pennsylvania?"

"She was contacted by the president of Howe University, who asked her to take over a project at their museum. Short version—they want her to set up some displays, exhibits, whatever, in time for the hundredth anniversary of an archaeological expedition that her great-grandfather led sometime after the turn of the century. He apparently found some lost civilization in Turkey and brought back everything he could get his hands on."

"Cool. Good for her." Connor smiled. *And good for me. She's within driving distance.* "So where's the problem?"

"The problem is that when she opened the vault where her great-granddaddy's stash has been kept for the past hundred years and started cataloging the artifacts, she discovered that some of the more important pieces were missing."

"Stolen?"

"She thinks so."

"So she called the FBI, that's good. We have a whole department dedicated to—"

"I told her all that. But she didn't call the Bureau, Connor. She called you. She doesn't want anyone else. She doesn't want the publicity—feels it will look really bad for the university at a time when things apparently aren't going real well."

"Okay, I'll drive up there, I'll look things over, see if I can confirm that there really was a theft. If these items have been stored away for almost a century, there's a chance that over the years, a piece was removed to go on display here or there."

"That's what I told her, but the president of the college says the last curator of the museum was a real stickler. There's no notation of that vault ever being opened. She doubts anyone presently at the school—including most of the trustees—would even recall that these items were in storage there." John shook his head. "She needs the art-theft team, is what I think. I can have that coordinated, but right now she just wants to talk to you."

"Did she leave a number?"

John took a folded piece of paper from his shirt pocket and passed it to Connor.

"I'll just give her a call, take a drive up there in the morning, see what's what. We can always hand off the case if necessary."

"Connor, you don't play well with others. If there's something there, you're not going to want to turn it over to someone else and walk away. I know you." John rested his arms behind his head and leaned back. "What I don't know is why you'd be so interested in a quiet little antiquities theft case. I admit I'm surprised."

Connor shrugged. "Change of pace. Maybe I'm tired of running all over the globe, chasing down informants."

"Nice try." John closed his eyes. "Next."

"Maybe I like art. Antiquities. Archaeology. Indiana Jones. All that stuff."

"Who is Daria McGowan, Connor?"

"She's an archaeologist."

"That much I know. I've got her background. Education, publications. Important digs. She's very well known on an international level. The Iranians invited her in as a consultant on a big dig. American and female. A very big deal. Not their SOP."

"Like you said, she's very well known internationally."

"How do you know her?"

"I met her in Morocco. Last fall."

"You're involved with her?"

Connor smiled. "I only met her once."

"You met her one time, in Morocco, and you told her you were an FBI agent?" John sat up, frowning. "A bit risky, don't you think? In that part of the world?"

"Nah. She's an old friend of Magda's." Connor smiled again. "Magda's been trying to fix me up with her for about two years. We finally met in November."

"And?"

"And what? We met the one time, and we clicked. It'd be nice to see her again."

The two men sat in silence for a minute. Finally, John said, "Okay. You drive up there, you check it out. Help her look around for these artifacts; maybe they're misplaced. Mislabeled. Maybe there's been no theft."

"That's what I just said." Connor nodded. "That's exactly what I want to do."

"And if you determine this is really an art-theft case, we'll turn it over to NSAF." The FBI's National Stolen Art Files unit. "They know the best way to track stolen antiquities, they're the experts."

"Sounds good." Connor stood. "You feel like taking a dip, John? I have some extra trunks."

"No, thanks. I need to be getting back. Genna's been out of town on a job and should be in soon. I'd like to be there when she gets home." He got off the lounge and stretched. "Next time, maybe."

"Sure."

John followed Connor up the steps and into the house. "I'll take a bottle of water for the road, though, if you have one."

"In the fridge," Connor told him and began to pull on a pair of khaki shorts he'd left on a chair in the sun porch. "Help yourself."

"Thanks. You want one?"

"Sure."

Connor joined John in the kitchen a few minutes later.

"I'll call you as soon as I have a handle on this case," Connor told him as he twisted the cap off the bottle John had left for him on the counter. "I don't expect we're talking about anything the art guys can't handle, but I'd be lying if I said I wasn't interested in seeing Daria again."

"Fine. Take a drive, check it out, give me a call. With any luck, you'll be able to turn the case over to NSAF within forty-eight hours and you'll still have time to take the lady to dinner."

"That's what I'm thinking." Connor grinned. "I mean, how complicated can it be to figure out if a few old statues or pieces of pottery or whatever have been stolen?"

. . . . .

Connor finished his meal just as the sun drifted behind the trees. He sat alone on the patio that surrounded his pool, at a table with four chairs. He tried to remember whether there'd ever been four people sitting at this table at the same time, and couldn't remember that there had been. The most people who'd visited had been a whopping three: his cousins Mia, Andrew, and Belinda. Which would have made four at the table, if they'd been sitting outside. Which in December, they had not been.

He settled back to finish off the beer he'd had with dinner and watch the sun set. When it was almost dark, he took the chairs into the garage where he stored them, and since sudden thunderstorms darkened many an afternoon this time of the year, he folded the table's umbrella. He watched the fireflies dance across the pool, and thought about seeing Daria again.

He'd been truthful with John when he'd said he'd only met Daria McGowan one time. What he hadn't told John was that after that one meeting, he'd dreamed about this woman over and over. This, he smiled to himself, after months of dodging the efforts of their mutual friend, Magda, to introduce them. It wasn't that he'd been avoiding her. It was simply that life was such these days that he'd rarely had the time to say more than hello to any woman who might have caught his eye. Which was just fine with him. Connor had an agenda, and he hadn't penciled in *find woman*. Maybe someday, but not now. Then again, maybe never. Life was too complicated.

He'd seen Daria from his balcony once before the night they'd actually met. She'd looked pretty and fragile and he'd been intrigued. He'd been on his way to the courtyard to meet her when he was called from the Villa to attend a meeting, and had returned after midnight. By the next morning, she had gone. His loss, Magda reminded him at every subsequent visit.

Then, last November, he'd arrived in Essaouira on a Wednesday morning, tired and dusty and craving a hot shower, a soft bed, and a meal such as Magda's chef delighted in preparing for the guests. He thought that Magda had smirked when he arrived at the front desk, but there was a group of French tourists behind him waiting to check in, and he let it go. He'd gone to his room and stripped off his clothes and went directly to the shower. A phone call brought a meal fit for a king, and he ate at the table on the balcony and watched the windsurfers out in the harbor. He fell asleep in his chair, and when he awoke, the tray was gone, his back was stiff, and his head hurt. He'd crashed on the bed, fully clothed, and slept straight through until the next morning.

He'd ordered an American breakfast—eggs, toast, potatoes—and a pot of coffee, and once again sat on the balcony to eat. After weeks traveling from desert to mountain and to desert once again, the view of the Atlantic had been as welcome as an oasis. He thought about borrowing a boat from Cyrus. He'd drop anchor in one of the coves and dive in and swim until his arms and legs wore out, then he'd climb onto the boat and return to the marina.

His eyes had strayed to the courtyard, and to the flash of white that moved to the corner table. He'd recognized the hat, white and flowing like the dress she'd worn the day they'd almost met. Smiling, he'd put down his coffee cup and leaned over the railing.

"Please be you," he'd said aloud. "Take off that silly hat so I can see if it's you."

The hat remained on her head, so he grabbed his sunglasses and headed for the door. On his way across the lobby, he ran into a Jordanian he'd once worked with, one of his old field contacts. Trapped, he'd chatted politely, even while he watched a swoop of white move from the courtyard to the gate and disappear beyond the Villa's outer wall.

He'd caught Magda's eye, and from the gleam he saw there, he knew that the woman in white was the woman he'd sought, and he knew, too, that she would be back.

"You win, Magda," he'd said as she passed by on her way to the kitchen. "What time is dinner?"

"The corner table in the courtyard at seven-thirty. Perhaps you will have company." She poked him in the ribs. "Then again, perhaps not."

She was already there at the table when he arrived, sipping water with a slice of lemon, looking as fresh as a flower after a gentle rain. She'd looked up at him with eyes the color of cornflowers when he approached the table, and all he could think of to say was a most original "Hi."

She'd extended a hand to him, and he'd smiled as he took it. Her appearance was very feminine and soft, despite her casual attire—khakis and a cotton shirt—and total lack of makeup. Her hands were hands that worked in the field, tough and calloused, the nails short and devoid of polish and she was deeply tanned from months in the desert. Images of every other woman he'd ever known flashed through his brain, but none were like her. She appeared to face the world without thought of fashion or embellishment, or even—he couldn't help but notice—a professional haircut. Hers looked as if she'd cut it herself.

Later, he'd been hard-pressed to recall much of the conversation, except that they'd talked about their families. He'd been surprised to learn that she, too, had lost a brother, but other than that, for the most part, he only remembered her eyes and the sound of her laughter.

Fifteen minutes into dinner, he'd been trying to think of a way to make the evening last beyond the meal when they'd been interrupted. A message had been left for him at the front desk: a meeting he'd expected to attend the following day had been moved forward and would take place in one hour. He'd have to leave the Villa immediately in order to make it on time. There was no question that he'd keep the appointment; it was the reason he was in North Africa. He'd had to make his apologies to Daria and cut their evening short.

He'd given her his card before he left, and asked her to call him when she was back in the States, or when she was planning on coming back to the Villa.

"Call that number and leave a message, it will get to me," he'd told her. "Anytime. Day or night. I'll get the message."

It had been with great reluctance that he'd left her there at the table, alone, on a beautiful Moroccan night.

He'd really expected that in order to see her again, he'd have to travel back to the Villa. But wonder of wonders, here she was, almost in his own backyard, just a little over an hour away. That she'd kept the card all these months, that she'd called him when she needed help, satisfied him deeply.

She remembered me, and she called.

He couldn't remember the last time anything had pleased him more.

FIVE

Daria stood by the window in Louise's office and watched the sleek sports car park in the first visitor's spot. Even before the door opened, she knew who was behind the wheel. The car looked like the man—sleek and dark, sexy and dangerous.

He stepped out and looked around the campus as if to get his bearings, one arm leaning on the top of the car. He wore dark glasses and a shirt open at the neck, well-fitting jeans, and had a light-colored sport jacket slung over one shoulder.

He looks like a government agent, she thought as she stared shamelessly. *Or a spy.*

"... wondering if you'd had a chance to look through those journals of your great-grandfather's," Louise was saying.

"Oh. Yes." Daria reluctantly turned from the window. "I did. Almost all of them, actually. It was quite fascinating, almost like being there."

"That's what I thought, too, when I read them. I was thinking if once we get the exhibit open, perhaps your family might give approval to have them published. In the hands of the right publisher, we might have a bestselling series."

"Well, the reading is certainly interesting enough, I agree. I don't know who you would have to get permission from, though." Daria frowned. "I don't know who actually owns them. It may be the university. If they were part of his estate, and the estate was left to the school . . ."

"We can have that looked into. I'd still want the blessing of the McGowan family even if Howe does legally own them. Maybe we could include a forward from you," she said thoughtfully. "The bridge between one generation and another. Perhaps your father would want to contribute, as well."

Louise was about to say something else when there was a knock on the half-opened door.

"Dr. Burnette?" The tall man filled the doorway. "I'm Connor Shields."

Louise walked to the door to greet him.

"Yes, I'm Louise Burnette. Please, come in, Agent Shields. We've been waiting for you."

"Good to meet you." Connor shook her hand and smiled, then looked beyond her.

"And you know Dr. McGowan," Louise stepped aside as Daria made her way across the office.

"Daria, it's good to see you again." Connor took her hand and held it warmly between both of his.

"Thank you for coming right away, Connor." Daria cleared her throat. "Especially since it's Sunday."

"When I said anytime," he lowered his voice, "I meant *any-time*."

"I . . . we appreciate it." A flush crept up from beneath Daria's collar to her cheeks.

"Let's have a seat, shall we?" Louise gestured toward the chairs near the window.

Connor let go of Daria's hand, and waited until both women sat before seating himself.

He is very well-mannered, for an American, Daria recalled Magda saying, and the hint of a smile crossed her lips.

"Daria explained your situation on the phone," Connor told Louise. "Frankly, I have to admit I'm having a hard time understanding how such valuable objects could have been kept here all these years, yet no one bothered to check on them."

"It isn't so unusual, Connor." Daria touched his arm. "There are many, many museums that have locked rooms with locked crates that haven't seen the light of day in fifty or a hundred years. New objects are acquired and the older acquisitions are moved farther back into the storage area—often a basement or warehouse. Curators are hired and fired, and sometimes their records are misplaced. Acquisitions are often forgotten over time."

"And here at Howe," Louise added, "in the last fifty years, dinosaurs became more popular than ancient cultures. As I mentioned to Daria, the last curator's interests lay in the area of American natural history. Professor McGowan's finds, along with those of another archaeologist who led an expedition about the same time, were locked away and pretty much forgotten as other items were acquired and put on display."

"What reminded you?" Connor asked.

"For the past few years, the financial picture here at the university has become increasingly grim. We have been considering different means of raising cash, and recently someone suggested selling off what few liquid assets we have." She smiled wryly. "It didn't take long to make a list of those. We have some land we could sell, but there isn't enough to make a dent in the budget. And this isn't really a high-rent district out here, as you may have noticed."

"The town looks all right," Connor noted.

"The town is *all right,* and that's about it. We're surrounded by farms, many of them Amish, and the price per acre is pretty low."

"So what you're saying is that selling off land wasn't the solution," he said.

"Right." Louise nodded. "And then someone started talking about selling off artwork—the university does have quite a nice collection of American primitive paintings—so we went around to the various buildings to take stock of what we had. On my way back home that night, I came past the museum, and it jogged my memory."

"I'd have thought it would have occurred to someone sooner than that."

"Agent Shields, no one has seen that collection in almost one hundred years. There was no official catalog we could refer to, because Professor McGowan died before his find was ever put on display."

"But if there was no catalog, why are you so sure something is missing?" he asked.

"He made an inventory when he first returned to the States," Daria told him. "He described everything in every crate in great detail. Some items he'd even sketched. Every crate was numbered, so we know exactly what should be in each one. He was in the process of designing his exhibits when he died, and his inventory reflects that. Louise— Dr. Burnette—and I have gone through the crates several times, double-checking and searching for the missing items. They are not in the vault."

"Where else have you looked?" Connor asked.

"We've searched the basement," Daria told him, "and last night, I started going through the house where I'm staying here on campus, where my great-grandparents lived. I thought perhaps there might be something there."

"I'm guessing you didn't find anything," Connor said.

"Only some letters he wrote to my great-grandmother from the dig. Unfortunately, romantic as they are, there's nothing that's going to help us figure out what happened to the missing artifacts."

"What about other buildings throughout the university?" Connor said, thinking aloud. "I'm assuming you've scoured the other houses, the science building, offices, storerooms?"

"Actually, I'm working on that this afternoon, along with the lone member of our archaeology staff who is on campus for the summer. Daria and I believe that the only items that might still be on campus and might have gone unnoticed would be pottery. Jars, vases, that sort of thing. Certainly any of the gold or jeweled items wouldn't be sitting out unnoticed on a shelf."

"Good point. Has anyone searched the museum?" he asked.

"Only Dr. Burnette and I."

"That's good, then. I'm assuming no one knows what's there, including members of your staff. I suggest we keep it that way for a while." He stood. "Daria, why don't we start by showing me the vault?"

"Yes, I'd like you to see the museum." Daria stood as well. "And I want to show you the inventory. I've entered everything onto my computer—crate by crate, item by item. We can stop at the house and I'll run a copy off for you."

"I have it, Daria," Louise told her as she rose. "I'll make a copy for Agent Shields."

Louise left the room.

"Thanks again for coming, Connor," Daria said. "I didn't know what else to do."

"Well, you know, this isn't really something I'd normally handle. The FBI has a dedicated team of experts in this field—art theft, cultural theft, that sort of thing."

"That's what Agent Mancini told me, but I was so uncertain what to do. I thought you . . . well, you said to call you, anytime."

"And I'm glad you did. I really am. I'm just saying that if there has been a major theft, it's in your best interests to have the best in the field working on the case. Our people specialize in this type of thing."

"And what do you specialize in, Connor?" she asked.

He appeared to welcome Louise's return to the room, as if Daria's question was one he hadn't really wanted to answer.

"Here you go, Agent Shields." Louise handed over a thick stack of paper in a brown folder. "The inventory Daria made and we both doubled-checked."

"Thank you." He glanced at it briefly before tucking it under his arm. To Daria, he said, "Ready when you are."

"Then let's get started." Daria gathered her bag and headed for the door. "I have my phone, if you need me, Louise. And you know where to find us."

"Let's take the shortcut," Daria said when they'd stepped outside into the oppressive heat of the afternoon. Overhead the sky was hazy, the sun a blur behind the clouds, the air heavy with humidity. "At least there will be some shade."

"I'm all for shade," he agreed. "But I'd think you'd be used to the heat, feel right at home, all the time you spend in the desert."

"Desert heat is one thing, this humidity is something else." She pulled dark glasses from her bag and slipped them on.

"Right, dry heat, and all that. Though frankly, when it gets to be a hundred or more degrees, it's just plain hot."

"True."

She rounded the side of the building and he followed her.

"We'll stop at McGowan House and pick up a few bottles of water," she said. "We'll need them."

"McGowan House, eh?" He smiled. "You've been here less than a week, and already they've named a building after you?"

Daria laughed. "The university uses the house my great-grandparents lived in as a guesthouse. Louise very kindly offered to let me stay there while I'm at Howe." She took a key from the pocket of her shorts. "It's the white building straight ahead."

They followed a crumbling brick path to the back of the house.

"This will just take me a second. Come on in."

"I'll wait."

She jogged up the back steps and unlocked the door. "Want anything besides water? I might have some pretzels."

"Just the water, thanks." He stood with his hands on his hips overlooking the gardens behind the house, where hydrangeas top-heavy with blooms fought a wild tangle of roses for space.

True to her word, Daria was back in a flash, the water bottles held against her body. She handed two to Connor.

"Great. They're cold. Thanks," he said.

"So," he said after taking a long drink from one of the bottles and replacing the cap. "Tell me about Shandihar. I have to admit I'd never heard of it. All I know is what you've told me, that it was a city in southern Turkey and was found by Alistair McGowan in 1908."

"What exactly would you like to know?" She began to walk.

"Who were its people? What was its culture?" He followed along the path.

"At first, it was little more than a crossroads on the Silk Road, populated by merchants from all over the region. Greeks, Turks, Mesopotamians, nomads. Shandihar was quite the melting pot, with religions and superstitions and cultures blending over time. As the years passed, the society became matriarchal, with the import of the goddess Ereshkigal from Mesopotamia, who somehow came to prominence. My great-grandfather's journals mention several temples dedicated to her, and writings that indicated that the priestesses who served her pretty much ran the city. Travelers passing through had to pay tribute—essentially, a toll—to come into the city."

"They couldn't have gone around it?"

"The walls of the city offered safety after dark," she explained. "Beyond the walls, at night, anything could happen. There were tales of wild animals that hunted at night and that were most fond of human flesh and blood. And of course, there were bandits."

"So, in other words, it was worth paying the toll to be able to sleep safely."

"I'm sure that was the idea. In addition to the tolls, the merchants who did business in the marketplace had to bring tribute to the temples twice each year. If you wanted to spend the next life in heaven, you paid up. The more you gave, the better your chances of a happy afterlife."

"What did the priestesses do to keep everyone in line? Surely there were some who didn't want to cough up their share."

"These ladies were pretty shrewd. Here's the thing about Ereshki-gal. She was the goddess of the underworld. The place where you do not want to spend your afterlife." Daria smiled, pleased by his interest. "When you died, you had to face the goddess at the junction between heaven and hell. If you wanted to get into heaven, you had to bring offerings to the goddess."

"They had to bribe their way into heaven?"

"Exactly. You were to appear at that gateway with something in each hand. Then you would tell the goddess all your good deeds, so she could judge your worthiness."

"So far, so good. You bring the bribe, you brag a little." Connor nodded. "Everyone can come up with something good that they did over the course of their lifetime. So where's the incentive to pay the tribute?"

"Those who refused to pay were brought before the priestesses, who would pass sentence on the offender."

"I have a feeling the punishment may not have fit the crime."

"One or both hands were cut off," she told him. "If you really pissed them off, they'd have your tongue cut out as well."

"Ouch. Why not just kill them?"

"It made more of a statement. Everyone knew you were marked for the underworld, and no one would assist you because you were the walking dead. It was just a matter of time before you starved to death or died of thirst, since no one was permitted to help you. And once you died, you'd go straight to the underworld, because when you showed up at the gate, you'd have no gifts for the goddess and because you had no tongue, you couldn't tell her about all the good things you'd done. So off you went, right into the pit."

"I imagine that made quite the impression."

Daria nodded. "Enough that the tongueless head is a recurring theme in Shandihar art. I found several pieces in the collection that depict the goddess or one of her priestesses holding one in her hand. Remind me to show you."

"Great. Looking forward to that."

Daria laughed.

"Why haven't I heard more about this city?" he asked.

"A few years after the discovery—around 1914, I think—an earthquake buried it under tons and tons of sand, so it's lost once again. I don't know if the site could even be located, since the landmarks are all gone."

"Has anyone looked?"

"Not that I know of," she told him as they approached the museum from the side. "Here we are."

"That's it?" They rounded the corner and faced the courtyard. "That's the museum?"

Daria nodded.

He scanned the front of the building.

"You said on the phone there's security."

"There is." She nodded.

"Where?"

"I guess the guard's inside. Let's go see." She took the key from her pocket and walked across the courtyard to the door, which opened with a push.

"Stan?" She called out.

"Right here." His voice came from the stairwell.

The guard, a tall, thin, balding man in his mid-forties, came up the stairs from the office level.

"Sorry, Dr. McGowan. I had to use the facilities," he told her.

"You leave the door unlocked when you take a break?" Connor asked skeptically.

"No one's around." Stan shrugged. "No harm, no foul, right?"

"Next time you leave your post, lock the door behind you," Connor told him pointedly.

Stan glanced at Daria.

"Stan, this is Special Agent Shields, from the FBI."

"Oh." Stan stared at Connor with no small interest. "Here to see if anything's been pinched, huh?"

"Here to assess the situation."

"I thought there were two guards assigned." Daria frowned.

"One of us takes the night shift, the other the day. This week I have day shift, next week we'll trade off."

"So at any given time there's only one guard," Connor noted.

"That's right."

"I guess if you'd noticed any activity around the building you'd have notified Dr. Burnette," Connor said.

"Sure. But there hasn't been any."

"Go on back to your post, Stan. But Agent Shields is right, the door should be locked at all times," Daria told him. "Starting now."

She locked the door with the key and slipped it back into her pocket.

"I'm going to be showing Agent Shields around for a while," Daria told the guard, "so you can go back to doing whatever it was you were doing." She gestured toward the folding beach chair inside the front door. A stack of paperback novels, several crossword puzzle magazines, and a large bottle of water sat nearby.

"Give a shout if you need me." He ambled over to the chair and sat down, and took the first book from the stack.

"That's your security?" Connor whispered to Daria.

"Don't knock it," she whispered back. "That's the most they've had here in almost fifty years."

"And Burnette wonders why things went walking out of the museum."

"Well, they did have the building completely boarded up for a while. It isn't likely anyone got in then."

Connor walked around the perimeter of the room, checking the wide, oversized windows that arched at the top.

"None of these open," he noted.

"They're really only designed to let in natural light for the exhibits. They're well placed, so only indirect light is allowed into the room, but no direct sunlight, which could have an adverse effect on the artifacts."

"Any windows on this floor that open?"

"I'm not sure. I didn't check them all."

"Let's do that now."

She led him from one room to the next. In each, he examined the windows, those that opened to the outside, and those that were fixed. When he finished, he said, "I don't see any sign that any of the windows were tampered with. No indication that anyone's tried to break in on this level."

They went back into the great hall, and Connor studied the door frame.

"I guess Dr. Burnette would know if this door or the frame had been replaced over the years?"

"I would think there'd be a record of the expenditure someplace or a copy of the work order. We can ask Louise to look into that."

"Let's check the windows downstairs," Connor suggested.

"There are none," she told him.

"No windows in the basement?"

"No."

"There must be another door to the outside, though," Connor said. "There couldn't be just this one and the one we found at the end of the hall. That one showed no sign of having been forced, and even when you opened it, the outside is obscured by all those overgrown shrubs."

"I've asked Louise to have those removed. They could provide protection for anyone who's looking for a way to get inside. And I'm afraid that as soon as the story gets out, there will be more interest in the building and what's inside it than there has been in a very long time."

"There's another door on the office level," Stan said without looking up from his book.

"Let's check it out." Daria headed for the steps leading to the half level below. "All the offices are down here. I think there are four of them. I haven't gone into them all, just this first one. If there's a door to the outside, I missed it."

She switched on the lights at the bottom of the steps.

"We left the flashlight here on the desk yesterday. And it's still here." She tucked it under her arm and stepped back into the hall. "Let's check out the door. I'm guessing it's at the very end of this corridor."

"Lead the way."

They passed three more glass-paneled doors leading to the other offices. Daria shined the light straight ahead, and at the very end of the hall was another door.

"Could I have the light?" Connor asked and Daria handed it over. He ran the beam around the door frame.

"Like the others," he said. "No sign of a break-in, at least from this side. Try the key, let's see if they used the same lock as upstairs."

Daria took the key from her pocket and tried the lock, but it wasn't a fit.

"Any idea where this opens?"

"I'd say at the back of the left wing of the building, assuming I haven't gotten disoriented somehow. We can take a look at the door from the outside when we leave, unless you want to do it now."

"We'll do it on our way out."

"Shall we take a look in the basement?"

"Lead on."

"Down this way." Daria beckoned Connor back to the stairwell, then down to the next level. She used the flashlight to find the lights for the hallway.

"It really is dark down here," he noted. "Dungeon dark."

"Louise's secretary thought it was quite creepy." Daria smiled.

"Don't you?"

"I've been in so many tombs and crypts over the years, it takes a lot to raise my hackles these days. Dark rooms don't quite do it anymore." She unlocked the door to the storage room and turned on the overhead light.

Connor followed her inside, then stood with his hands on his hips, taking it all in.

"Where shall we start?" he asked.

"Let's start with crate number one. It's there on your right." Daria walked past him and pointed to the number on the side of the crate. "This is the number Alistair painted on before the crates left the dig. He itemized the contents, sealed it, then marked it. The X up here is mine. It indicates that I have gone through the crate and examined every piece, and marked it off on my list. The list you have in your hand is the one I ran off my computer. It has both mine and Alistair's checks."

He placed the list on the top of the crate and studied it.

"So, this item here—necklace of solid gold with gold beech leaves and lapis beads—he packed into the crate and later unpacked, but it was missing when you checked the contents?"

"Right." She nodded and began to lift the lid.

"Here, let me give you a hand." Connor picked up the wooden top of the crate with ease and set it aside. "Let's see what's in here."

"Okay, first item here is a goblet, it's the third item on your list, see?" She unwrapped it carefully and held it up.

"Golden goblet with griffins set with carnelian?"

"Right. See, it's checked off on both lists."

"Got it," he said. "By the way, what is it with griffins?"

She smiled as she rewrapped the goblet. "They're wonderful mythological beasts. I actually went on an expedition to the Gobi Desert not too long ago in search of proof they really existed."

"You're kidding, right?"

"Nope."

"And you look so normal."

Daria laughed and set the wrapped goblet on top of a nearby crate, then reached for the next item, which was enclosed it its own wooden box.

"It was a spoof, of course, and wasn't something I'd ordinarily have spent time on, but the professor in charge of the expedition was a legend in the field, and I thought, if he could take a month off, I could, too."

"What did you do? I mean, you didn't actually find anything?"

"We found exactly what we expected to find. Sometimes animals die in proximity to each other, say, for example, an eagle and a lion. When archaeologists from the past century, century and a half, found them, they often put the bones together incorrectly."

"Incorrectly, as in, the eagle wings on a lion's body?"

"Exactly. There was a time when people really did believe that griffins had been found. Dr. Allen—Elwood Allen, from Cambridge— put together the expedition and invited several other archaeologists to go along. I was one of them."

"What was the point?"

"He was making a documentary for the BBC. It was quite clever, actually. We took bones from different animals found in the Gobi and made up the most fanciful beasts and put them on display. It was great fun." She carefully removed the next artifact. "Here we have something really unusual. It's a jar made from an ostrich egg."

"Ostriches in the Near East?" Connor frowned.

"They were not uncommon several thousand years ago. What is uncommon is that this is in such lovely condition. Old Alistair certainly did treat everything with kid gloves. I'm really impressed with the care he took to ensure that every item made it to the States intact."

Connor studied the jar for a moment, then referred to the list. "Here it is. Ostrich egg jar. With two check marks. What's next there?"

Daria took pains to wrap the precious jar securely before setting it aside.

"Let's see what else we have in here . . . oh, I love this one." She grinned and unwrapped what appeared to be carved stone. "This is an amulet, worn to protect against demons."

Connor leaned closer for a better look.

"I can't really tell what that is." He turned on the flashlight and examined the piece. "What are those things?"

"Demons."

"I thought you said this was supposed to ward off demons."

"It is. These are particularly fierce ones."

"My demons are more evil than your demons?"

"Something like that." She grinned. "They are ugly things, aren't they?"

"This never gives you nightmares?"

"Never. I don't do nightmares." She pointed to the list. "This is fourth or fifth on the list."

"Got it."

"Seen enough to get a feel for the situation?"

"I think so." Connor nodded.

Daria returned the items to the crate and Connor helped her to replace the lid.

"What's your next move here?" he asked.

"I almost don't know what to do first," she said. "I need to compile an official list of what I believe is missing, complete with Alistair's sketches, and the photographs that were taken at the site, if I can find them. Then I'll compile a similar list of the items that are still here so that an appraisal can be made of the collection. The university is hoping to use that as collateral for a loan to pay for the repairs to the museum and the preparations for the exhibits."

"Off the top of your head, what are we looking at here?"

"In terms of value?" She shook her head. "I can't put a number on it."

"Ballpark."

"There are some things that are truly priceless, things that are so unique and valuable that they cannot be reproduced. What is that goblet worth? It's hard to come up with a price. The gold is high quality, the carvings are beautifully done, add in the age of the item, the fact that there may only be that one in the entire world . . ." She shrugged. "How do you place a monetary value on that?"

"So you're saying the collection, in its entirety, could be priceless."

"In its entirety, absolutely. Priceless. This is all that's left of a civilization that existed thousands of years ago. Its people, its art, its history, its religion . . . this is all that is left of Shandihar," she told him. "There are individual pieces that could be considered priceless in their own right. This was a major find a hundred years ago, made even more valuable, I believe, because it's been hidden for all this time."

"Why are you not as nervous as I am about having only Stan up there guarding the door? At the very least, I'd have a couple of armed guards and the most sensitive alarm system money can buy."

"And if anyone knew what was here, I'd agree with you. But right now, no one knows. And as long as we keep it quiet and out of the public eye . . ."

"Daria, someone knew." He corrected her. "At some point over the past hundred years, someone knew and helped themselves. And that someone did not come from outside the university. Whoever stole from your great-grandfather's collection was someone on the inside, someone who had access to the building."

"You're probably right."

"There's no sign of a break-in anywhere around the building, and as you just pointed out, who else would have known what was here?"

"Louise said the building was boarded up until recently, so the thefts probably would have taken place before the building was sealed," she said thoughtfully. "Not much chance of catching the thief, then, is there?"

"Probably not, if that's the case. But I'm sure NSAF—that's the unit within the FBI that handles stolen art—will know the best way to track down the artifacts."

"I need to think about this."

"What's to think about? We have experts who handle exactly this type of case."

"Here's the thing. Generally speaking, there are only two places where the artifacts could be. In private collections, or in museums or galleries."

"So? The art guys will know where to look."

"But they're the *FBI*."

"And that's a bad thing because . . ?"

"It's bad because it will give the appearance that the collector, or the museum that acquired the piece, has done so illegally, and that is not necessarily the case," Daria told him. "It may be that the owners have no idea that the items were stolen. They may have purchased from a dealer who believed he was buying from a legitimate source."

"Or from someone who knew it was stolen and didn't particularly care."

"But if the artifacts are now in the hands of legitimate collectors, they could face tremendous embarrassment. There'd be a huge scandal. Keep in mind that if they purchased the items in good faith, they are victims, too." Daria shook her head. "I'd rather see if I can trace the items myself before we sic the FBI on them."

"How would you go about doing that?"

"I'd start on the Internet. I'd search the museum websites—many of them contain photographs of their collections and include the provenance. I'd also search for collectors. They often catalog their pieces and offer them on loan to galleries and museums." She smiled weakly. "Same way, I suspect, that your 'art guys' would begin."

"Let's assume you're successful in tracking down even a few of the pieces. Then what?"

"Then I contact the owner and explain the situation and give them an opportunity to return the items to Howe."

"Why would they be willing to do that on your say-so?"

"I have my grandfather's journals to back me up. They are very specific as to where and when certain pieces were found. He also indicated that many of the pieces were photographed in situ before they were touched. I'll get those from Louise. And we do have his inventories. I think we have enough to establish that the artifacts were discovered by Alistair McGowan on behalf of Howe University. It's a start, anyway. Keep in mind that most museums and private collectors try very hard to avoid scandals of this nature. It's very damaging to their reputations, not to mention the integrity of their other acquisitions. This sort of thing casts a very long and very dark shadow on everyone connected, from the dealer to the buyer to the curator. It's definitely to be avoided at all costs."

"And if you fail to convince them, and they refuse to hand over the artifacts?"

"Then we call in your art guys, and we let them fight it out."

SIX

"So, what you're saying is we need a game plan." Louise's fingers tapped impatiently on the arm of the sofa. On their way back across campus from the museum, Daria and Connor stopped at the president's house to discuss their findings with her.

"Right. I've given this a lot of thought over the past few days," Daria told her. "And after talking with Connor this afternoon, I do have a proposal."

"Let's hear it." Louise sat back against the cushions and waited.

"If the university is serious about reopening the museum by the fall of next year, they have to raise the capital now, and quickly. I think what you need to do is have the entire collection properly appraised by an art historian who is capable of putting dollar valuations on the artifacts."

"I thought you could do that." Louise frowned.

"I thought perhaps I could help you in that regard," Daria admitted, "but after seeing what's here, I've come to the conclusion that you need someone who is an expert in appraising large collections. I'm an archaeologist, Louise. I can tell you the cultural value of every piece in those crates, but I don't feel comfortable putting dollar signs on them. Is it enough to know that the collection is priceless?" She shrugged. "Would a bank find that sufficient documentation for a loan the size of what you're going to need to put that building into shape? I really doubt it."

Louise appeared to think it over.

"Can you recommend someone?" She asked.

"Off the top of my head, no."

"I have an idea," Connor spoke up. "You know that you're going to have to have this entire setup insured, the building as well as the artifacts. Why not contact your insurance agent, tell them you want coverage for the museum and ask them to send an appraiser to put a number on the collection as well as the building?"

"You think they have people on staff who do that?"

"I'm sure they have someone who can appraise the building, and as far as the contents are concerned, I think they'll find someone real fast. They're going to want the business, because the premium will be huge, but they're going to make certain that the amount of insurance is adequate so if there is a loss, they don't get raked." He rubbed his chin thoughtfully for a moment, then added, "I'll bet they even have someone in their risk management department who can tell you exactly what you need to do as far as the renovations are concerned to best safeguard the collections. I have a cousin who works in this field and he spends a lot of his time inspecting buildings and working with the security firms."

"Connor's got a really good point," Daria said. "And chances are, the bank is going to want to bring in an appraiser of their own, if you're going to use the collection as collateral for the loan."

"I can call our insurance agent and see what she suggests," Louise said thoughtfully. "I suppose it would save us considerably over hiring an independent appraiser. Plus, if they can send someone out to tell us exactly what to do in the building . . ."

"Be prepared to move the collection in the interim, though," Connor cautioned. "The bank may want to place it in one of their vaults until security has been brought up to date. I'm sure the insurance company will require specific improvements to the system—such as it is—that's in place now."

"All of which means you need to get to the bank as soon as possible," Daria told Louise.

"I'll put a call in to the vice president of our local branch first thing in the morning and see when he can meet with me," Louise said. "Maybe take a few of the flashier objects with me to give him an idea of what we're talking about here, see if we can get them to establish a line of credit for us so that we can start the improvements to the building as soon as possible."

"I'd do that first thing," Connor said. "In the meantime, I'm going to see what I can do about tracking down the missing artifacts."

"*We're* going to track the missing artifacts," Daria corrected him.

"I was hoping you'd come with me to the bank, Daria," Louise said. "I'm really not qualified to explain what we have here and why it's so valuable. I think it would have greater impact coming from someone with your credentials."

"Just let me know when."

"I'll call Jim Sanders, the bank VP we usually deal with, and see when he's available. This sort of thing may be out of his field of operations, but we'll start with him."

"Don't forget your insurance people," Daria reminded her.

"Alice Radell." Louise smiled. "Best agent in the state. I have a meeting with one of our department heads at eight tomorrow morning, but as soon as that's over, I'll start making my calls."

"While you're doing that, I'll get started on the search for the missing artifacts. I'll have my cell on, so just give me a call when you're ready to go." Daria stood.

"Thank you." Louise smiled. "I have to admit, I feel a little better, having a plan. I've been worried sick about this since learning about the missing items, and worried, too, about protecting what we have."

"Hopefully, we'll be able to find some of those items," Connor said as he rose from his chair.

"Well, Daria, you'll be pleased to know that help is on the way." Louise turned to her. "I spoke with Sabina Bokhari about an hour ago. She was shocked when I told her what was going on. She insisted on cutting her trip short, and will be here by Tuesday at the latest."

"Great. She'll be an enormous help. But I thought she was on a dig with some students."

"She is, but she isn't the only archaeologist on the site. She said she feels very comfortable leaving the dig in the hands of the other two. A Dr. Henning and someone else whose name I don't recall."

"Emmitt Henning, yes. I know him well. I wouldn't hesitate to leave my work in his hands, either. And I'm very much looking forward to meeting Sabina."

Turning to Connor, Louise asked, "Have you decided to bring in the FBI's art people?"

"Not yet," Daria replied before Connor could. "We will if we have to, but if Connor and I can handle this on our own, I think it would be better for everyone. I'm fairly confident that we can, at least for the time being."

Daria explained to Louise how even the hint of having purchased stolen antiquities could ruin the reputations of collectors as well as museums, not to mention tarnishing the reputation of the university.

"Well, if we can guarantee the return of whatever items you might be able to find without causing undue embarrassment to the owners, I'd certainly go along with that. Of course, if you're unable to locate any of the missing pieces, I expect we'll have to turn this over to the FBI."

"That's the plan," Daria assured her.

"How long do you suppose before you'll know if you'll be successful?"

"A few days, maybe. I expect to find some of the information we need on the Internet. It's either there or it isn't. In which case, Connor will call in his people."

"Go to it, then," Louise told her. "Daria, does this mean you've accepted our offer to reopen the museum?"

"First things first, Louise," Daria said from the doorway. "Without a commitment from the bank, there won't be a museum. Get your funding, and then we'll talk."

"But you're going to do it, aren't you?" Connor asked as they walked back to McGowan House.

"I don't want to get anyone's hopes up, mine included. If they can't renovate that building, and do it quickly . . . if they can't guarantee the security of the collection . . ." Daria shrugged. "It all depends on whether or not Louise can convince the bank to give the university a very large loan. I can't even begin to estimate what it would cost to do everything that has to be done to the museum. They'll need all new systems—new electric, new plumbing. Air-conditioning and a new heating system. You name it, that building needs it."

"It looks pretty good, though, considering its age. I guess boarding it up for a while preserved it somewhat," Connor noted. "I'll be interested to see what the insurance company recommends."

"That was a good suggestion, by the way," Daria said as they approached her temporary home. "Getting the insurance company to prepare the appraisal and assess the building. And since the bank will probably want its own expert to come in, that will give the university two appraisals. Hopefully, the two experts will agree."

She unlocked the front door.

"But, as Louise noted, at least we have a game plan." She pushed open the door. "Come on in. I'm sorry it's so hot and stuffy in here. There's no air-conditioning and only one fan in the house, and I put that in my bedroom last night so I could sleep. I tried to open the windows downstairs but haven't been able to get them to move."

They stepped into the quiet house.

"Maybe I can budge them," Connor offered. "Which ones would you want opened?"

"The ones in the kitchen, for starters, since I've been working in there at night." She gestured toward the hall that stretched out in front of them. "It's back here."

"This is some house," he said, looking around.

"Isn't it? Benjamin Howe built it as a wedding present for his daughter, Iliana, when she married my great-grandfather," Daria explained. "She was his only child, and I guess he wanted to guarantee that she stayed close."

"So I guess Pop wasn't disappointed when Iliana fell in love with one of his hires."

"Not at all. According to her journal, he was pretty damned pleased with her choice of husband. It worked out well for her, I suppose, in the long run. Alistair was quite a bit older than she, and he died when their children were still young, but at least they had a roof over their heads. Since her mother died when Iliana was a young girl, she served as her father's official hostess here at the university. She stayed until her death, actually, in the late 1930s. She died in this house." Daria smiled. "Louise says that some who've stayed here claim she's still around."

"No sightings?"

She shook her head and grinned. "Of course, I've only spent a few nights here, but no. Nothing's gone bump in the night, not even a knocking pipe to wake me. Of course, I sleep like the dead myself, so anything could be going on around me and I'd probably miss it."

She placed her bag on the table. "I'm going to run upstairs for my laptop. We should probably set it up in the library, if we're going to get on the Internet. They have wireless access there. Feel free to wander if you want."

She found him in one of the front parlors when she came back downstairs.

"I was admiring the tiles around this fireplace," he said when she came into the room.

"Mercer tile," she told him. "There are different tiles surrounding each of the fireplaces in the house. Whoever chose them had great taste."

"I agree." He straightened up. "Ready?"

"Yes." She turned a lamp on in the front window. "Just in case it's dark later."

"I'd like to stop at my car and pick up my own laptop," he told her as she locked the front door behind them.

"Because two heads are better than one?"

"That, and because I may be able to gain access to areas you might not."

"You have super-duper FBI powers?"

"Something like that." He fell in step alongside her. "And if we really need to call in the cavalry, I have a friend at the Bureau who has extraordinary computer skills. He can get into just about any place."

"How?"

"If he told me . . ."

She laughed. "Yeah, yeah, he'd have to kill you."

"That's what he tells me, so I don't ask. I just let Will do his thing." They'd reached the parking lot, and Connor unlocked his trunk. He opened it, took out a black leather case, and slammed the trunk lid closed.

"The library's just over on this side of campus," she told him. "It's not far."

"I'm not in a hurry. Besides, I like the company."

She couldn't think of a response, so she let it go.

They went into the library, which on a hot Sunday evening was deserted except for the lone librarian at the front desk. Not bothering with the pretense of a welcoming smile, she glanced pointedly at the clock above the door—no doubt noting the late hour—before gesturing in the direction of the cubicles where Internet access was available.

Connor and Daria took seats next to each other, then booted up.

"What's the procedure?" he asked.

"First, we go to our favorite search engine." Daria typed in an address and Connor did the same. She glanced at his screen. They'd chosen the same one. "Next, we type in . . . oh, let's try 'artifacts from Shandihar' and see what comes up."

The screen filled with a long list of choices.

"Look here, see the second entry?" Daria leaned over and pointed at his screen. "It's a link to a newspaper article from Westport, Connecticut." She clicked on the link on her computer. "Justin and Cloris Porter. Collectors of antiquities."

She began to skim the article.

"Here you go, third paragraph. 'Their collection contains a very rare ceremonial goblet from the lost city of Shandihar, an ancient settlement in what is now Turkey that was excavated in the early 1900s and later lost again when an earthquake struck the region.' "

Daria took a notepad and pen from her bag and wrote down the names and location of the item.

"See? Not so difficult," she told Connor cheerfully. "We don't need an FBI team to do this. We'll go through all these links, then we'll start on the museums."

"Don't get overly confident," he cautioned. "Maybe you just got lucky."

"And got lucky again." She tapped him on the arm and pointed to her screen. "It appears that Damian Cross from Centerville, Delaware, is the proud owner of a statue of the goddess Ereshkigal." She glanced over at Connor. "Centerville is really close, maybe a forty-five-minute drive. We could go . . . or should we try to get a number and call first?"

"I think we should just drop in on him. For one thing, if you call, maybe he doesn't like what he's hearing, he hangs up. If you cold-call, once you get your foot in the door, he's likely to hear you out."

"Okay, so let's go." Daria began to stand.

"Let's finish up first. I know you're eager to get going, but let's get all the info we can now, then we'll start tracking people down."

"All right." She sat back down. "You're right. It's going to make me crazy, though, knowing that there's a piece so close. Just down the road, practically."

"If he still has it, it'll most likely be there tomorrow."

"True."

"And this way, we'll track what we can, check off what we've found on the list, then maybe have this friend of mine see what he can do before we decide whether we want to turn over the list to the Bureau."

"Good point." She resumed her search. "Why don't you stick with the private collectors, and I'll start going through the museums."

"How will you know if a museum has any of the missing items?"

"Easy. Many of them list their exhibits by name and identify not only the artifacts, but where they came from." She typed for a moment, then sat back and said, "For example, here's the website for the Metropolitan Museum of Art. Over here on the left, we'll click on Permanent Collections. There, you have a listing of their collections. We'll click on Ancient Near Eastern Art . . ."

"You can see photos of what they have right online." He shook his head. "Why does this strike me as being too easy? Shouldn't someone have done this before?"

"Why would anyone? Who would have known to look? Remember," she lowered her voice to a whisper, "no one knows it's here but us."

"I hope you're right about that," he muttered.

"Well, they certainly have a wonderful collection, but I don't see any sign of what we're looking for. Not that I'd expect to, but I wanted to show you how easy it can be to track things. And see how under the photograph of each item they list the provenance of the piece. Where it came from, whether it's on loan from a private collection or donated outright or purchased, and the year of its acquisition."

Connor watched over her shoulder as she skipped from one item to another.

"Do all museums have their collections available like this?" he asked.

"There's one way to find out." She closed out the screen and typed the name of another museum into the search engine. "Let's see what they have."

They spent the next several hours searching the Internet, but came away with a mere six artifacts in private hands. Interestingly, four were within driving distance of Howeville.

"That's six more than we knew about this morning," she reminded Connor as they walked across a quiet campus. "And all very significant pieces, three of the collectors are almost in our backyard. One in Greenville, the other two here in Pennsylvania. Which makes me think there's a dealer—or was, at one time—close by. Maybe in Philadelphia or Wilmington."

"I want to get on this right away. We'll start tomorrow with Damien Cross," Connor said thoughtfully. "He's the closest, and he might know of other collectors and be able to direct us to someone else. We'll find out who sold him the piece, and when, and maybe we can track down the dealer or the party who sold it to *him*. Then we'll move on to the Blumes—Anderson and Kelly, they're the couple in Gladwyne, Pennsylvania—and from there, we'll go see Mrs. Sevrenson in Philadelphia. We'll leave the two parties in New England—the Westport couple and the woman in Marion, Massachusetts—for last."

"Sounds like a plan. I can't wait to get started."

"You're really enjoying this, aren't you?" Connor couldn't help but smile. "You're just beaming from ear to ear."

"Well, it was a successful search. We're close to at least a few of the missing artifacts, and maybe tomorrow we'll even get to see one of them. I'd say that was a good day's work."

"Agreed." They'd reached McGowan House and stopped at the end of the walk.

"You're not driving back to Maryland tonight, are you?" Daria asked.

"I don't have a reservation anywhere, but I noticed a motel on the main drive coming into town, right off the highway. I'm sure I can get a room."

"Great. I'll see you in the morning."

"See you then." He walked off into the night.

Daria entered the quiet house and locked the front door behind her. She dropped the bag holding her laptop at the bottom of the steps and went into the kitchen. It was closing in on eleven, and she realized that she hadn't eaten all day. She rummaged in the refrigerator and came out with an orange. She made a piece of toast and spread it with honey from the jar Vita had brought her that morning from one of the local farms and ate standing up. Her hunger sated, she sat at the table and went over her notes.

Six, she told herself. This morning she'd known only that they were missing. Now she knew where they were, or at the very least, where they had been. There was always the possibility that one or more items had been sold or gifted or loaned to a museum. For now, it was enough to know that these six artifacts existed and were almost within reach. And there was also the very real possibility that some of the owners might know of other pieces in other private collections.

She opened her bag and took out her notebook, prepared to check off the items which may have been located. She noticed that her phone, which she'd silenced in the library, was blinking to alert her to a new message.

"Daria, it's Louise. I couldn't wait until morning, so I called Jim Sanders. We have a meeting with him tomorrow morning at eleven. Please meet me at my office by nine-thirty and we'll go over to the museum together and select a few items to take with us. See you then."

Daria erased the message and scrolled the phone's list of calls received. When she found the number from which Connor had called her two nights ago, she hit send and waited while it rang.

"Shields."

"Connor, it's Daria. I just got a message from Louise about tomorrow. We have an appointment with the bank at eleven, and I'm meeting her at nine-thirty to go to the museum and select a few of the artifacts to take with us."

"Do you want me to come with you?"

"I don't know." She frowned. She hadn't thought of that. "I don't know if the presence of the FBI would alarm the banker or reassure him."

"In that case, go without me but let him know we're on the case if you feel you have to. I'll spend the morning trying to locate more of the artifacts. I've already put a call in to my friend at the Bureau to see what he suggests, so maybe we can add to that list we started tonight."

"Good idea. How about I call your cell when I get back from the bank?" Through the phone, she could hear sirens and traffic sounds in the background. He was still on the road.

"Great. Then you can let me know what the banker had to say and I'll tell you what the FBI's computers have been able to dig up."

"Deal. I'll see you then. Good night, Connor."

"See you tomorrow."

Daria disconnected the call and dropped the phone into her bag. She wondered if she should have offered him a room here at McGowan House. There were five empty rooms on the second floor. Funny, if he'd been one of her colleagues, she wouldn't have thought twice about having a man stay in the house. The men she spent time with in the field were all friends, and nothing more. They shared commonalities of education and philosophy and reverence for the past. They spent much of their days together on a dig, painstakingly sorting through the debris of the ages, and their nights gathered around a communal fire talking about the day's finds and frustrations. There had been the occasional fling, but other than a professor in Near Eastern studies she'd met two years ago at a symposium at Harvard, serious affairs had been few and far between. She thought of the men with whom she'd spent the greater part of her adult life in the field, and couldn't name one who had sparked more than a professional interest. Compared to Connor, they all appeared in her memory as dry and pale. Intellectually stimulating, perhaps, and comfortable companions, but not the sort of men who set your pulse racing.

There was nothing dry or pale about Connor Shields.

Stimulating, on the other hand . . . yeah, she could say that. Tall and rugged, a killer smile. Nope, nothing dry or pale there . . .

Careful, girl, she told herself as she got up and went to the back door to make sure it was locked. *He's probably not going to be around for that much longer, and even if he was, do you really think you're his type?*

She tried to close the windows, but except for one, once opened, it was as if they were resisting being returned to the position they'd been stuck in for God only knew how many years. Daria gave up and gathered her notes, her bag, and the phone from the table and turned off the kitchen light. She checked the front door, turned off the lamp in the parlor window, and headed up the steps.

In Iliana's bedroom, she paused and glanced in the mirror that stood on the dressing table near the window. Nothing flashy about that face, she told herself. She ran a hand through her hair, which had grown out since the last time she'd cut it. Good enough for the field, but maybe now a real cut from someone who knew what they were doing might be in order. Maybe even some makeup.

Forget it. She turned away from the mirror and went into the bathroom and turned on the shower. What was she thinking? Neither a new hairstyle nor a new face would make her anything other than what she was, and right now she was . . . well, field-weary, her mother would say. Tired from trekking over hills and mountains, with dark circles under her eyes and skin dry from too much desert sun.

"Yeah, I'm a real glamour girl," she said softly as she stripped off her clothes and headed for the shower. "Chances are there's a woman in his life anyway, so don't set yourself up for a fall."

All the same, she thought as she began to shampoo her hair, she could use a cut with a little style. After all, if she stayed at Howe for a while, there'd be meetings with the bankers and the trustees and members of the archaeology department, and eventually the media, if they really got this project off the ground. She would need to look a little more polished—all right, a lot more polished—and less like she'd just crawled out of a tent.

She made a mental note to ask Louise if she could recommend a salon.

SEVEN

"**H**ow'd you make out at the bank?" Connor asked when Daria opened the door to McGowan House around one the next afternoon.

"We caused quite the commotion." She grinned. "Louise's banker took one look at the pieces we'd brought with us and immediately called in the branch manager and several others. Long story short, they're preparing a vault and will have an armored truck pick up the crates as soon as humanly possible. In the meantime, they've hired armed guards, the first of whom should arrive by three."

"Pretty much as I thought. They're not going to take any chances. I figured they'd want the entire collection safely under lock and key."

"Right. Their lock and key. Which is as it should be. If they're going to loan such a huge amount of money to the school, they're going to want to protect their collateral. They've already locked up the artifacts we took with us. We left them in one of the vaults." Daria walked toward the kitchen and Connor followed. "There's a meeting scheduled at the bank's main branch in Wilmington on Wednesday, to show the finance guys some of the collection."

"So the loan looks like a go?"

"They're giving Howe a modest line of credit to start out, but I'm sure that getting money for the building repairs isn't going to be a problem." She was still grinning from ear to ear. "There was so much excitement in that room when we started unwrapping the pieces we'd brought with us. I've been handling antiquities for so many years, I'd forgotten how it feels to see something like that for the first time."

"I take it they were blown away."

"Totally. And I have to admit I got just the tiniest kick out of the drama, you know? Building the suspense by telling them about my great-grandfather's quest; reading to them from his journal; slowly unwrapping each piece . . ."

"Sounds like an archaeological striptease."

Daria laughed. "And every bit as provocative, I assure you."

"I never would have suspected it of you, but it sounds as if you got the job done."

"There was an audible, collective gasp when I unwrapped the goblet and let them pass it around the table."

"You should have your own TV show, like that guy on the Discovery Channel."

She looked at him blankly.

"Guess you don't watch a lot of TV," he said.

"Not so much. By the way, Louise has already spoken with her insurance agent. They're lining up an appraiser for the artifacts and one of their property people is coming to look at the building ASAP. Maybe as early as tomorrow."

"So all she needs now is a number and an okay from the bank." Connor took a seat at the kitchen table.

"Cutting to the chase, yes. Of course, the bank is going to want to have everything authenticated. Fortunately, there is someone at the

Philadelphia Museum of Art who is qualified, and they're going to try to get her down here quickly. Hopefully, she and the insurance appraiser can work together. It's very hard to put a dollar value on some of these artifacts, and I'm hoping the art historian from the museum can help the appraiser understand that."

"You know, even if you decide not to take the job, you've already done the university a great service."

"Are you kidding? If they get the funding, no way I'm walking away from this." Daria leaned against the kitchen counter. "There will never be another opportunity like it. Besides, I feel this is something I'm *supposed* to do."

"Because Alistair was your great-grandfather?"

"If I said I didn't feel that connection, I'd be lying. I've read all his journals. I feel as if I know him. I understand how and why his imagination was captured by the poets who'd written about the City Ruled by the Queen of the Night—that's how Shandihar was known in antiquity. I understand, because I was drawn to the field by similar stories, stories told by my own father. And I understand how his curiosity grew into obsession, and how he felt when he stood on that mound of rocks and sand and knew that the object of his quest lay beneath his feet. I felt as if I was there with him. When he described how it felt to touch the past with his own hands, I knew the feeling intimately."

"Because you've felt all those things, too."

"A thousand times." She jammed her hands into the pockets of her shorts. "I've brushed away dirt from the face of a hundred idols, and uncovered the bones of kings and priests, farmers and potters. When you live in that world—the world where the past surrounds you—you experience life in a different way. You see what's important, what lasts and what falls away." She paused, as if gathering her thoughts. "You see the evolution of society through countless eyes, and you see the patterns of society that emerge over the centuries, the advancements, how one society builds upon the discoveries of a previous one. How knowledge is shared, how religions spread. You develop a deep respect for those who lived in ancient times, believe me, when you've uncovered their homes and seen how they lived, who they loved. You hold the cups they drank from, the combs they used to dress their hair, a statue of the deity they worshipped, and you *feel* them."

"I imagine being the daughter of both an anthropologist and an archaeologist, you would be as mindful of the individuals as you are of the civilizations you've studied."

"You remembered that, about my parents?" She smiled, pleased that he'd recalled their conversation over dinner the night they met.

"I remember everything you said," he told her. "I remember you were going to give me some information about your brother—Jack, right?—and I was going to see if some friends of mine could get a lead on him."

"Yes, Jack." She nodded. "If you're serious, I can get copies of the reports written by the investigators my parents have hired over the years. That's probably the most accurate way to bring you up to date. My parents have a full file of reports."

"Of course I'm serious. Get them to send you copies of those reports and we'll take a look."

"Thank you. I'd really appreciate that. And I know my parents will. I'll give them a call right now." She patted her pockets for her phone. "I must have left my phone upstairs when I changed after the meeting with the bank. Hang on for a sec while I run up and get it."

She was almost out of the room when he asked, "Daria, do you ever worry that you spend more time in the past than you do in the present?"

"Why would you ask that?"

"Because you never talk about your own life in terms of today or tomorrow."

"I never think about it. But I suppose it's because the past is my job, my career."

"But it doesn't need to be the focus of your life," he said softly. "What do you do when you're not working? What do you do for fun? Who are your friends?"

"There aren't too many times when I'm not working, and frankly, I think my work is fun."

"And your friends?"

"Mostly people I've worked with." She crossed her arms defensively. "How many of your friends are in the FBI, Connor? How much of your life do you devote to your job?"

"Point taken." He nodded. "Most of my friends are in the Bureau, and I do spend much of my time working on my cases."

"So what's the difference between you and me?"

"The difference is that I live my life in the present," he told her. "You seem to live a lot of yours in the past."

She reddened but did not reply.

"Don't you want a here and now?" he asked. "Don't you want a story of your own?"

She stared at him for a long moment, then left the room.

Good move, Shields, he chastised himself as her footsteps echoed down the hall, then seconds later on the stairs leading to the second floor. What had he been thinking, saying such personal things to her? And who was he to question how she lived her life?

"No one," he answered himself aloud. "No one at all."

Daria was an intelligent woman who'd made her choices a long time ago, and appeared to be happy with those choices. She was well-known, had published widely, and was successful on an international level.

Connor wryly thought that he, too, could make this last claim, though his success was certainly on a far different level than hers.

"The eagle and the dove," he muttered aloud.

"What?" Daria walked back into the kitchen, her shoulder bag over her arm and a folder fat with paper in her hands.

"Listen, I'm sorry. I had no right to say what I did. It's your life and one you're obviously happy with, so just forget what I said."

She waved a hand dismissively. "My parents are going to send me a copy of their file on Jack. I'll let you know when it comes. They said to tell you thank you. But right now, we have other things to talk about. Was your friend at the FBI able to locate any of the missing artifacts?"

"Yes, he was." Connor opened his briefcase and took out several pieces of paper. "Quite a few, actually."

"Yes!" She grinned and reached for the papers, her previous pique apparently forgotten.

Connor handed them over, saying, "There are several galleries that have objects on loan, and two or three that have purchased pieces outright. Assuming that these are authentic and are in fact from Shandihar . . ."

"Easy enough to check." She opened her folder. "Here's the list of items we're missing. Let's see what matches up."

Daria took the chair next to Connor and handed back his papers. "What's first on your list?"

Connor picked up the top sheet of paper and read, "Bronze and gold figure of woman believed to be high priestess of Ereshkigal. Circa 1000 b.c. Shandihar. Gift of Celina Shaw, 1965."

Daria scanned the list she'd made of the missing objects.

"Bronze and gold priestess. Check." She glanced up from the list. "Where is it?"

"In the Raines Gallery in Boston."

"Great. What else?"

"Large silver jug. Circa 900 b.c. Shandihar. On loan from a private collector, 1998. The William Joseph Peaks Gallery, St. Louis."

"Silver jug . . . large. Yes, got it." She tapped her pen on her bottom lip. "I wonder if we can get the gallery to tell us who the owner is."

"If you can't, we can." He leaned against the back of the chair. "I'm still not sure we shouldn't turn this over to the art-theft people. I understand all your reasons, and I respect the fact that you want to protect the owners. But the more I think about it, the less I think anyone is going to simply hand something over to you. I mean, why would they?"

The pen continued to tap away on her lip.

"Because somewhere along the line, these artifacts came into the mainstream through the back door. At some point, there was an illegal sale, and no respectable collector or gallery wants their name sullied. No one wants to be suspected of having bought from the black market, or from a shady dealer."

"These people, who probably paid large sums of money for the pieces they bought, are going to believe you . . . why?"

"Because I'll have the journals with me, I can show them—"

"Yeah, yeah, the journals. The inventories. Daria, that sort of thing can be faked."

"Well, then, I'll have you with me."

"You are very naïve if you think that you're going to walk out of anyone's house with any of these artifacts in your hands."

"I never expected that to happen. What I expect is that people will call their lawyers, who will then call the university, their lawyers will talk to Howe's lawyers, and things will go from there. There will be meetings, negotiations, that sort of thing. In the end, I suspect that some of the pieces will be 'donated' to the university by the present owners. Besides giving them the cachet of being donors, it gives them a healthy tax write-off and the opportunity to get some very positive press when the museum is ready to open. Howe is more likely to see the return of at least some of the items that way."

"That makes sense. I think."

"Look, you have to understand the people who collect these things. They invest a lot of money to have something that no one else has."

"All the more reason not to hand it over because some very pretty woman rings the doorbell and asks for it."

"They'll respond better to me—someone who understands the

piece, who understands the way the market works—than they will to having a couple of badges waved in their face. One badge makes it official business. More than one badge makes people think they're about to be arrested. Plus, when given the choice between having your reputation damaged and the chance to come out looking like a philanthropist, most people are going to choose door number two."

"All right. We'll try it your way and see what happens." His eyes dropped to the report. "A pair of bronze griffins . . . are these the ones you mentioned earlier?"

"No, those were gold. Where are the bronzes?"

"The Hollenbach Gallery in Chicago. Purchased through the gift of Emory and Doris Wilcox, 1951."

"They're not going to want to give those back if they purchased them. That one might have to go to your team of experts," Daria told him. "If the piece is on loan, the gallery or museum doesn't have to make a decision; they can just refer back to the owner. But if funds were spent to purchase the item, you have a board of directors to be dealt with, and you might have corporate issues. Those pieces could end up in litigation."

"So let's put together a list of the items we're going to go after, and I'll turn the others over to the Bureau."

"All right," she said with some reluctance. "It's probably for the best. Let's see what else you have."

They worked through the rest of the list and by two-thirty, Connor had called John Mancini, explained the situation, and promised to e-mail a list of the items and their present locations when he got back to his motel room.

When he got off the phone, he told Daria, "I know you hated having to do that, but look at it this way, once the Bureau gets involved, you can use that to reason with the private collectors."

"You can deal with me quietly now and we can resolve this, or I'm going to have to turn it over to the FBI. They're already on the case, but

I thought it better for you personally if we handled this matter between you and the university . . ." She talked it out. "Makes them feel as if they're being given special treatment."

"Exactly."

"All right. We'll try that." She slid the folder into her shoulder bag and said, "So we're headed to Centerville first, right? Damian Cross and his statue of the goddess?"

"That's a good place to start. You know how to get there?"

"Roughly."

"Roughly, eh?" He stood and gathered the papers from the table. "I don't suppose that rental car of yours has GPS?"

She frowned. "What does GPS mean?"

"It means we're taking my car."

EIGHT

The main road leading to Centerville, Delaware, was tree-lined and cool, even under the August sun. Many of the houses Connor drove past were set on wide lawns, the air of wealth and privilege more pervasive than the humidity. Here and there, private lanes led over gently rolling hills that hid handsome homes from curious eyes. Large estates, their boundaries marked by the ubiquitous split-rail fences, sat quietly in the distance.

"I've been through this area before," Daria noted, "when I was younger. One of my aunts took Iona and me."

She pointed to a sign on the left side of the road.

"That's Winterthur, down that lane. It's a museum. It was the home of one of the DuPonts, but I don't know which one," she told him. "It houses a world-famous collection of American art and furniture. The grounds are magnificent."

"Open to the public?"

"Yes." She turned in her seat as they passed what seemed to be endless fields surrounding the old estate, which wasn't visible from the road. "I'd like to go back while I'm in the area. I'd like to see it through adult eyes. I imagine I'll have a different sort of appreciation for their displays. I remember being so impressed with the house, the one time I was there. I must have been nine or so, and we'd just come back from a summer trekking around some ruins somewhere in the Mediterranean, I can't even remember which ones. So when our aunt told us she was taking us to see a famous old American house, well, of course, we were expecting something completely different."

"You expected to find ruins." Connor's mouth tilted in a smile.

"Exactly." Daria grinned. "Imagine our surprise when we arrived at this very elegant, gracious manor house, surrounded by beautiful gardens and woods. And inside, the loveliest furniture, paintings, china. My sister and I felt like total bumpkins."

"Maybe we'll get to go sometime soon. You can take me on a tour." Connor glanced at the GPS monitor. "We take the next left."

"Amazing little device, isn't it?" Daria stared at the small screen. "Like having a tiny person in your car who always knows exactly where you're supposed to go."

"That's the idea." Connor put on his turn signal and waited for a truck to pass.

"This is one zippy little car, isn't it?"

He smiled. "Would you like to drive home?"

"Uh-uh. My most recent driving machines have been a centuries-old Honda and that little Ford I got from the rental place. Very basic transportation. Nothing at all like this." She touched the dash appreciatively. "I've never driven a Porsche before."

"Then you should take the opportunity while you have it."

"Maybe another day." She pointed to the monitor. "If I'm reading this correctly, Damian Cross's house should be right up there on the left."

"I believe you're right." Connor slowed and turned onto a cobbled drive. He parked in front of a stand-alone garage and turned off the ignition. "Let's see if Mr. Cross is around."

"There's no car, but he has"—she counted—"four, five garage bays to park in. He must own a lot of cars."

Connor inspected the outside wall of the garage.

"A lot of cars or a lot of something he likes to keep at a controlled temperature." He pointed to the gauges. "Looks like it's air-conditioned and heated. Must have something good in there."

"Too bad the windows have those pesky shades, otherwise we could see." Daria looked around. "And he sure does like these cobbley stones. Not just the driveway, but the walkway, and it looks like a patio out back and that area around the pool are all made of the same stones."

Connor followed her gaze. "He's got quite a place. Old restored farmhouse set nicely off a narrow country road, pretty gardens out back, looks like fruit trees on the other side of the house. Mr. Cross seems to have his own little Eden here."

"I can't wait to see the inside of the house." Daria smiled and tugged on Connor's arm. "As beautifully restored as the exterior is, I bet the inside is just gorgeous."

They walked around to the front of the house.

Daria pointed to the foundation plantings. "The landscaping is impeccable. I'd say Damian Cross is a man of some means. Probably has lots of really nice antiques in there."

"We'll know in a minute," Connor said as he rang the doorbell. Immediately, a dog began barking wildly on the other side of the door.

When no one answered the door, Connor rang the bell again.

"I don't think anyone is home, Connor," Daria told him. "Between the doorbell and the dog, I think anyone inside would know we're here."

The dog continued to bark and scratch at the door.

"Dog doesn't sound too friendly." Connor noted. "Think I should leave a card?"

"I think coming home and finding a business card from the FBI might spook him. He might not call. Why don't we just drive up to

Gladwyne and see if the Blumes are home, then check again on our way back?"

"Cross could be at work at this hour. Let's see how far we are from the Blumes."

They walked back to the car and got in. Connor turned on the engine, then entered the Gladwyne address into the GPS system.

"A little over an hour," he said. "It's almost three. Want to give it a try?"

"Sure."

He started back the way they'd come, and Daria said, "I guess the new security people should be arriving at the museum right about now."

"Were you supposed to be there?"

"No. Louise and Stefano Korban, the only archaeology professor on campus this summer, will be meeting them. Louise thought my time was better spent tracking down the artifacts at this point, and I totally agree."

"Have you met Korban?"

"No. I'm sure I will soon, though. Louise thinks highly of him." She watched out the window as the scenery changed from country fields and quaint antiques shops to restaurants and gas stations. Up ahead was the Brandywine Battlefield, and farther still, several more restaurants and a small strip mall. Connor swung into the left lane to turn onto a highway that led northwest.

"It's interesting that for a small school with no money and no real reputation to speak of, Howe has several people on staff who are well-known in the field of archaeology."

"This Korban guy?"

"Yes. He and the head of the department, Sabina Bokhari. You'd expect to find professors with their credentials at places like Penn or Yale. Not Howe."

"Why do you suppose they're here?"

"I don't know."

"You could probably ask them."

"Maybe I will." She smiled and leaned back against the seat.

Forty minutes later, Connor pulled up in front of a large colonial-style home situated on a wide, grassy lot in a very upscale neighborhood. A for sale sign spelled out the name of a real-estate company in red letters, above which a likeness of the realtor, Nancy Keenan, beamed. A phone number ran across the bottom of the sign.

"Well, at least we caught them before they moved," Daria said as they got out of the car and started across the lawn.

"I'm not so sure of that," Connor replied. "The house looks vacant. You can see through the front windows clear to the back of the house."

They walked up to the front door and peered through the side lights.

"You're right, I spoke too soon," Daria said. "The house is totally cleaned out."

"Let's walk around back." Connor gestured for her to follow him.

The Blumes' backyard was a peaceful oasis consisting of a stone patio with a wall on three sides and a koi pond at one end, and quiet, lush gardens in shades of cool greens.

"It's lovely," Daria said. "I'd sure be hard-pressed to leave a house like this."

Before Connor could comment, a car pulled into the driveway at the house next door.

"Let's see if the neighbor knows anything," Connor said as he took off across the lawn.

Daria caught up to him just as he was introducing himself to the neighbor, a petite blond woman wearing a short denim skirt and a coral T-shirt. Her face was mostly hidden by very large dark glasses, and she wore sandals of braided leather.

The woman placed a shopping bag bearing the name of a tony-sounding store on the ground next to her car. "I'm happy to see someone looking at the house. We'd love to have new neighbors. With the houses spread out the way they are here, and us being one in from the corner, it's gotten a bit lonely. We'd love to see the house inhabited again."

"Did you know the previous owners well?" Connor asked.

"I'd say we knew them fairly well," the neighbor seemed to choose her words carefully. "They were about twenty years older than we are, so we didn't socialize a whole lot, except for holidays. Someone in the neighborhood always had a big open house, so we'd see them then. And sometimes I'd see her out on the patio and she'd invite me over for a cup of coffee or something, and we'd chat. So we were friendly, but not the best of friends, if you follow. Still, we really do miss them. They were lovely people."

"How long ago did they move?" he asked.

"They didn't exactly move," she said with some apparent discomfort.

"What do you mean?" Connor frowned.

"Look, the realtor said we shouldn't talk about it to anyone, that we should just direct potential buyers to her. That's probably what I should do."

"We're not potential buyers," Connor told her. "We're trying to track down the Blumes. Do you know how we can contact them?"

"Really, you need to talk to the realtor. Her name and number are on the sign." She picked up her shopping bag and went through a service door into her house.

"Well, that was odd," Daria said. "What do you suppose that was all about?"

"Maybe there was some scandal, maybe the Blumes went bankrupt and the bank took the house." Connor found his phone in his pocket and walked toward the sign. When he got close enough to read it, he punched in the numbers for the real-estate office, and hoped that Nancy Keenan was around.

He was in luck. She was not only there, but willing to show the house right away if Connor could wait five minutes for her.

The realtor drove up the driveway in a brand-new sedan and

parked at the end of the drive. She was very fashionably dressed in a short black linen dress and sandals with kitten heels. Her dark hair was expertly cut—a fact that did not go unnoticed by Daria—and she carried a large black bag of pebbled leather. All in all, her appearance was very upscale, as befitted the neighborhood.

"Thanks for waiting, Mr. Shields." She extended a well-manicured hand. She turned her attention to Daria. "And Mrs. Shields. Nice to meet you."

"Oh, I'm not—"

"We appreciate you dropping everything and coming over to show us the house," Connor said smoothly, placing a hand on the back of Daria's neck and giving it a very gentle squeeze. "We were just passing through and saw the sign."

"It's a wonderful neighborhood, isn't it? Did you look around the outside while you waited, as I suggested?"

"We did, yes. Very nice." Connor nodded.

Fishing her keys from her shoulder bag, Nancy waved them on to the front door, which she unlocked and held open so that Daria and Connor could enter.

"Don't you love the chandelier here in the foyer?" She stepped past them and went straight to the kitchen. "Let me turn on the air and cool the house down. I usually try to do this before buyers arrive. Would you prefer to wait outside until it cools off a bit?"

"No, we're fine," Daria said and winked at Connor. *If Nancy thinks this is hot, she's obviously never been in the Sahara in summer.* He got it, and winked back.

"Then let me show you around the first floor. As you can see, the foyer floor is marble—that's Italian marble, by the way, hand-selected by the previous owners."

"Really?" Daria said, feigning interest.

"Oh, yes. They oversaw every bit of the renovation, just three years ago," Nancy assured them. "Everything was replaced, and I mean everything."

"I noticed the living room has a lot of niches built into the walls," Connor said.

"The people who lived here were collectors. They had a very valuable collection of ancient pottery and things of that nature."

Connor went up the steps ahead of Nancy and Daria, looking through every room until he found the master bedroom.

"This is a wonderful space," Nancy said, coming into the room a few minutes behind him. "Large bedroom, sitting room with a fireplace, two dressing rooms, baths, and walk-in closets."

"It looks like the carpet in here is brand-new," Connor noted. "Here in the bedroom, and in the hallway."

"Yes, it was replaced before the house went on the market."

"Funny," he said, "you'd expect the downstairs carpet to have more wear, and require replacing before the bedroom carpet. Especially since everything in the house was replaced within the past three years. Isn't that what you said?"

"Yes." She shifted her gaze to the pull shade in the front window and pretended to fuss with it. "It was an odd color."

"Was it red?" he asked.

She turned to him and, all the charm now gone, asked flatly, "Who are you?"

He held out his badge. "We're looking for the Blumes."

"If you're really with the FBI, you shouldn't have any trouble finding out what happened to them. I'm sure you can get the reports—"

"Let's say we want to hear your version."

"The Blumes were murdered in this house a few months ago. It's made it a real hard sell."

"What can you tell me about it?" Connor asked.

"Very little. Just what was in the papers, actually. The son listed the house, and he didn't want to talk about it, so I didn't pump him for information. All I know is what everyone else knows. The Blumes were at the Academy of Music in Philadelphia on a Saturday night, they came home and apparently caught someone in the act of burglarizing their home. They were both killed."

"The killers ever caught?"

"Not as far as I know. It really cast a pall over the neighborhood, though," Nancy told them. "Everyone was very nervous for months afterward, though the police said the Blumes were most likely targeted because they had a lot of valuable things in their house and never made any effort to hide that fact."

"Things from their collection?" Daria asked.

"Yes. They often loaned things to the museum in Philadelphia, that's how important some of their items were. There was a big article about them in *Philadelphia Magazine* about a year ago."

"You mentioned a son . . ."

"Yes, Martin Blume." Nancy took a card from her purse and a small notebook. "I can give you his number if you give me a minute, Agent Shields."

"Take your time."

"Here we go." Nancy wrote on the back of the card and handed it to Connor.

"Thanks, Nancy," he said as he pocketed the card. "We appreciate it."

"How did you know?" Nancy asked as they started down the steps. "About the blood on the carpet?"

"I could smell it," he told her when they reached the bottom.

"Great." She grimaced. "No wonder the house isn't selling . . ."

"Who's next on the list?" Connor asked when he and Daria were back in the car.

"Elena Sevrenson." Daria's seat belt closed with a click. She read off the Philadelphia address to him. "Could you really smell blood in that bedroom?" she asked as he programmed the address into the system and started the car.

"Nah. But I could smell the chemicals they used to remove it. That smell lingering in the room for so long, well, that says blood-soaked carpet and the floor underneath to me."

"Guess that wasn't such a good idea, having a magazine feature your collection of valuable antiques and artwork," Daria said. "You think that's what happened? Someone read about it and decided to rob them while they were out?"

"I think that's probably how the thief or thieves found out about their collection, but I doubt the robbery took place while the Blumes were gone. They would have had a killer security system in place. As a matter of fact, I recognized the name of the company on the keypad by the front door. They handle a lot of specialty security on the East Coast. I doubt your local burglar could have gotten around it. I think it's more likely someone was waiting for the Blumes when they returned home that night, made the Blumes unlock the house, robbed them, then killed them."

"I wonder what they took—and how the Blumes died."

"We're about to find out." Connor speed-dialed a number and waited for the call to be answered. "Will. Connor. How's it going? Good, good. Listen, I need you to put those legendary computer skills to work for me. Here's what I need . . ."

Elena Sevrenson's eighteenth-century town house was located on the fringe of Philadelphia's Society Hill. Like the Blumes' neighborhood, it was strictly upscale. Connor made several trips around the block before he found a parking space on the narrow city street.

"This is so pretty here. All the houses are so tidy, and so colonial-looking." Daria's admiring eyes went from one house to the next.

"These are some of the oldest continuously inhabited streets in America. They've been lived in since the 1700s," he told her.

"I feel as if I should be giving you the history lesson. After all, I'm supposed to be the expert."

"But probably not in American history." He smiled. "Which was one of my minors."

"What was the other one?"

"Political science and English lit." He checked the address and pointed to the house two doors down. "That's the place."

"You had three minors?" She frowned. "What did you major in?"

"Statistics."

"How the hell did you end up in the FBI?"

"It was sort of the family business," he said as he rang the doorbell.

The door was answered promptly by a tall, willowy woman who appeared to be in her mid-thirties.

"Yes?"

"Are you Elena Sevrenson?" Connor asked.

She surprised them by asking in return, "Who are you?"

Connor showed her his credentials and repeated the question.

"No. I'm Lily DiPietro, her niece. My aunt died four months ago."

"Ms. DiPietro, I'm so sorry," Connor told her. "May we come in for a moment?"

"Sure." She stepped back. "Agent . . . Shields was it?" She turned to Daria. "And you're?"

"Daria McGowan."

"Please, come in." Lily DiPietro led them into a living room that was perfectly furnished in a style consistent with the architecture. "May I ask why you're looking for my aunt?"

"We have reason to believe she owns an artifact that may have been stolen from a museum," Connor told her.

"That's impossible." Their hostess's stare went cold. "My aunt would never have purchased anything that had been stolen. She was very careful who she bought from, and she had very strong feelings about the black market."

"She wouldn't have known the piece was stolen, and the piece did not come into this country illegally," Daria assured her. "And depending on when she bought it, the piece was probably presented to her with credible provenance. The dealer may not have known."

"What piece are we talking about?" Lily asked. "Although it hardly matters, since everything was sold after Aunt Elena's death."

"May I ask how she died?" Connor ignored her question for the time being.

"She was murdered, Agent Shields. Right here in this house." Her eyes filled with tears.

"Was it a robbery?" asked Daria.

Lily nodded her head and lowered herself to the sofa.

"What was stolen?" Daria sat next to her.

"Just two objects."

"Would you happen to know what those pieces were?" Daria asked.

"A pair of gold griffins. Turkish, I think they were."

Daria's heart jumped in her chest.

"The funny thing was," Lily continued, "she always had something on display in three cases in the dining room. I've been telling her forever that wasn't smart, that she was asking to be robbed, but she was very stubborn. Her attitude was that she didn't collect these things to keep them locked away. She wanted to look at them, enjoy them, every day."

"May we see the display case the items were stolen from?" Connor asked.

"I can show you the cases," Lily told him, "but the items that were stolen weren't on display at the time. That's what's so strange. My aunt rotated the items every six months. The griffins hadn't been out of the vault for over a year."

She led them into the dining room and pointed to glass cases, all of which now held china birds.

Connor stood in front of the first case. There was no lock on the glass door, and he couldn't help but wonder what a person could have been thinking, keeping something valuable in so seemingly careless a manner.

"There were objects in these cases, but nothing was touched. Just the griffins from the vault. Why they took them and nothing else . . ."

"Where was the vault?" Connor asked.

"In the basement. She had it built years ago. It was even supposed to be bombproof." Lily shook her head in disbelief. "Can you imagine going to the expense of building such a thing, and then just putting things on display in your dining room? If I told her once, I told her a million times, Aunt Elena, put it all in the vault or in the bank or give it all away."

"What pieces did she have on display at the time of the theft?" asked Daria.

"Some pottery jars, I think. But the police have a full report. You can get all this information from them."

She looked across the room to where Connor stood. "Why were you looking for her anyway? What brought you here?"

"There was a theft from Howe University," Connor explained, "and though we don't know exactly when it occurred, we do know what items are missing. We identified your aunt as the owner of two of those pieces—the gold griffins—and we wanted to talk to her about how they came to be in her collection."

"The griffins were stolen?" Lily frowned. "But I'm sure my aunt had no idea . . ."

"We're equally sure," Connor assured her. "We believe she most likely purchased them from a dealer who could have acquired them from another dealer. That's one of the things we're trying to find out."

"For the past thirty or so years, she—and my uncle, when he was alive—bought from Cavanaugh and Sons on Rittenhouse exclusively. I can't imagine her acquiring any objects through anyone else. As a matter of fact, they bought the pieces I sold after her death." Lily walked them back to the living room.

"You sold her entire collection?" Daria asked.

"Except for several Egyptian items she had previously placed on permanent loan to the museum at Penn, yes. I called Mr. Cavanaugh and asked him if he was interested in helping me sell the collection, and of course he was. He sold every single piece. I couldn't bear to look at any of it. I know that's what attracted those bastards who killed her."

"How would anyone have known what she had?"

"The *Philadelphia Inquirer* ran an article last year about something she'd loaned to the art museum. When they interviewed her, they asked about her collection, and she told them. I said at the time that it wasn't a smart thing to do, but . . ." She raised both hands, palms up.

"Would you happen to have a receipt from the dealer you sold to, Ms. DiPietro?"

"Yes, Agent Shields. Would you like to see it?"

"Please."

When Lily DiPietro left the room, Connor turned to Daria. "Is there a pattern here, or have I been in this business too long?"

"The hair on the back of my neck stood straight up when she said her aunt had been murdered," Daria whispered. "Connor, who would be—"

"Here." Lily handed a sheaf of papers to Connor. He glanced at it, then passed it on to Daria. "Take a look."

Daria studied it page by page. When she reached the end, she looked up at Connor and said, "Mrs. Sevrenson had a most impressive collection. Any one of these pieces would bring a small fortune at auction. It's hard to believe that thieves would come in, ignore all this, and only take two items."

"That's what I told the police," Lily said, "but they didn't know what to make of it, either."

"Ms. DiPietro, are you absolutely certain that the griffins were stolen? Are you positive she hadn't disposed of them some other way?

Could she have sold them and not mentioned it to you? Could she have sold to a different dealer?"

"No, Agent Shields, there would have been paper on a sale." Lily shook her head emphatically. "There was nothing in her desk about a sale of the griffins."

"The pieces she loaned to Penn—are you certain they were all Egyptian?"

"Yes."

"And you're sure she didn't loan anything to any other museums or galleries?" He continued to question her.

"I'm absolutely positive. My aunt was meticulous in her record keeping. Even at seventy-nine, she kept all her books in order."

"In that case, maybe she left a record of where the griffins came from?" Daria asked hopefully.

"I'm afraid not. My uncle began the collection many years ago. Many of the pieces were purchased by him. He was apparently a very astute collector, but unfortunately, he didn't keep records very well."

Lily dabbed at her eyes with a tissue. "This whole thing has been so terrible. She was an old woman. Defenseless. They didn't have to kill her, torture her the way they did. They should have just taken whatever it was they came for and left her alone."

"May I ask exactly what happened to her?" Connor asked gently.

"It's in the police report, so I'm sure you can get a copy, but they never did make it public, it was just too grisly." Lily was openly crying. "The bastards cut off her hands." She sat on the nearest chair, as if her legs had given out. "And then they cut out her tongue, and left her to bleed to death."

NINE

Daria's hand flew to her mouth.

"Oh my God!" she gasped. White-faced, she turned to Connor. "Connor . . ."

He reached for her arm and grasped it firmly, as if he thought she needed to be held up.

"Ms. DiPietro, I'm so sorry to have upset you," he said gently. "We had no idea . . ."

The dead woman's niece said tearfully, "It was such a horrible way to die, and she was such a sweet woman. Why would anyone do such a thing? Where would someone even get the idea to do something like that?"

Connor had thoughts on that, but didn't think now was the best time to share them.

Lily turned to Daria. "I can see I've shocked you. I'm sorry, I shouldn't have been so blunt. I just should have said she was killed during a break-in and left it at that."

"No, no," a still-pale Daria insisted. "I'm glad you told us. It's important that we know."

"Why?"

"Because I can enter the killer's MO into our computer and see if there have been similar murders," Connor said before Daria could open her mouth. "We might be able to learn something about the killer or killers."

"I think the Philadelphia police already tried that," Lily told him.

"Sometimes our computer people can dig things up that someone else might miss," he said smoothly.

"If you find anything new, you'll let me know?"

"Absolutely," he promised.

"Then if there are no other questions, I really need to get going. I have theater tickets tonight and I'm supposed to meet a friend for dinner. I was just getting ready to leave when the doorbell rang."

"We're sorry to have detained you, and sorrier still for your loss." Connor shook her hand. "I apologize again if we've upset you."

"Agent Shields, I've been upset since the day she died," Lily assured him as she walked them to the door. "She was my only relative, and I hers."

"At the risk of sounding insensitive, may I assume you were the beneficiary of her estate?"

"Except for her bequest to Penn—the pieces on loan became theirs upon her death. As I said, neither of us had anyone else."

Before he left, he handed her his card. "If you think of anything at all, or if you have any questions, give me a call."

"I'll do that, Agent Shields. Thanks." Lily did her best to smile as she closed the door behind them.

"You okay?" Connor put a protective arm around Daria, and even in the summer heat of the early evening, felt her shiver.

"Connor, did you hear . . . did you get that?" She stumbled over her words.

"Yes. I got it." His jaw tightened and he slowed his step until they arrived at his car. Once inside, with the engine running, he said, "You know, I'm liking this less and less, the more I think about it. We need to know how the Blumes died. There's obviously a connection between Elena Sevrenson's death and the fact that she had those griffins."

Daria nodded. "I don't know of any culture other than Shandihar that punished in that specific manner. Her death was clearly a punishment. A condemnation." She swallowed hard. "But it's almost too crazy to be true. I mean, who outside of a few scholars would even know about any of this? This story isn't at all well-known; it isn't like Tut's tomb. And who would even know that she had the griffins?"

"Anyone who read the *Inquirer* article her niece mentioned."

"Crap. I forgot about that."

"First things first." He took the phone from his pocket and hit redial.

"Will, it's Connor. Where are we with that information I asked you for?" He reached across the front seat and gave Daria's shoulder a comforting squeeze. "Yeah, I know it's only been two hours since I called, but I'd appreciate it if you'd really turn the heat up. I need to know the cause of death . . . sure, I understand. Tell her she has to wait her turn."

He placed the phone on the console and checked the rearview mirror for traffic. He pulled out of the parking spot expertly, and headed for the center of the city.

"You agree, though, right? This is all connected?" Daria turned in her seat to face him. "Why else make Mrs. Sevrenson open the safe but only steal the artifacts from Shandihar when there were so many other valuable items right there under their noses? Why kill this woman in exactly that manner unless it's to make a statement?"

She thought that over for a moment, then said, "No, it wasn't a statement. It was a punishment."

"A punishment for owning something that was stolen from Shandihar?"

"For owning something that was stolen from the goddess," Daria said. "Those griffins were from one of the tombs in Shandihar, a tomb where one of the high priestesses was buried."

"Who the hell would know that?" Connor frowned.

"Someone who read Alistair's journals would know," she replied. "He went into quite a bit of detail about finding them and how he removed them from the tomb. I'll show you the passage when we get back to Howe."

"How many other people do you think might have read that same passage over the years?

"I have no idea. I don't know where they were kept, or how accessible they were."

He took a left turn instead of heading toward the expressway.

"We're going to make a quick stop at Mr. Cavanaugh's and see if he sold those griffins to either Mr. or Mrs. Sevrenson. If he was the dealer, he'd remember where he got them."

"And when," she pointed out. "The when is important. I think the farther back in time we go, the harder it's going to be to figure out who stole them originally, and how many hands they've passed through since then."

"Like I said, first things first. And the first thing we need to figure out is where Cavanaugh got the griffins. Next up, did the person who sold them to him realize the significance of the pieces? Where they came from, and that somewhere along the line they were stolen?"

Rush-hour traffic had just eased up, and within minutes, Connor was driving around Rittenhouse Square, looking for a sign for Cavanaugh and Sons.

"I don't see it," Daria said. "Go around again."

"Do you remember the address?" Connor asked.

"I didn't really notice," she admitted. "I take it you didn't, either."

"I figured Rittenhouse Square, how hard could it be to find?" He pulled into a parking spot on Walnut Street that was just at that moment being vacated. "Let's just get out and look around. It has to be here someplace."

The hazy August stew of heat and humidity clung to even the smartly dressed women who passed by on their way to the corner where they crossed the street. Nearby, a genteel-looking storefront announced the home of Cavanaugh & Sons, Purveyors of Antiques, in tasteful gold script. In the window, an elegant Victorian settee with red silk upholstery stood next to a delicate candlestick table, upon which sat a Deco-era vase.

"Looks like Cavanaugh's tastes pretty much run the gamut," Connor observed.

"I guess the antique-furniture market might be a little busier than the market for antiquities these days, especially since there's less and less available in the legitimate marketplace. Most collectors really are ethical when it comes to what they buy. They want to know it's come cleanly, so I'm not surprised to see dealers mixing up their stock. I would imagine one would have to, in order to make a living."

They walked to the door and as Connor reached for it, a young woman opened it and collided with him in the doorway.

"Oh! Sorry!" she exclaimed, looking up. "I didn't see you."

"My fault." Connor smiled at her.

"I was just about to lock up." She flushed red and glanced at her watch. "We close at seven on weekdays. Would you mind stopping back tomorrow?"

"Actually, we would." Connor nodded and reached into his pocket for his credentials. He held the ID up for her inspection.

"Oh. FBI?" She glanced from Connor to Daria and back again. "You're with the FBI?"

"Yes. We were hoping to speak with Mr. Cavanaugh," he told her.

"Which one?" the young woman asked.

"How many are there?"

"Three. David, Colin, and Mr. C."

"David and Colin are the sons, Mr. C. is the Cavanaugh?" Connor guessed.

"Right."

"I'm thinking Mr. C. might be the one I'm looking for. Would he have handled any dealings the shop had with Mrs. Sevrenson?"

"Oh, Mrs. Sevrenson." The woman's face clouded. "Yes, she and Mr. C. went way back. It was just terrible what happened to her."

"It was. How can I get in touch with him?" Connor asked.

"He's in Maine, on vacation. Is there something I might be able to help you with?"

"We just wanted to ask him a few questions about some pieces from Mrs. Sevrenson's collection."

"I helped Mr. C. catalog the items. I helped pack and unpack them, too, so if there was something in particular you were looking for . . . ?"

"Ms. DiPietro mentioned that there were two items stolen from her aunt's house the night she was murdered. We were hoping Mr. Cavanaugh could tell us something about those two items."

"I know that something was stolen, and I know he had to fill out something for the insurance company about the theft, but you'd really have to talk to him about that. I'm afraid I wasn't that familiar with the pieces." The young woman seemed to backtrack from her previous statement. Clearly, this was something she didn't want to be involved with.

"Do you have a phone number for him?" Connor asked.

When she hesitated, he took a card from his wallet and handed it to her. "Could you give him a call and ask him to contact me at this number?"

"Sure." She glanced at the card. "I'll let him know."

"Please tell him it's very important that we speak as soon as possible."

"I'll be sure to do that."

"Thanks. I appreciate it." Connor took Daria's arm and walked back to the car.

"Connor," she said when they'd set off for the Schuylkill Expressway, "I'm wondering if maybe we should talk to Damien Cross. Maybe he should know what's going on, what's happened to the Blumes and Mrs. Sevrenson."

He handed her his phone. "His number should be under last numbers dialed. If he answers, just let him know we'd like to speak with him."

She scrolled through the numbers until she found it. She dialed, then waited.

"I got the answering machine," Daria whispered. "Should I leave a message?"

Connor shook his head. "Let's just head back there. I have a really bad feeling . . ."

"I was hoping it was only me," she said as she disconnected the call. "What if . . ."

"Like I said, let's not get ahead of ourselves. For all we know, Damien Cross took a week at the beach."

"I don't think he would have left his dog alone inside the house if he went away for that long."

"A day trip, maybe." He didn't sound convinced.

Connor made a call to his boss, but had to leave a detailed voice mail. He hung up hoping that John wouldn't pull him off this case just yet. It was just starting to get interesting.

By seven-thirty, they were back at the Cross property and ringing the doorbell once again. And once again, the only sound of life came from the barking dog on the other side of the door.

"Let's walk around the back," Connor suggested. "Maybe there's a door unlocked."

"Are you going to go in?"

"Depends."

"On what?"

He didn't answer.

Daria followed him around the corner of the house. At the rear, they found a patio with French doors that led from the kitchen. The brown-and-white dog scratched wildly on the other side of the glass.

"Connor, that dog wants out badly." She walked to the door and leaned down to the dog's level. "What's wrong, pup? Have you been locked inside the house all day?"

I'd bet money it was more than one day, Connor thought, as he took in how skinny the dog looked.

Daria was just about to say something else when she jumped back from the glass. "Oh, God. Look at the glass."

Smears of red streaked down the outside of the door like ribbons. Connor knelt down and studied it.

"It's on the outside of the glass. Looks like a really clear handprint right here, but there's nothing on the handle." He took something from his pocket, turned his back on her and did something to the door.

"Do you have a tissue?" He asked.

She looked through her bag. "Here's a napkin."

She handed it to him. "Are you going in there?"

"No, that would be breaking and entering. Not a good idea. But at the same time, I can't help but think Cross might be in there, and he could be injured, or worse." He held the napkin over the door handle and gave it a turn. "I'm thinking maybe I'll just open the door and call inside. If he answers, I'll go in."

"And if he docsn't?"

"Then we go to plan B." He hesitated, the whining dog now appearing ready to lunge. "Pit bulls aren't known for being all that nice. I hope this one is friendlier than most."

"Not pit bull. American Staffordshire terrier," she said. "My parents used to have one, and she was an absolute lamb. I think this poor thing just wants out." She peered over Connor's shoulder. "See, the dog isn't snarling, it's just whimpering and scratching at the glass."

"Stand back anyway, just in case."

"Connor, did you pick that lock?"

"Of course not. I'm a federal agent."

"How do you know how to do that?" She ignored his halfhearted indignation.

"Spy school."

"Stop it. Even I know that FBI agents aren't spies. Seriously, where did you learn—"

The napkin still covering the handle, he opened the door and tried to grab the dog's collar. The animal was faster than Connor, though, and shot past them to the yard.

"Boy, that dog really wanted out in the worst way." Daria followed the dog toward the back of the property. "He didn't even pause to give us a sniff. And it looks like *he* is a *she*."

"Oh, man." Connor closed the door quickly.

"What?"

"Didn't you smell it?"

"Smell what?" Daria, a hundred feet into the yard, was distracted by the dog.

"Guess you weren't as close to the door as I was." He started around the side of the house. "Stay here for a minute, and don't touch the door."

"Where are you going?"

"To look for something."

Connor had gone three quarters of the way around the house before he found what he was looking for: a window where the drape was covered with an inordinate number of flies.

But only one window. Which meant the body was most likely confined in one closed room. Otherwise, there would be flies on every window, and a surge of them would have tried to escape when he'd opened the door for the dog.

He walked the rest of the way around the house but found no

other signs of anything amiss. When he returned to the patio, he found Daria filling a metal bowl with water from an outside spigot.

"Where'd the bowl come from?" He frowned. "You didn't go inside, did you?"

"No. It was on the grass." She placed the bowl on the ground. "This poor dog is so thirsty. This is her second bowl. You don't think she'll get sick, do you?"

She turned and found Connor sitting on the stone wall that surrounded the patio.

"Did you find what you were looking for?" she asked.

"I'm afraid so."

"From the look on your face, it doesn't appear to be good news."

"Not for Mr. Cross. Assuming he's inside."

"You think he's dead?"

"Yes. Well, someone is."

"Why would you think that? You didn't even go inside." She walked to where Connor sat, the dog at her heels, and sat beside him. "You didn't go inside, did you?"

"No."

"If you think he's in there, why not just go in and look?"

"Because I suspect it's a crime scene. One that I have no jurisdiction over."

"A crime scene? Jesus, this is scary. You really think Cross could be dead?" She paled. "What do we do now?"

"We're going to start by calling 911." He got up and started toward the car. The dog began to growl.

"It's all right," Daria snapped her fingers and called to it. "Here, come sit. Can you sit for me? Good girl."

Connor reached inside the car and grabbed his phone, then dialed 911.

"This is FBI Special Agent Connor Shields," he said when the dispatcher answered. "I want to report a possible homicide . . ."

· · · · ·

"She's really hungry, Connor," Daria told him. "I think she's trying to behave, but she probably hasn't eaten since, well, probably since the day Cross died. Do you think I could go inside? Maybe get her some food?"

"Sorry, but no. At least, not now."

They were sitting on the stone wall, waiting for the arrival of someone from the New Castle County, Delaware, police department.

"How long do you think Cross has been . . ." She had gone pale again. "Cross or whoever is in there."

"My best guess, based on how thin the dog is, and the number of flies on that drape, I'd have to say he's been dead for a couple of days." He stood, his hands on his hips, and walked to the end of the patio, where he remained for a moment before walking down the driveway. He watched the road for a while, then walked back toward his car.

"Maybe Cross isn't in there at all," Daria called to him. "Or maybe he's dead but he died of natural causes. A heart attack, maybe. Maybe it's not what we think."

"Maybe," he said without conviction.

The dog approached him, wagging its tail tentatively. He reached down and let it smell his hand.

"She's a sweet thing, don't you think?" Daria joined them, as restless as both Connor and the dog appeared to be.

"Yeah, she is." Connor agreed. *And maybe our only witness to what happened here,* he was thinking as he rubbed the dog's head between the ears.

A patrol car pulled into the driveway and parked behind Connor's car. A uniformed officer got out of each side in what appeared to be synchronized moves.

"You Agent Shields?" the driver asked Connor as the dog began to bark. The officer stopped and eyed it warily. "That your dog? Get it under control."

Connor held the dog's collar and unsuccessfully told it to sit. "Yes,

I'm Shields. And no, it isn't my dog. I believe it belongs to the owner of the house."

Daria grabbed the dog from him and coaxed it back onto the patio. When she told it to sit, it sat immediately.

"Good girl," Daria said softly, and tried to fade into the background. This was Connor's game.

"You called in a possible homicide?" the second officer, the younger of the two, said as he approached Connor.

Connor explained why he and Daria had been looking for Damien Cross, and what they found when they arrived at the house, from the whimpering dog to the hideous telltale smell when he opened the back door, to the flies that crawled on the drape covering the window on the far side of the house.

"Let's take a look at that." The driver, whose name plate identified him as Patrol Officer Eugene Hill, watched as Daria took control of the dog. "Why don't you show us . . ."

Daria gave up the hard stone wall in favor of one of the cushioned chairs that matched the glass-topped table on Damien Cross's patio. Over the past ninety minutes, she'd watched the sun turn the sky coral and purple as it set behind the trees at the far end of the property. It was closing in on nine o'clock, and her patience had just about run out. She was hungry, she was hot and tired and thirsty, and she had work of her own to do. She'd given her statement to the officers and had watched Connor give his. At her request, one of the officers had brought out some of the dog's food and her bowl, and Daria had fed her in increments, a little at a time, so she wouldn't eat too much too fast and get sick. She passed the time tending to the dog and trying not to think about what was going on inside the house. She was also trying not to think too much about the murders and what they could mean. The Blumes. Elena Sevrenson. Now Damien Cross.

She watched the endless stream of law enforcement personnel arrive. Forty minutes or so after the medical examiner got there, the body was brought out of the house. Crime scene technicians came, carrying lights and cameras and black bags, and from time to time, Connor would be called into the house by one of the officers. Two more patrol cars and one unmarked vehicle had pulled into the driveway since the body of Damien Cross had been discovered lying in a pool of blood in the first-floor library.

The mosquitoes were the next to arrive, and to Daria's mind, they were the last straw.

She'd made several phone calls to Louise and they brought each other up to date. She'd called her sister, Iona, and her brother, Sam, and was greatly disappointed at having to leave messages for both.

The next time Connor came out of the house, she waved him over.

"I'm really sorry that we've been held up here for so long," he apologized as he approached her, "but I think we should be able to leave very soon."

"I never knew a crime scene was so complicated, so many people coming and going."

"I suspect what they're doing here isn't so very different from what you do." He pulled out the chair next to hers and sat. "What do you do when you find a tomb to excavate, for example?"

"We go layer by layer, photographing, drawing diagrams. We number whatever we find, note the layers of soil or rock. If we find remains, we note their condition and study them thoroughly before they're moved. We make sketches, we photograph everything in context."

"Same here. The entire scene is photographed, evidence is numbered and photographed in situ, marked and tagged and placed in evidence bags. The body is carefully examined before it's moved. Not much difference, really."

"The difference is that the remains I deal with are often thousands of years old, not newly dead." She felt uncomfortable with the admission. "Actually, I've never seen a newly dead body. My experiences with

death have all been secondhand, in that I study the context of the remains, I study what's been left behind. But I don't have to study a flesh
and blood body. For me, the experiences have been more intellectual
than emotional."

"Ahhh," he said softly. "I understand. I can see why this must be
very upsetting for you. I'll check inside, see if anyone needs anything
else from me."

When Connor was halfway to the door, she called to him. "Do you
think we could take Sweet Thing with us?"

"What?"

"Sweet Thing. That's her name." Daria pointed to the dog's collar.
"It's on her tag."

"I'll ask."

"What would they normally do?"

"Probably take her to a shelter."

"I'd hate to think of her being in one of those places. She's probably confused enough. I'd like to take her back to Howe."

"Let me see what Vince Coliani, the lead detective, thinks about
that."

He disappeared into the house. When he returned ten minutes
later, he had a leash in one hand and the bag of dog food in the other.

"He said it was okay?" Daria's eyes lit up when she saw what he
carried.

"He said just take her and go quietly. If any next of kin show up
and want the dog, he'll give me a call. Frankly, I think he was glad I offered. His life just got very complicated, so it's one less detail for him
to handle. So we'll just take Sweetie Pie—"

"Sweet Thing," she said.

"Right. Let's just get in the car and go on back to Howe."

He opened the passenger-side door for her, and she got in.

"You're going to have to make room for her somehow. She's
probably going to have to sit on your lap," Connor told her. "Are you
going to be all right with that?"

"Sure." Daria somehow managed to get the seat belt on and the dog situated on her lap.

She heard the trunk slam and a moment later Connor slid in behind the wheel.

"I put the rest of her things in the trunk," he said, handing her the dog's leash. "I hope Louise is all right with you bringing her back."

"I already asked. She doesn't mind."

"You spoke with her?" Connor started the car and backed out between two police cruisers.

"Several times. My dance card wasn't exactly full tonight."

"Sorry. Crime scenes take a while to process."

"I know. I don't mean to complain. And I realize that poor Mr. Cross—they're still assuming it was him, right?"

"Yes. His wallet was in the pants pocket."

"It was the same, wasn't it? The same as Elena Sevrenson?"

Connor nodded and turned onto the road.

"This is really frightening. Two people—"

"Actually, four. I got a call back from Will Fletcher, our computer geek. It appears the Blumes died the same way."

"Dear God." Daria leaned back against the headrest. "You told the detective back there about the others?"

"Of course. I had to."

"I guess he'll contact the Philadelphia police and the police out where the Blumes lived."

"He already has. Which is what I meant when I said his life just got complicated. And the press hasn't even gotten hold of the story yet. I expect we'll be hearing from them very soon."

"Good Lord, I hadn't thought about that." She frowned. "Do you think it will all come out, even about the thefts?"

"I'd bet my life on it."

"Do you think it will hurt the school?"

"Are you kidding? This story is going to guarantee that once the museum is opened, Howe won't be able to handle the crowds. The public eats up this sort of thing. They're going to want to know more about Shandihar, about Alistair, about you."

"Ugh." Daria grimaced. "Next thing you know, someone's going to be talking about a curse."

"If there isn't one, someone will invent it."

The dog tried to get off her lap and onto the floor, so Daria moved the seat back as far as it would go.

"I can pretty much shoot that down. I certainly read no such thing in Alistair's journals, and I never heard about anything like that from my father."

"Your father read the journals?"

"Years ago. He lectured at Howe as an adult and he had an opportunity to read them, but most of what he knows he learned from talking to his father."

"His father being one of Alistair McGowan's sons?"

"Yes."

"We need to find out who else could have known about the artifacts in the museum basement. And who knew enough about Shandihar to know about the wicked punishments the priestesses meted out when they were pissed off."

"I asked Louise who else might have read the journals."

"And?"

"The journals have been kept in the president's office in a glass case all these years, for at least as long as Louise has been at Howe. She said they were in the case when she took the job, and thinks they might have been there all along. She noted that the condition of the bindings and the paper is exceptional for books that old, which they would be if they'd been kept behind glass and out of the sunlight all these years."

"Which doesn't mean they hadn't been removed, read, and returned over the years."

"Well, they have been, several times that she knows of. Members of the archaeology department have borrowed them, but never for any length of time."

"I'm assuming she knows who those department members were?"

"Only the ones during her tenure. Not before that."

"She can't be certain that they've always been kept in her office. There's always the chance that someone else had them. Maybe they were even in the library."

"That's highly unlikely." Daria shook her head. "I've seen these books, and I've seen books of that same age that have been circulated even in a very limited way. I agree with Louise."

"By the way, I spoke with John this afternoon. He agrees with me that it's time to turn the entire theft issue over to the NSAF."

"He's probably right." She looked out the window. "I thought it would be better to do this quietly, but with all these people dying . . ." She shook her head. "I think it's best if someone who knows what they're doing takes over from here."

"I was hoping you'd say that."

They drove several miles in silence.

"So, I guess you'll be going on to another case."

"As soon as John has something for me. Right now, I'm sort of between jobs."

"What exactly do you do?" she asked.

"A little of this, a little of that." His eyes never left the road.

"You're very evasive, you know that?"

He smiled as he pulled up to the stoplight, but he didn't respond.

"Louise said Dr. Bokhari will be back tomorrow night. Maybe she'll have some insights." Connor hadn't talked about his job so far, and probably wasn't going to now. And it really wasn't any of her business, so she let it go.

"Dr. Bokhari, the archaeology professor at Howe?"

"Yes. I'm looking forward to meeting her, plus it will be interesting to see what she thinks about all this."

"What do you suppose will happen with the plans to reopen the museum? Do you think they'll go ahead with it?"

"That's one of the things I spoke to Louise about. They're definitely moving forward. They have armed guards at the museum now, and the meeting with the insurance people is scheduled for tomorrow. You were right. They are sending someone out to assess the building. Along with the risk manager, they're sending a mechanical engineer to look over the systems, as well as a structural engineer. At the same time, a contractor hired by Howe is going to go through and see what renovations will be required."

"Sounds like a full house."

"I guess for me, the next logical step is to start planning the exhibits. What to put with what, how best to tell the story. Alistair's as well as Shandihar's. Their destinies were so closely tied together." She smiled in the darkness. "And it's such a romantic story, you know? Him getting sucked in by the ancient epics, struggling for so many years to find someone who believed in him, being turned down repeatedly."

"Until he met Benjamin Howe. How did they meet, by the way?"

"Howe attended a lecture Alistair gave at the Wilmington Society for the Preservation of Antiquities. He'd always been interested in the past, and was looking for something that would give his college instant cachet. He spoke with Alistair after the lecture, and offered him a position, right there on the spot."

"Lucky break for Alistair."

"In every way. He found the funding he wanted and he found Shandihar. And he found the love of his life in Iliana. In one of his journals, he wrote about the first time he saw her. 'My heart leapt within me at the very sight of her. It always would, ever thereafter.' Isn't that the most romantic thing you've ever heard?"

"Romantic, yes, but Alistair died young, didn't he? Before he got to see his find placed on exhibit to the public?"

"He wasn't so young; I think he was close to sixty when he died. Iliana was quite a bit younger than he was. And while he never did see his precious artifacts on display, he must have died knowing that he'd realized every dream he'd had. He left quite a legacy, in his work and in his family. I think he would have been very proud to know that his only grandson followed in his footsteps."

"Not to mention his great-granddaughter."

"Yes." She turned her face to the window. "I like to think he'd have been proud of that. I'd like to think he'd have been proud of all of us. Dad, Sam, Iona, Jack. Me."

"That reminds me. We need to talk about your brother Jack."

"My mother is sending me copies of all the reports. Maybe the package will be here tomorrow."

"In that case, maybe you can steal a little time away tomorrow to look it over with me. Just to see if there's anything else I need to know that's not reflected in the PI's reports."

"Are you sure you don't mind? It could get complicated."

"Complications don't scare me. Besides, I've been thinking about taking a few weeks off. Now's just as good a time as any."

"I'll bet you could think of better places to spend your vacation than Howeville, Pennsylvania."

"Oh, I don't think so." He glanced at her across the front seat. "I think I'm exactly where I want to be . . ."

TEN

I t was close to midnight when the Porsche parked in the visitor's lot. The lights were still on in the president's house and the museum, but Daria was too tired to care too much about what might be going on in either. With the exception of those two buildings, the campus was totally dark.

Before she opened the car door, Daria snapped the leather leash onto Sweet Thing's collar. The dog hopped out eagerly and immediately began to sniff the ground. Connor went to the trunk and retrieved the bag of dog food he'd taken from Damien Cross's home.

"I'll walk you down to the house," he told Daria as he took her arm.

"I'm not afraid to walk back alone," she replied. "After all, I have a 'pit bull' here to protect me."

"I think you were right about her personality. She really is more of a lamb than a lion."

"It will be nice to have her in the house. We always had dogs when we were growing up."

"What did you do with them while you were all globe-trotting?"

"My mom's sister kept whatever menagerie we had at any given time. She never had kids of her own, and was a really good sport about stuff like that."

"I guess it's hard for you to have a pet these days."

"Actually, I have a parrot. I had him when I was in grad school. He got passed around from my brother to my sister and back again when I started spending more time out of the country than in it. These days, H.D. spends most of his time with my parents."

"H.D.?"

"Hound Dog." She grinned. "I was a big Elvis fan when I was younger."

"These days?"

"Not so much."

They reached the end of the path leading to her door. Set between two enormous evergreens, the house appeared forbidding in the dark.

"Let's get you and the dog inside and get some lights on." Connor stared up at the big house.

"I'm fine, really, Connor. I'm not afraid of the dark. But I could use a hand getting the door open," she said, as the dog strained at the leash.

"Give me the key, and I'll unlock the door."

It took him a minute to find the lock and then the keyhole in the dark, but he managed to turn the key and open the door. Once inside, she snapped on the overhead light in the hall.

"Want the dog food in the kitchen?" he asked.

"Yes, but you don't have to—"

"Sure I do." He smiled and walked ahead of her toward the back of the house.

Daria unhooked the dog's leash and let her roam free to investigate her new home.

"Do you have anything to use for dog dishes?" Connor asked when she came into the kitchen.

"I think there are some glass bowls in this cabinet," she told him. She found two—one for water, one for food—and turned to place them on the floor. She hesitated for a moment, a curious look on her face.

"What?" He followed her gaze to the back window where Sweet Thing was sniffing with great purpose.

"Nothing." She shook her head. "I just thought . . ."

She waved a hand dismissively.

"What?" he asked again.

"I thought I closed that window when I went to bed last night. I don't remember opening it this morning. Of course, after the day we've had, I guess I'm lucky to remember my name."

He went to the window and peered out.

"The screen's gone," he told Daria. "It was definitely on the window when I opened it last night."

Connor unlocked the back door and went outside, the dog trotting at his heels. When Daria started to lean out the window, he looked up and said, "Try not to touch anything around the window. We're going to want to dust it for fingerprints."

He pointed to the ground. "Here's your screen. It didn't jump out of the window by itself."

"You think someone broke in?" She frowned.

"Looks that way to me. Sweet Thing, too, judging from her reaction."

The dog was scratching and clawing at the screen. When Connor lifted it by a corner to keep her from shredding it completely, the dog leaped into the air to get to it. Connor had to hold it above his head to keep her from grabbing it.

Connor came back into the kitchen holding Sweet Thing's collar with one hand and the screen with the other. When he put the screen in the butler's pantry and closed the door, the dog became agitated.

"Why is she acting like that?" Daria frowned.

"I think she smelled something she didn't like," Connor told her as he locked the back door. "Like maybe whoever handled that window."

"You think he's gone? Whoever was in here?"

"Yes, but I think he's only recently gone. Like maybe he went out the back when he heard us coming in the front."

"That's a pretty creepy thought. Not as creepy as thinking he might still be here, though."

He closed and locked the window carefully. "We'll take a look through the house and double check just to make sure, and we can check to see if anything is missing."

It took them a half an hour to go from room to room, but they found nothing disturbed. No one in the closets, no one under the beds, no one in the attic.

"Strange that someone would go to the trouble to break in to a house but not take anything," Daria noted. "I wonder what he was looking for."

Maybe not what, but who, Connor couldn't help but think.

Connor went back into the kitchen where Daria's laptop sat on the table.

"Daria, do you remember what file you were working on today before we left for Centerville?"

"Was that really only this morning?" She blew out a long breath. "It seems like days ago now."

"It sure does. But do you remember?" he persisted.

"Sure. I'd made a list of the artifacts that we thought we might have located, and where they might be."

"You're positive?"

"Absolutely."

"Do you mind if I look at something on your computer?"

"Go right ahead."

He sat at the table and pulled up Daria's documents. A few clicks of the mouse, and Connor was looking at the list. "Yes, this was the last file opened," he nodded, "but it was last opened at 10:37 P.M."

"I wasn't here at . . . oh." She sat in a chair across from Connor. "Someone else opened the file."

"And someone else now knows where the rest of the artifacts are, if they didn't already know."

"We're going to have to warn those people." She looked at him with frightened eyes.

"I can take care of that right now." He began to type. "Shit. I can't send e-mail from here. I forgot, you don't have Internet service here in the house."

"Maybe you can send it from the library in the morning."

"Maybe I can just call in the names right now." He took out his cell phone.

"It's after midnight."

"John Mancini seldom sleeps," Connor said as the number began to ring. "John, hey, it's Connor. I've got something for you . . ."

It was another hour before Connor ended his call. Exhausted, Daria was half asleep, her head resting on the kitchen table, her eyes closed.

"Daria," Connor whispered.

"I'm awake," she told him. "I just couldn't keep my eyes open any longer."

She sat up and yawned. "Did you give John all the names and addresses?"

"Yes. He'll take care of it."

"Good. I hate the thought of anyone else being tortured like that." She shuddered.

"We'll do everything we can to keep that from happening. In the meantime, you need to get some sleep. You look as if you're going to fall over."

"That's exactly how I feel." She looked at the old clock on the opposite wall. "But what about you? It's really late. How far is the motel from here? Do you still have your room?"

"I checked out this morning."

"Then stay here. There are several guest rooms upstairs. I'm afraid there's no air-conditioning, so you won't be as comfortable as you would be at a motel, but it's a lot closer."

"Hey, I sleep in tents, too, remember? There is no air-conditioning in most of the places I sleep." He grinned. "And frankly, I would have slept on your front porch if I'd had to. There's no way I'd leave you alone here, knowing that someone has already broken into your house once tonight."

"Do you really think he won't be back?"

"I really think he's done here." *At least for now.*

"Maybe we should call the police." She paused in the doorway. "At least make a report."

"I already told John. He agrees that the break-in here must be part of the whole picture. First thing in the morning, I'm going to see if I can lift prints off the windowsill and the screen. John's going to get someone from NSAF up here ASAP. And in the meantime, I think you need to get some sleep."

Daria nodded. "I have a meeting with Louise at nine in the morning." She waved for him to follow her, but first he rechecked the lock on the back door.

"I'll go look for some sheets for your bed," Daria said, yawning as she made her way up the stairs, "if you wouldn't mind locking up down here."

"Fair enough." He checked all the windows, the basement door, and the front door before turning off the lamp on the table in the hall. As he climbed the steps to the second floor, he heard a low rumble. Looking up, he saw Sweet Thing on the top step, her ears back, her upper lip curled.

"Hey, girl. It's me. No need for that." He held his hand out to her. "We're old friends, remember?"

"Who are you talking to?" Daria walked out of the room near the top of the steps.

"The dog forgot for a moment that we're buds," Connor told her.

"She growled at you?"

"Yeah."

"I think maybe you startled her. I don't think she would have at-tacked you."

"I don't think she would either, but it's good to know her protec-tive instincts are in full swing."

"I have sheets for the bed in here, and if you'll give me a minute, I'll have the bed made for you."

"Thanks, Daria, but don't bother. I can do that."

"Really. It's no bother."

He took the pile of sheets from her hands. "No bother for me, ei-ther. You're exhausted. Get some sleep. I'll see you in the morning."

"Okay. Thanks. I am pretty much wiped out. But I don't mind telling you I'll sleep better knowing you're here." She stifled a yawn. "See you in the morning. Come on, Sweet Thing," she called to the dog, who had positioned herself at the top of the steps once again.

Connor closed the door to the bedroom and stripped the white coverlet from the bed. From the room next door, he heard Daria talk-ing to the dog, and he smiled to himself. She and the dog had taken to each other like long-lost friends, and there was no doubt in his mind that the dog would be a most protective guardian. Not that Connor had any intention of leaving Daria unprotected.

He finished making the bed and went into the adjoining bath-room. He noted gratefully that Daria had left several towels stacked on the side of the sink. He turned on the shower and stripped down. It had been a busy day, but his mind was still in overdrive and he had a lot to think about before getting into bed, including how to prolong his stay here at Howe. He turned down the hot water until it was al-most off, and stood beneath the cold spray until his tanned skin was almost red. His head clear and his body cooled, he turned off the shower and wrapped one of the towels around his waist. Quietly, with only the light from the hall to guide him, he crossed the room and opened all three windows to the slight breeze that passed through the trees alongside the house. He peered out the window at the campus.

He could see Louise's house and noted that it, too, was now in darkness. The student body was still on summer hiatus, and the campus was eerily quiet. Connor watched the shadows for a long time, but nothing moved. Still, he knew that somewhere out there was someone who knew a lot more about the treasures hidden in the museum's basement than he was supposed to.

From the beginning, Connor suspected that someone from the university was involved in the thefts. Now he had to wonder if that person was also a murderer.

The only thing Connor knew for certain was that he would not be leaving Howe until he found out.

ELEVEN

"I thought I smelled coffee." Daria came through the swinging kitchen door.

"I hope you don't mind." Connor looked up from the folder he was reading. "I'm used to getting up early."

"I'd be crazy to object to someone making my coffee in the morning." She smiled when she noticed the mug he'd left next to the pot for her. "Thank you. This was thoughtful of you."

"Just as easy to make enough for two." He shrugged without looking up. "Did you sleep?"

"Not really. I kept thinking about the break-in, and what happened to those people. But I was glad you were here." She filled the mug and took a sip. "This is really good."

"Thanks. You know I'm armed and can handle anything that might happen, right?"

"I really hadn't thought about you being armed. I just figured you could handle it." She paused. "Are you armed right now, this minute?"

He reached a hand behind his back and held up a black handgun.

"Oh."

"Does it make you nervous?"

"Not as nervous as thinking about having my tongue cut out."

He smiled and slid the gun back into the holster at the small of his back.

"Have you seen Sweet Thing?" Daria leaned back against the counter.

"I took her out earlier. She heard me moving around and came into my room, so I brought her down with me and we took a little walk. Last I saw her, she was sleeping on the top step."

"She's outside alone?" Daria frowned. "What if she runs away? Or chases someone?"

"She has been extremely well trained. When you tell her to stay, she stays."

"You think she's still there?"

"Go on. Take a look. I will bet you anything she's still right there on the top step." Connor slid several sheets of paper from the folder and appeared to be studying them.

"Anything?" Daria stopped halfway to the door. "You're that sure?"

"I am."

"Good. We'll bet your car."

"Wait a minute—"

"Hey, your idea." Daria peeked out through the glass. The dog was standing on the top step, looking up at her. "And oh, my, that idea is certainly going to cost you."

"You're bluffing." Connor was in the doorway behind her.

"You think?"

"If that dog wasn't right there, you'd already be outside looking for her."

"I'm that transparent?"

"Sorry, but yes."

"Damn." She opened the door and the dog came in, wagging her tail. "I did get your attention though, didn't I?"

"Daria, you got my attention a long time ago." He was leaning against the doorjamb, coffee mug in his hand.

She tried to think of something clever to say, but could not. When she realized she was blushing, she put her head down and fussed with the dog. By the time a response had come to her, he'd gone back into the kitchen alone.

"What is on your agenda today?" Connor was at the table, acting as if he had not just thrown a pitch she hadn't bothered to take a swing at.

"I have a meeting with Louise in about twenty minutes." Daria filled Sweet Thing's water bowl at the sink.

"Then what?"

She shrugged. "Just work. I expect the museum will be a busy place with all the inspectors and insurance people, so I'll work here. And since someone from the FBI is going to go after the missing artifacts, I can go about my business."

"Which business is that?"

"Designing the exhibits. Deciding what to showcase, what should go where. How best to display certain pieces."

"So you decided to stay."

"I think I've known since day one I'd be staying. I guess I just wanted to believe I was making an intellectual decision rather than an emotional one."

"What's wrong with making decisions based on your emotions?"

"I'm a scientist," she said, as if that should explain it. "Anyway, I'm eager to start. I need to put a lot of thought into how I want to present things. This will be the debut of Shandihar's culture to the rest of the world, so I want to get it right. And I want to convey Alistair's joy in having found the city. I want people to be able to see Shandihar the way he saw it."

"Sounds like fun."

"It will be." Her eyes darkened. "At least, it would be, if we didn't have these murders . . ."

He placed the papers on the table before him in a neat stack. "Regardless of what has happened, you still have a job to do. You have a lot of responsibility. Getting the museum reopened is the goal, right? To help keep the school going?"

She nodded.

"Then focus on that, and only that."

"I can't. I thought about this a lot last night." She sat across the table from him. "About Alistair and his search for Shandihar. Finding it. Packing up everything he could get his hands on and bringing it back here. He was so proud of himself, that he'd found a place that no one else believed existed. He couldn't wait to show the world what he'd found. And then he died. Now that the university is finally going to display the Shandihar artifacts, once again, people are dying."

"I thought you said Alistair died of a lung infection."

"He did. But I was remembering last night that Iliana wrote in her diaries about several others connected with the expedition who'd died after Alistair. Three of his assistants died within the next two years."

"How?"

"The same vague 'lung disease' that Alistair died from."

"Maybe they all picked up the virus at the same time."

She looked doubtful.

"Seriously. Think about it. They were all in the same part of the world together. They might have picked up a virus or some sort of bacteria."

"And it lay dormant in all four men for two, three, or four years?" She shook her head.

"Right. I'd forgotten that Alistair returned to Howe two years before he died. And if the others died within two years, that would have been . . ." He tried to recall the dates.

"Anywhere from 1911 to 1912. My great-grandfather died in late 1910."

"So what are you saying, Daria?"

"I don't know. You're the investigator. You tell me." She stole a look at the clock. "I have to get going or I'll be late for my meeting with Louise."

She rinsed her mug out in the sink. "Thanks for the coffee. And for letting Sweet Thing out. I apologize for not being able to offer you breakfast."

"I'll pick up something later. I'm pretty resourceful."

"Will you be here when I get back?" She paused with her hand on the kitchen door.

"Would you like me to be?" His eyes held hers for a long moment.

"Yes. I would."

"Then I'll see you later."

"Great. See you later." She pushed through the door and as it swung back, he called to her.

"Daria. Where are Iliana's diaries?"

"Upstairs on the table next to my bed."

"Do you mind if I take a look?'

"Not at all," she called back as she unlocked the front door. "Go for it."

Daria stepped out onto the front porch and drew in a deep breath of sheer mugginess. It had been years since she'd experienced an American summer in this part of the country, and she'd forgotten how oppressive the humidity could be. She had become accustomed to the dry desert air.

Instead of her usual work clothes—shorts and a T-shirt—she'd put on a khaki skirt that fell to her knees and a sleeveless cotton shirt because she wasn't sure if anyone else would be at her meeting this morning. She hoped it wouldn't be the bankers. Or the insurance people. She wouldn't mind the contractors who were going to work on the building, though; she'd like to have some input if they were going to alter the interior design. She made a mental note to ask Louise about that. The Great Room had been perfectly designed for exhibitions like the one she had in mind. There was no need to mess with what worked.

Vita was on the phone when Daria stepped into the reception area. She waved Daria in, pointed to Louise's open door, and mouthed the words, "Go on in, she's waiting for you."

"Louise?" Daria entered the inner office.

"Over here." Louise was at a small conference table that was set up by the windows on the right side of the room. "I was just looking over some of the notes I made when the security firm was here yesterday."

"Has anything been decided?"

"Yes. The bank is refurbishing a large secure space in the basement of their main branch in downtown Wilmington. They're hoping to have it completed by the end of the week. In the meantime, there are several guards at the museum keeping an eye on things."

"Why move the collection at all, if bringing in more guards works?"

"The bank feels that the artifacts will be safer if they're locked away in a vault."

"That's probably what Mrs. Sevrenson thought, too."

"What?" Louise frowned. "Who?"

"Elena Sevrenson. The woman in Philadelphia who was murdered. Her niece told us she had a vault in her basement. That's where she kept the griffins."

"And yet they were the only things stolen. Odd that nothing else was taken." Louise took a seat at the table and motioned for Daria to do the same.

"Particularly since there were other highly valuable objects on display in the dining room at the time."

"That couple out in Gladwyne—do we know what was stolen from their home?"

"I suspect I do, but I'm sure the FBI will let us know for certain."

"And the gentleman from Delaware?"

"Someone will be searching the house to confirm what was stolen. The piece he owned from the university's collection—a statue of the goddess Ereshkigal that's almost two feet tall—should be easy enough to spot."

"Good Lord, you'd have to be an idiot not to see the connection." Louise swore softly under her breath. "It's only a matter of time before this story breaks and the phones start ringing off the hook."

"Louise, does Howe have a public relations person?"

"We did." Louise sighed. "She left at the end of the semester and we haven't replaced her yet."

"Is there anyone on staff you could call upon as acting public relations director to at least see you through the next few weeks? Unless you have the time to deal with the media yourself, it could get ugly."

"Good point. Let me think on this for a while. Maybe there is someone . . ." She bit her bottom lip. "In the meantime, I have some things to give you."

Louise got up and walked to her desk, where a cardboard box sat on the chair. She carried the box to Daria at the table.

"In here is a copy of the catalog from the Oliver Jacobs exhibit."

"The one that marked the opening of the museum?" Daria's eyebrows raised in interest.

"Yes. Vita is still searching for the records Casper Fenn kept, detailing his acquisitions and sales. I haven't had time to help her look more thoroughly. I imagine you would welcome the opportunity to see what transpired back in the 1940s and 1950s."

"I would, thank you. Can I take the catalog back to the house?"

"Yes, of course."

"I should tell you that I may have had a break-in at McGowan House last night."

Louise frowned. "And you waited until now to tell me? Did you call the police? What was taken?"

"I meant to tell you as soon as I arrived this morning, but we started talking about other things. As far as I can tell, nothing was taken, but Connor thinks somebody got some information from my computer."

"Why? And what?"

"I made a list of the artifacts I think were stolen. The file had been opened before I got home last night."

"Did you call the police?" Louise asked pointedly.

"No. Since there was an FBI agent at the house, and the case has been turned over to them, we—Connor and I—didn't think it was necessary to call the local police."

"This is very serious, Daria," Louise got up again and began to pace. "Our museum has been robbed. People who owned some of the stolen artifacts have been murdered. And now there's been a break-in on our campus. I'm not sure what to do about any of this. I thought reopening the museum would be the answer to our problems, but it seems to be turning into the catalyst for more problems."

"Do you have a choice?" Daria asked. "As upsetting as all this has been"—Daria touched Louise on the arm—"is there really a question of whether or not the museum should be reopened?"

"No." Louise sighed. "I don't know what else to do. We went over every other conceivable option weeks ago. The trustees and I agreed that there's nothing else that will be of any lasting benefit to the university. So we will have to proceed, in spite of the murders and the thefts."

She tapped her pen on the tabletop. "Of course, there's no press like sensational press."

"I'm afraid that's true," Daria agreed. "Which is why you're going to want to find someone who can start fielding questions and act as a liaison between the university and the media."

"As much as it pains me to say it, we will need the press when it's time to open the museum. Yes, you're right. I need to address this as soon as possible."

"The sooner the better, I'm afraid."

"About these art theft people from the FBI . . . when might we expect them?"

"Connor is arranging that. He spoke with his office yesterday."

"Good, that's good." Louise nodded. "The security people have been at the museum since yesterday afternoon. If you're thinking about getting in the building, you're going to need this."

Louise took a badge from an envelope that lay on the table and handed it to Daria. "No one's getting in without one of these, so make sure you have it on when you go down there."

"Thanks." Daria put the badge in her bag. "By the way, what arrangements have been made to appraise the collection?"

"Penn is sending someone next week on the bank's behalf." Louise brightened. "At least we're making progress in that quarter. Oh, and more good news. Dr. Bokhari will be back tomorrow evening, so you'll have some help with the exhibit, if you want it."

"That is good news. I'm looking forward to meeting her." Daria pushed the chair away from the table. "If there's nothing else, I'd like to get to work on those displays."

"There is something." Louise got up and opened the office door. "Vita, do you have those envelopes . . . yes, those."

Daria followed Louise into the reception area where Vita was removing several large brown envelopes from her desk.

"I found this in one of the file cabinets downstairs when I was searching for Casper Fenn's records." Vita handed the envelopes to Daria.

"The photographs that were taken at Shandihar," Louise told her. "They might help you plan your displays, since the artifacts themselves will be going into the vault soon. Not that you won't have access to them, but having these right in front of you might make your job a little easier."

"Definitely. Thank you. I can't wait to look at them." Daria opened the lid of the box and dropped the envelopes inside. "I'll take good care of them."

"Let me know when the FBI's art people get here," Louise called after Daria who was already on her way out of the office.

"I will."

Daria closed the door behind her, her heart pounding. She fought an urge to dance down the front steps of the building. She couldn't get back to McGowan House fast enough.

"Connor?" she called as she entered the house. From the kitchen, there was music playing softly, and she hurried toward it.

When she pushed through the swinging doors, she found Connor still seated at the table, Sweet Thing at his feet and a sweet thing with long blond hair sitting in the chair she herself had occupied just an hour or so ago.

"Daria." Connor smiled when he looked up at her. "Meet Special Agent Polly Kingston. NSAF. Here to save the day."

"Oh. Hello." Daria exhaled a breath she hadn't realized she'd been holding. "Nice to meet you."

"You as well." Polly looked over her shoulder and met Daria's eyes.

Polly Kingston was older than Daria had first thought. Maybe early fifties, but she'd kept herself together very well.

Sweet Thing greeted Daria enthusiastically, and she leaned over to give the dog a pat on the head.

"Connor was just bringing me up to date on the case. I have to admit, this is more complex than what I've handled in the past."

"How so?" Daria took the chair between Polly and Connor.

"Well, our art-theft cases don't generally have this element of murder running through them. Yes, of course, there are cases where people dealing in stolen art or antiquities have been killed, but I've never seen a case like this. We were just discussing the best way to handle it. I think my first priority will be to recover the artifacts that are still in the hands of private collectors. Hopefully before someone else is killed."

"The people in Connecticut and Marion, Massachusetts," Daria noted. "And then you'll contact the museums and galleries?"

"Yes, though I'll have another agent working on the institutions," Polly told her. "As luck would have it, we are really shorthanded right now. There was a big theft at a gallery in California over the weekend, and some Picassos were stolen in Michigan on Friday, and there's an ongoing investigation of some Internet sales that's just heating up. So we're stretched pretty thin right now. I was just thanking Connor for doing some of the legwork for me. I appreciate having the list of stolen items and their probable locations handed to me." She smiled at Connor. "You've saved me a great deal of time."

"Actually, Daria was the one who knew to use the Internet to locate the collectors. We found the collectors, but unfortunately, someone else found them before we did."

"Shouldn't someone be warning the others?" Daria asked.

"That's already being done," Polly assured her. "John Mancini has contacted agents in each of the locations to make contact with the individuals ASAP."

"And then you'll go in and see about getting the university's property back?"

"We'll do our best," Polly assured Daria, "but Howe could very well end up in litigation if any of the institutions don't want to cough up important pieces. Especially since Howe is planning on placing a very bright spotlight on Shandihar over the next few years. The museums that have artifacts to put on display are going to want to keep them for a while."

"Actually, Agent Kingston, right now I'm more concerned about the people who possess the artifacts. Having them returned is secondary at this point."

"The plan is to arrange for them to be protected," Connor told her.

"So whose job is it to figure out who is stealing the artifacts, and who is killing the collectors?" Daria looked from Connor to Polly and back again.

"The homicide investigations are being handled by the police departments where the murders took place," he told her.

Daria frowned. "I'm sure they're all very competent, but let's face it, the Blumes and Elena Sevrenson were murdered months ago. Connor, do either of the investigating departments have any leads?"

"None that I know of."

"Who is coordinating the investigations? If there are two departments involved, who's on first here?" Daria stared at Connor. "And if there's another death, that brings in another police department. Why isn't the FBI taking over the case?"

"I'll be coordinating the theft portion of the case," Polly told her, "and I'll have agents working with me in each city."

"But shouldn't someone be looking over the entire thing? The thefts *and* the murders? Shouldn't the left hand know what the right hand is doing here?"

Connor glanced at Polly, then told Daria, "That's what we were discussing when you came in. John's asked me to hold the reins on this one, to do exactly what you just described. Liaison between the Bureau and the various police departments."

"Is that the sort of thing you usually do?" Daria asked him.

"Not in this context, but I serve as middleman, so to speak, quite often." He smiled faintly. "In this case, I'll be working here, at Howe, since this is the hub."

Daria turned to Polly. "Will you also be handling the theft here? The original theft from the museum?"

"Yes, once we've located and secured the missing artifacts, but that aspect of the case will be much more complicated, and might never be solved. No one knows when that theft occurred. The perpetrator may well be deceased. Right now, given the fact that someone else is hunting down the collectors, and has a head start, we need to make them our priority."

"I agree completely," Daria said, "and I do appreciate how hard it's going to be to—"

Polly's phone rang. She excused herself and answered, then listened intently. Finally, she said, "I should be there by three o'clock. Secure the scene and keep out everyone except the ME until I get there."

She closed her phone with a snap.

"I'm afraid we're a day late in Connecticut."

"My God, not another one!" Daria gasped.

"Two, actually." Polly Kingston's relaxed demeanor had disappeared in a heartbeat. "The preliminary report indicates Cloris Porter was home alone when the killer or killers entered her home." She looked at Connor. "They killed her in the manner you previously described, then apparently waited in the home until her husband, Justin, arrived. Their son-in-law went to the house around ten-thirty last night when he was unable to contact either of them by phone. It's believed that theft was the motive, but it's unknown what was taken from the home."

"Connor, do you have the list of collectors and the pieces they own?" Daria asked.

He opened the folder and skimmed the list until he found what he was looking for.

"One two-handled ceremonial goblet, gold, encrusted with emeralds."

"Well, at least I'll know what to look for when I get there." Polly made notes in a small notebook she took from her bag.

"What about the woman in Massachusetts?" Daria asked.

"We have someone trying to contact her right now. I hope we get to her in time." Polly was all business. "I have a plane to catch in an hour. Tell me everything you know about this Shandihar culture, everything you know about the missing artifacts, and who you think might have a reason to be killing these people and why. I also need a description of the artifacts you think the Porters might have had."

"I can do better than a description." Daria went to the counter where she'd placed the box she brought back from Louise's office and opened the lid. She took out the envelope. "These are photographs that were taken at the site. Many of the artifacts were photographed as they were discovered. With luck, we'll have pictures of the missing items. If not, we still have the drawings Alistair made."

Her heart was pounding as she opened the envelope and carefully removed the many photos, none of which she had seen yet. The first photo was of a man standing between two stone pillars. He wore field clothes, a large straw hat, and an enormous smile. Daria lifted the photo and stared at it intently, as if taking in every detail, before placing it on the table.

"If my guess is correct, this is Alistair McGowan at the portals of Shandihar. Let's see what wonders he found, shall we?"

Daria passed the photograph to Connor, who gave it a cursory glance before passing it on to Polly. She studied it momentarily before placing it to one side on the table.

"And here we have a bronze statue of a woman. Maybe one of the priestesses." Daria said. "I think we saw this statue the other day."

She handed the picture to Connor and went on to the next. "Some sort of chalice. Looks to be of gold, judging from the way the light is reflecting off it on the side." She glanced across the table at Connor. "We've seen this one, too. Let's look for the artifacts we haven't seen."

Daria went through the first envelope, then the second. With each stack of photographs she set aside, she became more confused. When she'd gone through all the envelopes and had passed along each photo, she turned to Connor and said, "No large bronze statue of Ereshkigal, no golden griffins. No gold necklace . . . there must be another envelope of photos somewhere."

"You're sure?" Polly asked. "Maybe you should take another look."

"Daria's right," Connor said. "The photos of the missing artifacts are missing as well, and I don't think that's a coincidence. I don't think you're going to find another envelope that just happens to have all those pictures in it."

"What do you think happened to them?" Daria asked.

"I think whoever is behind the thefts has the photos," he told her.

"So there's no proof that the items even existed." Polly thought aloud.

"Alistair wrote in his journals about every item he found, and he even sketched many of them himself. We know they existed. We know he brought them back," Daria said.

"I think it's more likely that the person who took the photos passed them on to whoever had been sent out after them," Connor said, "so that the killers would know what they were looking for."

"That would explain how they knew to take only the Shandihar pieces." Polly said thoughtfully. "Doesn't it make you wonder, though, why someone would kill to recover these specific pieces, but completely overlook other very valuable artifacts? The Blume's house was reported to have had a fortune in artwork. Why didn't they touch anything else? A common thief wouldn't have left it all there."

"These aren't common thieves," Daria told her. "Whoever is doing this believes he's on a holy mission to recover the artifacts that were stolen from the museum."

"Frankly, I have a hard time with that 'holy quest' thing, Daria. If that's true—if the point is to return the artifacts—where are they? Nothing's been brought back." Connor shook his head. "Forgive my skepticism, but I think there's more to it than that. I'm a lot more comfortable with the common thief thing."

"Well, unfortunately, holy crusader or common criminal, I don't think they're finished. There are still several artifacts out there," Polly reminded them. "I just hope we can track them down before someone else does . . ."

TWELVE

Daria spent the rest of the day in an almost religious state of bliss in the museum basement, matching photos to artifacts and envisioning where and how this piece or that might be displayed for the reopening. The photos themselves were nothing short of miraculous. To be able to see, one hundred years later, exactly what her great-grandfather had seen just as he'd first seen it was an experience Daria would never forget. Once she got past the fact that the photos of the missing artifacts were missing as well, the importance of matching the original photographs to the artifacts had Daria's heart and head pounding for hours. In her mind's eye, she saw the sepia photos enlarged greatly and serving as the backdrop for the display of the corresponding pieces. Had any such exhibit ever been possible in the past? She was unsure. She knew only that the Shandihar exhibit at Howe University would be a magnet for the public as well as for scholars for years to come.

And to think she'd scoffed when Louise mentioned the possibility of a book. Daria had no doubt that the university would benefit financially from the venture. With visions of a handsome coffee-table book dancing in her head, Daria lost all track of time.

"So how'd it go today?"

Daria was startled by the voice coming from the doorway.

"Oh, Connor. Sorry. I was tuned out for a minute."

"More than a minute, I'd guess. Any idea what time it is?" He walked into the room, and immediately the room seemed smaller.

"None." She stood and found her legs stiff. "But my knees are telling me that I've been here for more than an hour or two."

"Try six hours."

"Really? That would make it—"

"Six-thirty." Connor nodded. "Are you hungry yet?"

"I guess I am." She stood and stretched. "I just got wrapped up in all this." She waved her hand around the room. "The photographs are amazing. Just to see so many of the artifacts exactly where they were first found—I felt as if I were there with him. It's almost over-whelming."

"I thought you were going to work from the house today?"

"I was, but with the photos in my hands, I had to come look at the real deal. I thought having people upstairs would disturb me, but it didn't. I hardly knew anyone else was in the building, except for when the plumbers and the electricians were poking around."

"Can you stop for some dinner?" Connor leaned on one of the taller crates.

"I'm going to have to. The guard told me I had to be out by seven o'clock, so it's a good thing you came for me. I might have gotten locked in." She began to pack the photographs back into their envelopes. "How did you get in, by the way? Were you able to get a badge?"

"Yes," he told her. "It says FBI on it."

"Ah, yes. Opens doors everywhere, I would guess." She rolled her shoulders to work out the kinks.

Connor picked up the pack of envelopes from the desk. "Is there anything else you need to do here?"

"I just need to lock up." She looked around the room. All the crates had been repacked and secured. She dug in the pocket of her skirt for the key.

"Polly got to the airport on time?" Daria asked as she locked the door.

"I assume so," Connor said as he followed Daria up the stairs. They waved to the guard when they reached the main floor. "Glad to see there's some real security here."

"They were hired by the bank," Daria told him. "There is another one around here somewhere, and I think I saw the university's security guard outside as well."

"Any idea when they're going to move the collection?"

"Louise said they were going to try for the end of the week."

They walked outside into the remnants of a summer shower that was spending its last few drops of rain. The sky was clearing as they walked back to McGowan House.

"I took the liberty of ordering a pizza and some salads to be delivered," Connor said when they reached the back steps. "I probably should have asked first."

"No, no, pizza's fine. I've hardly eaten anything else since I got to Howe. I love it." She unlocked the door and caught Sweet Thing by the collar as she was about to bolt.

"It's not ideal, but they deliver. And I figured the pizza would get here right around the time we did, since there was such a long wait for delivery tonight. Something about one of their drivers not showing up."

"That should work out just right, then. And I'll have time to take care of Sweet Thing." The dog jumped up to greet Daria, and she stroked the dog's head affectionately.

"She's been fed, watered, walked."

"Oh. Thank you. Well, then, maybe I'll have time to clean up a little. I've been in that hot basement all afternoon, and I'm covered in dust."

"Go ahead. Sweet Thing and I will wait for the pizza guy out on the front porch."

"I'll make it quick." Daria disappeared into the house and ran up the steps.

She was dying for a quick shower. She was hot and sweaty and dusty. She closed the bedroom door behind her and stripped off her clothes as she headed for the bathroom. She turned on the shower and let it run for a minute or two, then stepped in. The water was cooler than she liked, but it was welcome after hours in the stale, stuffy basement. She scrubbed her body quickly, washed and rinsed her hair in record time, and emerged from the shower feeling like a completely new woman.

Seven minutes later, she was back downstairs, wearing fresh clothes, her short hair tucked behind her ears. She hadn't taken time to dry it, so a few still-wet strands fell across her forehead. Connor and Sweet Thing were still sitting on the front porch, the pizza box and a brown paper bag on the floor between them.

"She is the best trained dog I've ever seen," Connor told Daria when he heard the screen door behind him close. "She is dying to see what is in that box but she won't go near it because I told her not to." He ruffled the dog's fur. "She is one good dog."

"Do you think one of Damien Cross's relatives will want her?"

"I guess that's always a possibility." Connor picked up the box and the bag and stood. "But for now, she's yours."

Sweet Thing wagged her tail and licked Daria's bare leg below the cuff of her shorts.

"I love her. It's going to be tough to give her up," Daria admitted. She opened the front door and held it for Connor.

When she and the dog had entered the house, Connor turned and said, "Throw the bolt. We don't want someone to let themselves in while we're eating."

"Good point." Daria locked the door and followed Connor into the kitchen.

She took plates down from the cupboard and placed them across from each other on the table.

"Knife? Fork?" She paused, her hand on the drawer where the flat-ware was kept.

"For pizza?" He frowned. "What's the point?"

"Well, you never know. My sister cannot bring herself to pick up a piece and just take a bite. She says she always gets sauce on her face."

"That's why napkins were invented."

"I don't think we have napkins, but I do have paper towels." She ripped a few sheets from the roll and folded them.

"We do need forks for the salad, though," Connor said as he re-moved the Styrofoam boxes from the paper bag and opened the pizza box. "I asked them to send several kinds of dressing, since I didn't know what you liked."

"I can use anything. Or nothing, for that matter." Daria brought two bottles of water and two forks to the table. "God, that smells so good. I didn't realize how hungry I am."

"Dig in," he told her, and she did just that.

"How did you know I love pepperoni?"

"There were too many choices, so I went with an old standard."

"This is really good, Connor. Thanks. I'm sorry for being such a crappy hostess. It's just that once I get into something that really inter-ests me, I lose track of time. Not that I'm much of a cook under the best of circumstances."

"I guess you don't get much practice."

"Every dig I've been on for I don't know how many years has al-ways had a cook. Meals were always prepared for us, three times a day. I guess maybe you're the same, since you travel a lot?"

"I'm a pretty good cook." He grinned. "Actually, I'm damned good. If I'd had time to get out today to the grocery store, we would not be eating pizza."

"Maybe while you're here, I'll get to judge just how good you are."

"Count on it."

"Feel free. My kitchen is your kitchen."

"I'll remember that." He nodded. "So you had a good day, did you?"

"I had a great day. I feel guilty about having such a wonderful day in light of everything that's happened. I can't stop thinking about how those people died, and all because of the art objects they bought. Objects that have a direct tie to me. To my family. And yet, just to see these artifacts in the state in which they were discovered . . ." She shivered slightly, a look of awe on her face. "To see a statue that's wrapped and crated, standing where it had originally stood, centuries ago, in a temple wall. Inside one of those wooden crates is a golden diadem that the photos show was taken from the wrapped remains of a woman who had died over two thousand years ago. Unfortunately, her remains were left behind, so we don't know anything about her, except that she was wealthy enough or important enough to have owned this wonderful golden crown."

"Maybe she was the queen of Shandihar. You said it was a matriarchal society."

"I don't think they had royalty the way we think of it. I think the priestesses were the only 'royalty' in this society. Maybe by studying the artifacts I'll learn more about the culture." She sighed. "That's one of the problems with removing artifacts from their place of origin without taking into consideration the context. I know from reading Alistair's journals that he felt he was way ahead of others of his time in trying to preserve as much as possible."

"That's why he had a photographer along with him, why he wanted so many pictures taken."

"Absolutely, and that was brilliant on his part, to use the latest technology in that way. Modern archaeologists might argue with some of his other methods, but he was ahead of his time in that regard. Much of what we'll learn about Shandihar, we'll learn from studying the photos."

"Photography being what it was back then, it must have taken forever to take them all."

Daria nodded. "I really admire my great-grandfather for having the patience to wait while each piece was photographed several times before he moved it. I can only imagine how his hands must have been itching to touch, to hold . . . but he did the right thing. The photographs taken in context along with his journals and his letters to my great-grandmother give us a picture of this expedition that is pretty much unheard of for that time."

"I'll bet it would make a fascinating book," Connor said. "Even better, one of those TV documentaries."

"That's exactly what Louise is hoping for." Daria grinned. "She's thinking along just those lines, hoping to cash in as much as possible for the university."

"You can't blame her. She's faced with a daunting task."

"I don't blame her. My first reaction was, this is history, these were real people with real lives, and I'm not sure we should be profiting from them." Daria sipped her water. "On the other hand, it's nothing that museums and galleries don't do all the time. And if the university is to keep going, they'll have to use whatever resources they have. Alistair's find is a fantastic resource. It wouldn't make sense not to capitalize on it."

She opened a foil pack of dressing and drizzled it on her salad.

"So what did you learn today that you didn't know this morning?" she asked.

"I learned that Cavanaugh will be back in town by the end of the week, and will meet with me then. He said he didn't want to discuss his dealings on the phone, especially since he had no way of knowing whether or not I was who I said I was. Smart on his part, actually."

Daria nodded. "Especially in light of what's been happening to people with a connection to the Shandihar artifacts. Did you ask him about the acquisition of the griffins?"

"Yes, but again, he declined to talk about it on the phone. So we'll see what he has to say when we sit down with him."

"We? I get to go with you?"

"You know more about these artifacts than I do. I think we'll learn more if you're along."

"Great."

"I'm having a report run on Casper Fenn—when he left Howe, where he went, how he spent his days."

"You think he was the one who stole the items in the first place?"

"I think he's the place to start."

"You've been busy. Anything else?"

"I learned that Madeline Cathcart of Marion, Massachusetts, is alive and well and under guard at this very moment," he told her. "And I had the computers from all of the victims confiscated and sent to my office for our computer whiz to check out."

"You think maybe they were contacted by the killer?"

"It's worth a look." He shrugged. "You never know what you'll find, or what you'll learn about a person when you start following their footsteps down the old information highway. Polly is still interviewing Mrs. Cathcart. If anyone has contacted her, we'll know who, and how the contact was made. She called to let me know she was at the house and Mrs. Cathcart was unharmed, and the cylinder was still in her possession." He paused, then asked, "What exactly is this cylinder, anyway?"

"It's like a regular cylinder. Thin, hollow tube?" When he nodded, she said, "But this one is made out of clay. When the clay was wet, someone—probably a scribe—wrote on the cylinder. It could contain a description of an event or a person, or a story, or it could even contain laws or customs."

"So it was sort of an early book."

"Yes. It was a written recording of something. In the absence of paper, they made use of clay. This was very common in early civilizations. Most did not have paper. There are quite a few cylinders still packed in the crates. I'm dying to get to them."

"Can you read them?"

"I don't know. I haven't really had time to study the inscriptions and symbols. As far as I know, they've never been translated." She thought about that for a moment, then added, "I doubt anyone can read them, actually. To the best of my knowledge, these are the only written records from this civilization to have survived."

She thought about it some more.

"Of course," she said almost to herself, "since Shandihar borrowed so much from other civilizations, there's a very good chance their language was borrowed as well. Or maybe they borrowed a bit from the Mesopotamians, a bit from the Persians, something from the Greeks . . ."

"I see those wheels spinning in there."

"Sorry. I can't help it." Daria laughed self-consciously. "Maybe tomorrow I'll pull one of those cylinders out and take a closer look."

"I thought you were designing exhibits."

"I am, and I have the best idea for those." Her hands were suddenly animated as she described what she had in mind. "Picture this. In the Great Room, huge blowups of the photographs of, say, one of the goblets, just as it was found at the site, before it was touched. Then, on a pedestal, in front of the photos, there sits the real thing. And in those big glassed-in display cases—again, the great enlargements as background, juxtaposed with the actual artifacts. We'd use the smaller cases for some of the larger individual pieces—say, the big statues of the goddess—to display them separately, and then use the larger cases for things that are related. Maybe all the ceremonial items."

"Very impressive. I like it." He touched the paper towel to his mouth. "It sounds like a hit to me."

"And if I could translate some of the writings"—she was smiling without even realizing it—"I could have them reproduced and incorporated into the displays."

"You're really enjoying this, aren't you?"

"More than I ever thought I would. I mean, I knew it would be a great experience, and that it would be, well, fun. But I didn't expect to feel this . . . *connected* to the project. I didn't expect it to mean so much to me."

"Sometimes the best things in life are unexpected."

"Yes. I suppose that's true." She could feel his eyes on her face and avoided meeting them, though she wasn't sure why.

Sweet Thing pawed at her leg, and she looked down at the dog.

"She wants us to share. I think she has her eye on the pepperoni. Do you think that would be bad for her?"

"Maybe a little bit of the crust wouldn't hurt. Though you might want to think about whether or not you want her begging food from the table."

"I don't think I do. At the same time"—she broke off a piece of the crust and gave it to the salivating dog that sat so prettily at her feet—"I'm having a hard time resisting her."

"I know exactly what you mean." Connor's phone rang and he swallowed his last bite of pizza before answering.

"What do you have for me, buddy?" he asked.

Connor got up from the table, his facial expression unreadable, and walked through the swinging kitchen door into the front hall. Daria could hear his pacing footsteps on the hardwood floor. After about ten minutes, he came back into the kitchen.

"Anything important?" Daria asked with more nonchalance than she felt.

"Several things," he told her. "The hard drives on all the computers belonging to the victims have been removed."

"Which probably means the killer had contacted them and wanted to hide the fact?"

"That would be a good guess. Especially since Mrs. Cathcart's computer is intact." He smiled. "Want to guess what our man Will found?"

"E-mail, maybe from the killer?"

"Several e-mails, actually, all concerning an item in her collection."

"The cylinder?"

"Good guess." He nodded and sat down. "But more importantly, Will traced the e-mail to the computer where the contacts originated."

"So that's great, right? You can find the computer and arrest the killer," Daria said excitedly.

"It's not going to be quite that easy," he told her. "The e-mail was traced to a computer in the library."

She stared at him as if not quite understanding.

"The library? Wait, you don't mean here?"

"That's right. The e-mails were all sent from the Howe University Library."

"The computers we used the other night?"

"Unless there are others somewhere else in the building, yes."

"How would he have found their e-mail addresses?"

"In Mrs. Cathcart's case, she contacted him. She'd seen a mention of Shandihar in an electronic newsletter she receives. There'd been an article warning about fake artifacts, and someone had posted that there are all sorts of bogus items being offered online from civilizations that never actually existed—like Shandihar. The next issue carried Mrs. Cathcart's response setting the record straight. She knew for a fact that Shandihar had been a real city, that she herself owned an artifact from Shandihar and that she'd acquired it from a highly reputable dealer in Boston."

"So he got the victims to come to him. He smoked them out."

"Exactly. He got them to confirm that they did have the pieces in their possession, then asked them to e-mail him privately, which they did. Very clever of him. And before you ask, yes, there is a response from Kelly Blume in the same issue."

"But not Sevrenson or Cross?"

"No, but he could have located them some other way, maybe through Blume or Cathcart. Polly is still interviewing her, so there may be more information to come."

"Can your guy tell which of the computers in the library was the one the e-mails were sent from?"

"Sure."

"So, if we went over there right now, and sent your friend an e-mail from each of the computers, he could tell which one was the right one?"

"Yes. But—"

Daria was already out of her chair. "Let's do it, right now. We'll send him an e-mail from every one of the computers and we'll know right now which one matches. And you could take the hard drive and read the messages that are on it, right?"

"Uh-uh." Connor shook his head. "That's not the way this is going to work."

"How's it going to work?" Daria gathered up the plates and the paper towels and the water bottles and set everything on the counter along with the empty pizza box.

"Sometime very soon, several of my colleagues will arrive, and they're going to handle this. They'll secure the computers and they'll do what they can to determine who the sender was."

"How exactly would they do that?" She frowned. "Lots of people use those computers."

"They can see who signed in at what time on what day, and which of the computers had e-mail sent at approximately that time."

"What if the killer didn't sign in with his real name?" Daria thought that over for a moment. "Why *would* a killer sign in with his own name?"

"As I recall, there are surveillance cameras in the library. I highly doubt that the person we're looking for came in, browsed the stacks, then took his time at the computer stations. My guess is that he came in, sent his e-mails, and left. I think we'll find the times all line up."

"You're assuming the killer is a man. You said *he*."

"The killer has to be one strong son of a bitch. Anderson Blume was six feet four inches tall, his wife was five-nine. They were both in excellent physical condition. Whoever killed them had the strength to handle them both. I think in the end, we'll find there were two killers, both men."

"How did you come to that conclusion? And what if the killer had a gun? Why couldn't it have been a woman with a gun?"

"One person—even with a gun—would have a devil of a time tying up two people and doing what was done to them. And experience has shown us that women don't kill the way these people were killed."

Sweet Thing whimpered and scratched at the back door. Connor found the leash he'd earlier left on the counter and snapped it onto the dog's collar. "I'll be right back. She wants out."

Daria washed the plates and forks and got rid of the paper trash. She had just dried her hands when her cell phone rang. By the time she located it in her bag, it had rung several times.

"Oh, Louise. I was just thinking about you." Daria told her about the e-mails and the FBI's imminent seizure of the library's computers. "Yes, it's definitely shocking, but you're right. Yes, of course I'll tell him . . . Oh. Please give her my best and tell her I'm looking forward to meeting her. I agree, now would not be a good time . . . I'm sorry this is breaking up your meeting . . ."

She hung up as Connor came back inside with Sweet Thing. "This dog would walk all night if someone would walk with her."

"She's an outdoor girl at heart, I guess." Daria set her phone on the counter. "That was Louise on the phone. She was calling to ask me to come to her office for an impromptu meeting. Dr. Bokhari's plane was earlier than expected, and she stopped in to Louise's office just as Louise was meeting with the head trustee and one of the members of the board. She wanted to know if I could run over and meet everyone. Of course, after I told her about the FBI being on the way—"

"You told her that the computers were going to be confiscated?"

"Well, yeah. Don't you think the president of the university de-serves a heads-up?"

"Daria, we don't generally do the heads-up thing," he said.

"She's concerned about the librarian on duty tonight. She wanted me to tell you that she's an older woman and very excitable. Louise is afraid she could have a heart attack if a couple of FBI agents came in waving their badges and grabbing the computers. What's the harm in letting the woman know?"

"It's just not a good idea, Daria." Connor appeared to think it over. "Actually, I think the library ought to be closed now. Would you mind getting Louise back on the phone? I think she's probably the only per-son who has the authority to put the building on lockdown, and I think sooner, rather than later, is the time to do exactly that."

THIRTEEN

"**A**s I told you on the phone, I'll close the library as of nine tonight instead of eleven, and keep it closed until your people have finished doing whatever it is they're going to do," Louise told Connor when he and Daria arrived at her office. "Luckily, there are hardly any students on campus right now, and few faculty members stayed around over the summer, so we won't have too many people to deal with."

"I appreciate your cooperation, Louise. I've been assured that the Bureau will handle this as quickly and efficiently as we can and with as little disruption to the university as possible."

"Thank you. I think we have more than enough to deal with right now, with these deaths. How long do you suppose that will stay out of the news?" Louise appeared concerned.

"Not much longer, I'm afraid. The detective investigating Damian Cross's murder is holding a news conference tomorrow. He'll be joined by representatives of the Philly and Radnor township police departments."

"The departments that investigated the other two cases?" Louise asked.

"Yes. Radnor township investigated because Gladwyne doesn't have its own police department. And it won't be long before we hear from the department in Connecticut, so the press should have a busy week."

"Which makes the appointment of a PR person all the more pressing. That was one of the issues we were going to discuss in our impromptu meeting tonight." Louise sighed and reached for the phone. "I'll try the library again. I've been attempting to get in touch with Gloria Weathers since we spoke earlier, but she's not picking up. She must be away from the desk."

"She isn't the only person working there tonight, is she?" Daria asked.

"No, but she usually stays at or near the front desk. There should also be two student interns, the assistant librarian, and at least one guard. We generally have two during the school year, but we moved one to the museum."

"I thought the bank had two guards on duty at the museum around the clock now," Daria said.

"They do. But Nora Gannon—she chairs our board of trustees—thought we should have someone on the school's payroll there as well." Louise dialed the number and waited almost a full minute. "There's no answer. I wonder if the phone is out."

"Does the librarian have a cell phone?" Daria asked.

"If she does, I don't have the number. And I don't have the pager number for the guard." Louise tapped her fingers on the desktop. "It's time I left here for the night anyway. I suppose I could just stop there on my way back to the house and tell Gloria to send everyone home and to close up early."

"We'll walk over with you," Connor offered. "It's not out of the way."

The campus was quiet, most of the buildings dark except for exterior lights. Those few students at Howe for summer school were all housed in the same dormitory at the opposite side of the campus. In the haze around the lights along the paths and in the parking lots, clouds of flying insects gathered. Across the common areas, fireflies winked in the darkness. As Connor, Daria, and Louise made their way from the administration building to the library, they passed only three students.

"I imagine you're looking forward to the fall semester, when the campus is livelier," Daria said to Louise as they neared their destination. "It's almost a little eerie here at night, don't you think?"

"You get accustomed to it after a few weeks," Louise replied. "It's almost welcome after the long school year. Our attendance has dropped over the past decade, but Howe is still a pretty busy place from the end of August right through the beginning of June. The summer months are a nice break."

They walked together up the library steps and into the building.

"Louise," Connor called to her as she started toward the main desk, "these surveillance cameras are operating, aren't they?"

"We'll have to ask security about that. I would think they would be, but how often they're checked . . ." She looked around and said, "Well, I would ask security, but I don't see the guard at his station. He must be making his rounds." Louise continued on her way.

By the time Connor and Daria reached the front desk, Louise had already walked behind it, and into the stacks that lay beyond.

"Gloria?" she called. "Gloria, are you back there?"

Daria walked into the room to their right, where comfortable-looking chairs formed a circle and a pair of worn black leather sofas faced each other. The room was inviting and well lit and obviously designed to encourage discussion, but other than Daria, it was empty.

"You rarely see a room in a library designed for conversation," Daria said when Louise joined her. "You always think of libraries as places where you never speak above a whisper."

"It was designed for the occasional informal lecture," Louise told her. "There are pocket doors that close the room off from the rest of the library. Another of Benjamin Howe's ideas."

"Any luck finding your librarian?" Connor asked when he joined the two women.

"No." Louise frowned. "She could be in the basement, or on the second floor. Though on second thought, Gloria has problems with her knees. She rarely goes upstairs."

"You said there were two students and an assistant working tonight as well?" Connor asked.

"That's the usual arrangement." Louise was still frowning. "I'm going to check around the desk. Maybe there's a note or something."

"I'll run down to the computer lab. If the two interns are students, maybe they're working on something for one of their courses." Connor headed toward the stairwell.

"I'll check the other rooms here on the first floor, then I'll run upstairs," Daria told Louise. "Maybe you should stay here, in case the librarian or one of the interns returns. Sooner or later, someone is going to have to come back to the front desk."

"Good point. In the meantime, I'll see if I can find the sign-in sheets from today."

Daria left Louise at the desk and went through an arch to her left over which a plaque read THE ILIANA HOWE McGOWAN READING ROOM. The room was dimly lit, and as far as she could see, as empty as the others. An oil portrait of a woman hung over the fireplace at one end of the narrow room, and she walked over to take a closer look.

The subject was a small woman with gray hair pulled back from her face to display her delicate features, a small heart-shaped mouth and wide blue eyes. She wore a black dress and sat demurely, her hands in her lap, a small, sad smile on her lips.

The nameplate below the painting read ILIANA HOWE McGOWAN, 1930.

Daria stepped forward to take a closer look.

So that's what you looked like. I'd been wondering. You were lovely, even in your later years. I imagine life was a bit lonely for you by 1930, with your husband already gone for twenty years, your father for ten, and your children all grown and gone.

Why did you stay on all that time, after everyone you loved had died or left you? And whose idea was the portrait? Was it yours? A small vanity on your part, lest your name be forgotten?

Daria stood in front of the painting, her arms folded over her chest, studying the face of her great-grandmother. She wasn't sure, but thought she might have seen a different portrait of her at one of those long-ago visits to her grandfather's home, or perhaps at one of those infrequent family reunions when she was a child. She hadn't known the woman's name, but she'd known she was a relative from long ago. In that painting, the woman had been younger, and wore a gown of light blue, the color set off by a gold necklace set with blue stones. To Daria and her sister, the woman had appeared regal, and both she and Iona had coveted that necklace.

Daria was so absorbed in the painting and the memories it stirred that by the time she heard the swift footsteps, it was already too late to react.

From out of nowhere, something struck her from behind with such force and speed that she was propelled forward. The last thing she remembered was raising her hands to cover her face as she flew toward the marble fireplace. The side of her head struck the mantel, and the world went dark.

"Son of a bitch." Connor stood in front of the bank of computers in the library basement, his hands on his hips. There wasn't much doubt as to which of the computers the killer had used. It would be the third from the left, the one that now lay shattered and in pieces.

He banged his hand on the low wall of the nearest cubicle.

"Anyone down here? Mrs. Weathers? Hello?" he called out before running back up the steps.

"Did you see anyone downstairs?" Louise asked when Connor approached the desk.

"No. But we won't need an FBI team to figure out which computer the e-mails were sent from." He told her what he'd found.

"Should I call 911?" Louise asked.

"The Bureau is going to be handling the vandalism of the computer, since it's part of an ongoing case, but give campus security a call and have them track down the guard who's supposed to be on duty here tonight."

"Where are you going?" she asked.

"I'm going to check upstairs. You said Mrs. Weathers didn't like the steps because of her knees, but if she's not downstairs, and she's not here, there's only one place left."

He was halfway up to the second floor when he turned back and called down, "Where's Daria?"

"She was in there." Louise pointed toward the room into which Daria had disappeared.

"Would you ask her to wait with you here until I come down? I'm not getting a good feeling."

Louise dialed the number for campus security. On the third ring, it was picked up.

"This is President Burnette. Was a guard assigned to the library tonight? Did he check in? Has he been in touch since? I'm over at the library and there's no one here . . . yes, I'm positive. There's no one at the guard's post, and the building appears to be empty. Yes, please, page him. I'll hold."

She looked up to see Connor running down the steps.

"I found your Mrs. Weathers. At least, I'm assuming that's who she is." He grabbed the other phone from the desk and dialed 911. "I'm afraid we're going to need the police here after all."

"You don't mean Gloria . . ." Louise went pale. "Is she . . . ?"

"Someone is." He looked around. "Louise, where's Daria?"

"She was in there. I was going to check after I called security—"

He shoved the phone into her hands. "Tell the police we need them now. Probable homicide."

He hurried to the doorway where Louise had last seen Daria.

"Oh, sweet Jesus . . ."

Seconds later he was bending over Daria, checking for a pulse, his own heart all but stopping at the sight of the blood that puddled under her head.

"Please be alive . . . please, please be alive."

He located a pulse and began to breath again. "Come on, baby, hang in there. Hang in there . . ."

"The Howeville police are on their way . . ." Louise stopped three steps into the room. "Oh my God, is that—?"

"Call 911 back. Tell them to send an ambulance immediately," he said without looking up.

All of Connor's instincts told him to seek, to find, to break the attacker. But he continued to kneel at Daria's side, wanting to touch her, afraid to touch her, until he heard the sirens stop in front of the building. When the EMTs appeared in the doorway, he waved them over and stepped back, and watched while her vital signs were checked and she was gently lifted onto a stretcher.

Then he left the room without a sound and disappeared into the night. For Connor, the game had just become personal. The killer had no idea just how dangerous a move that had been.

"How are you feeling?"

The unfamiliar voice was soft and melodious, with a slight accent Daria could not readily identify. She opened her eyes but could not get them to focus.

"Daria?" the voice asked. "Are you coming back to us now?"

A face floated in front of her. Daria tried to raise her head, but the pain was like a bolt through her brain.

"Easy, Daria." The mouth on the face moved. "Don't try to sit up."

"Who are you?" Daria whispered through very dry lips.

"I've been sitting here with you for so long, I'd almost forgotten we hadn't been introduced." The face moved closer. "I'm Sabina Bokhari."

"Sabina." Daria's voice was weak. "I've heard so much about you. I've wanted to meet you . . ."

"And I've wanted to meet you, too. I'm a great admirer of your work."

Daria tried to wet her lips.

"You need water, don't you?" The woman rose and walked away, then returned seconds later with a glass of water and a straw. "Here. Let's see if you can take a sip."

Daria sucked on the straw, grateful.

"Thank you," she said.

"More?"

"Please."

"Not too fast, though, all right?"

Daria nodded slightly and took a few more sips.

"Thank you," she said again. "How . . . why . . . ?"

"I was on my way to the library—my office is in the basement—when the ambulance pulled up. I saw Louise on the steps, so I went to find out what happened. I thought perhaps Mrs. Weathers had another heart attack." She swallowed hard. "Anyway, Louise told me what happened. She didn't want you to be in the hospital alone, and since the police needed to question her, she couldn't leave the university grounds. I offered to accompany you and wait with you until you woke up."

"Connor . . ." Daria frowned.

"Connor?"

"Connor Shields. He was with us, in the library."

"The man from the FBI?"

"Yes."

"I didn't see him, but I heard Louise tell the police he was in the building. Perhaps he was looking for whoever did this to you."

"Did they find the librarian?"

"Mrs. Weathers, yes. Yes, they did." Sabina's dark eyes clouded.

"What?" Daria asked.

"She was found on the second floor. She was . . . "

"She's dead?" Daria struggled to sit despite the pain. "Dear God, Sabina, is she dead?"

"I'm afraid so."

"How?"

"I'm not sure," Sabina said. "She was such a nice woman. I'd gotten to know her well over the years. I spent a lot of time in the library. I considered her a friend."

"I'm so sorry." Daria reached out for Sabina's hand.

Sabina nodded her thanks. "The last time I saw her, in June, before I left for the summer, she mentioned that she was planning a ten-day trip to Tuscany in the fall with her sister. They were going to attend a cooking school and go on a wine tour. She was very excited about it."

"Did she have other family?"

"Besides the sister, I don't believe so. Her husband passed away some years ago, before I came to Howe. She never mentioned any children. I imagine Louise has already called the sister."

"I feel as if we've opened a massive can of worms and all of these horrible, ugly things are crawling out." Daria covered her face with her hands.

"You mean because of the museum?"

"Yes."

"Louise was explaining to us—to me and the others who were with us last night—about the murders. About how the collectors who'd acquired the pieces that had been stolen from the museum had been killed so brutally." She shivered. "It almost makes you believe in the curse, doesn't it?"

"What curse?" Daria frowned.

"The one about the goddess seeking revenge on anyone who stole what belonged to her."

"Where did you hear that?" The woman had Daria's complete attention.

"I read about it several years ago. It was in a book I'd picked up somewhere while traveling."

"What was the book?"

"I don't recall the title, but it was an old volume about the oral tradition of storytelling in ancient times. The author related several versions of the same tales and demonstrated how they were altered to reflect the different cultures as they were passed along the Silk Route."

"What did the book say about this supposed curse?"

"That the Sisters of Shandihar—the high priestesses who ruled the city—had been anointed by Ereshkigal to take her place on earth, to speak for her. Their decrees were her decrees and were to be obeyed without question, or the transgressor would be punished."

"We know the preferred method of punishment," Daria interjected.

"According to the author of the book, if a guilty party died before they were punished, their descendants would be cursed, stalked by the *gallas*."

"The *gallas*." Daria was sitting straight up now. "The demon spirits sent to earth by Ereshkigal to pull sinners down to the Underworld."

"Yes, the sinners, or their descendants. It's that whole *sins of the father* thing."

"Or in my case," Daria murmured, "the sins of the great-grandfather."

FOURTEEN

"Who is Gail?"

Daria opened her eyes slowly and blinked against the bright lights above her bed in the hospital room.

"What?" She turned her head to find Connor seated there. "What did you say?"

"I asked you who Gail is." He got up and sat on the edge of the bed. "You were muttering something in your sleep about Gail."

"The *gallas.*" She forced herself to sit up. "The demon spirits of Shandihar."

"And you said you didn't do nightmares." He leaned forward and pushed several errant blond strands behind her left ear. "How are you feeling?"

"Like I plowed headfirst into a wall." She raised a hand to touch the side of her head, then thought better of it. "They said they had to shave part of my head for the stitches. How bad do I look?"

"You look beautiful." He took her hand.

She rolled her eyes and tried to laugh it off.

"Yeah, I'm a real beauty. My face is black and blue and my hair is—"

"Stop it," he said gently. "You are beautiful, bruises, stitches, head shaved or not. Actually, there's just a tiny bald spot there, but once the stitches are out, your hair will cover it. Doesn't matter to me."

She felt herself blush, and the knowledge that she was blushing turned her even redder.

"Don't even try to make me believe that no one's ever told you how pretty you are."

"Connor, I . . ." She bit her bottom lip. "Thank you. For the compliments. It means a lot to me, coming from you."

"That's better."

"What day is it?"

"It's Wednesday."

"Morning or afternoon?"

"Afternoon. It's three o'clock," he told her.

"Can I go back to the house?"

"That's what we're waiting to find out."

"I feel a lot better. I really do." She eased herself up a little more. "I really would like to leave."

"Let's see what the doctor says."

"How's Sweet Thing?"

"She's fine. She'll be happy to see you."

"Where's Sabina? She was here a while ago."

"I told her she didn't have to stay, since I was here, so she left."

"Oh. You met her then." Daria sighed. "She really is beautiful, isn't she? I mean, she's the classic exotic dark-haired beauty with the smoldering eyes and the fabulous smile."

"What? Oh, yes, she's pretty. She said to give her a call if you need anything. She also said she'd like to get together with you as soon as you're feeling better." He reached into his pocket and took out a card and handed it to Daria. "She left her phone number for you."

"Thanks." She took the card and closed her hand over it. "Tell me what happened in the library."

"As best we can piece things together, our man—the killer, or someone working with him—came into the library around eight-thirty last night. Disconnected the surveillance camera, somehow lured the guard into the basement where he bashed him over the head and apparently left him for dead. We found him on the floor near the back door after the ambulance took you to the hospital."

"His hands . . . ?"

"He's a lucky man. He's still alive and in one piece. After that, the killer managed to get the few students who were in the library to leave—we're not sure yet how—but once everyone left, he removed the hard drive from the computer and smashed the machine. According-ing to the two interns, they heard all of this, but didn't see the killer. When they heard Mrs. Weathers running up the steps screaming and heard the man running after her, they locked themselves in a supply closet under the stairs. That's where the police found them, huddled in the closet, scared out of their minds."

"Where are they now?"

"On their way back to their homes. The police took their statements and let them leave with their parents about an hour ago."

"Poor kids."

"Smart kids. They'd have been added to the body count, if he'd known they were there."

"There was supposed to be someone else there, wasn't there? A second librarian?"

"An assistant had been scheduled for last night, but she had car trouble and never did make it in," he told her.

"He was still in the building, then, when we arrived," Daria said softly.

"It looks that way. He was probably on his way out when we got there, most likely took the back steps down from the second floor when he heard us come in. The steps come down into a small hall behind the room you were in. He must have seen you there and figured he'd take you out before you could turn around and see him."

"You think it was an accident? That he only attacked me because I happened to be there? You don't think he was after me, specifically?"

"Knowing that someone broke into your house the other day makes me inclined to say yes, he was after you specifically. But I think if he was going to kill you, he would have."

"How would he have known I'd be in the library?"

"I don't think he did. I don't think he knew who you were. I think he just wanted to make sure you couldn't ID him." He squeezed her hands and asked, "Have you thought about maybe going back to your parents' place until we catch this guy?"

"No. If someone's going to come after me because of my connection to this, it won't matter where I am. If he went to Connecticut to get to his last victims, there's nothing to stop him from coming to South Carolina."

"I'll send people with you. I'll make sure you're safe."

"I won't put anyone in my family between me and him. I don't want them involved in any way."

She tugged on his hand. "Besides, you're here, right? You're not leaving Howe yet?"

"I'm not leaving until this bastard has been dealt with." His eyes narrowed to dark blue slits. "One way or another."

"Because, if he comes back . . . well, next time, he might get lucky."

"I'm afraid his luck has run out. He blew the only shot he's going to get at you." He raised her hand to his lips and kissed it. "Believe it."

"Ahem." The figure in the doorway coughed before entering the room. "Have I just ruined a moment?"

Connor looked over his shoulder. "Yes. Go away."

"Not on your life." The tall dark-haired woman laughed and came in anyway.

He sighed. "Daria, meet my cousin Mia Shields."

"Hi." Daria reached out to take the hand Mia offered.

"Good to meet you." Mia smiled.

"When I said 'Come now,' I didn't mean *right* now," Connor complained.

"Well, then, perhaps next time you could make that distinction before I drive two hours to answer your call for help." Mia sat on the opposite side of Daria's bed from Connor. "Isn't there someplace you need to be?"

"Yes." He turned to Daria. "I didn't have a chance to tell you I'd asked Mia to drive up and hang out with you while I tend to a few things."

"By hang out, you mean babysit," Daria said flatly.

"No, no," Mia said before Connor could open his mouth. "There are no babysitters in our family. Armed companions, when the situation calls for it, but no babysitters."

"There are some things I need to do. I can't leave you without protection, whether you're here or at the house."

"There's a policeman outside the door, isn't there?" Daria asked.

"Yes. And I'm sure he's competent. But he isn't . . . he isn't one of mine. And right now, I need one of my own with you. Someone I trust."

"Why, Connor, that's one of the nicest things you've ever said to me." Mia put a hand over her heart. "I'm truly touched."

"On the other hand, if her sarcasm becomes too much for you, you can boot her ass out and bring the cop back."

"I'm sure we'll be fine." Daria smiled. "Thank you for being concerned about me. And thank you, Mia, for coming here on short notice."

"You're welcome. And much more gracious than Con." Mia turned to him. "See? We'll be fine. You can go . . . do what you were going to do."

Connor stood and leaned over Daria and placed a kiss on her forehead, then hesitated before placing another on one side of her mouth.

"I'll see you later. You have my phone numbers if you need me."

"How long will you be?" she asked.

"Not sure. I just need to talk to a few people." He pointed to Mia as he left the room. "Behave yourself."

Mia rolled her eyes and turned to Daria. "Now, tell me how you got that lump on your head."

"I need the names and phone numbers of the people who were in your office when you spoke with Daria on the phone last night." Connor stood in front of Louise's desk, his hands on his hips.

"Connor, have a seat and I'll—"

"With all due respect, Louise, I don't have time. I have a lot of ground to cover."

"All right. Dr. Bokhari was here—you already met her in the hospital. I saw her when she got back to campus earlier; she said Daria is doing better."

"She's doing much better. Who else was here?"

"Nora Gannon, she's the chair of the board of trustees. And Olivia Masters. She's a long-time member of our board and a former television journalist. She's agreed to take on the role of public relations director until this nightmare is over. Oh—and Stefano Korban, one of the archaeology professors."

"I don't recall that you mentioned he was here." Connor frowned.

"He picked Sabina up at the airport. The other two were already here. I was bringing them up-to-date on my dealings with the bank and the insurance company when Sabina and Stefano arrived."

"Where can I find him?"

"He lives on campus, as does Sabina. I can give you their phone numbers, as well as Nora's and Olivia's. But I'm not sure I understand why you need to talk to them." Louise thumbed through her Rolodex.

"Other than Daria, me, my boss, and two FBI agents who were en route to Howe, no one knew that the e-mails to the victims had been sent from the university library. Until you called Daria and she told you. I'm assuming you repeated the story to the others when you got off the phone."

The color drained from Louise's face.

"I . . . I did." She sighed deeply. "Dear God, I did. It never occurred to me not to."

Her eyes met Connor's across the desk.

"You couldn't possibly think that one of them had anything to do with what happened in the library."

"You tell me how else the killer could have known so quickly that the FBI was going to confiscate the computers. Someone had to have tipped him off. It wasn't Daria and it wasn't me." His face was unreadable. "That brings me back to the little group in your office."

"I can't believe . . ." She shook her head.

"I need their phone numbers, Louise."

She wrote down the names and looked up the numbers and handed them over.

"Thank you. Now do me one more favor." He glanced at the note before tucking it into his shirt pocket.

"What's that?"

"Don't give anyone a heads-up this time."

FIFTEEN

Connor walked up the library steps, his ID in his right hand. He showed it to the Howeville police officer at the top of the steps, and again to the state trooper inside the front door. On his way to the basement, he ran into the two FBI agents who'd been sent to deal with the computers.

"Hey, Jason. Claire." He greeted them from the top of the steps, about to go down as they were about to come up.

"Connor, this your gig?" Jason Taylor called from the bottom of the stairwell.

"Not officially." He reached the last step. "You finished with the computers?"

"Yeah. He only used that one." Claire Mitchell told him. "And that one . . . there's nothing left. He smashed it but good, took the hard drive with him. He left nothing behind."

"Prints?" Connor asked.

"The computer's in a public place, who the hell knows how many people have used that machine? I don't think prints are going to help."

"You're finished here?" Connor started walking to the cubicles.

"Yeah. There's nothing we can extract, with the hard drive gone."

"You're sure none of the others were used?"

"Positive," Claire told him. "This guy stuck to the one machine. We ran them all six ways to Sunday and back. They're clean."

"You taking what's left of the computer with you?"

"Yeah. It's evidence." Jason pulled a plastic toothpick from his pocket and chewed on the end of it. "It's ours."

Connor stood over the demolished computer. "I want prints run."

"Connor, hundreds of people have used this machine."

"Yeah, but only one person beat the crap out of it. Maybe he got personal with it, maybe picked up a piece or two and smashed it against something else." He got down on one knee and stared at the cracked edge of the laminate desktop, then looked up and smiled. "Let's get the evidence guys in here to dust everything. Every piece of the machine, every inch of the desk, the chair. I have a feeling he left more of himself behind than he'd intended."

"Chief Thorpe," Connor called to the head of the local police department.

"Agent Shields." The older man nodded politely. "You're not going to gum up my works, are you?"

"The murder investigation is all yours." Connor held up both hands in a hands-off gesture. "But I did have a few questions."

"Shoot."

"The surveillance camera . . ."

"He took the tape with him when he left."

"Your people dusted for prints?" Connor asked.

"Hell, yes."

"And on the railing going up the steps?"

"Uh-huh. Just in case he grabbed it as he ran up after Miz Weathers."

"Okay, so where else did you dust?" Connor walked with the chief to the front desk.

"Handrails in all the stairwells. The front and back doors. Hell, even the men's room door," Thorpe told him. "I'm guessing you're going to want to see all the matching prints."

"Just want to see where he's been. I want them run against some prints I lifted off a window frame the other night. I figure if we can match those prints to the ones from the camera, to those from the computer, and to prints taken from the victim—assuming you find some latents and can lift them—we'll know something about him."

"What's that?" Thorpe frowned.

"We'll know he was in a big hurry. Didn't have time to worry about his prints. And we'll know that he can be panicked into acting foolishly. A good thing to know."

Thorpe studied Connor's face. "What else do you need?"

"Cause of death for last night's victim?"

"The ME isn't finished with the autopsy yet, far as I know, but the EMTs said it looked like strangulation. Marks on her neck suggested a rope or something similar. She was found facedown—"

"I know. I found her," Connor reminded him.

"Right. So facedown on the floor, strangled; I'm thinking he comes up behind her, chokes her till she stops breathing, then just drops her right there."

Connor nodded. "The interns said last night they could hear him chasing Mrs. Weathers up the steps, then it got quiet. Maybe he was stalking her through the stacks, then grabbed her from behind, like you suggested."

"Makes sense to me."

"Were you able to get the names of any of the students who were here when the killer came in?"

"Got a list of 'em. Spoke with them myself. You're wanting to know how he got them to leave."

"Yes."

"He told them there was a problem, some short in the electrical system, and they were going to have to shut off the power," Thorpe told him. "They thought he was university security, since he was wearing a uniform."

"Did it look like what the real guards wear?"

"They said it was the same color, but whether or not it was the same, they couldn't tell. They just knew it was brown."

"Did you point out a real guard to them?"

"Don't make me roll my eyes at you, Agent Shields." Thorpe sighed. "Of course we did. They just weren't paying attention. They're studying, a guy comes up in a uniform, he looks like a guard, as far as the kids are concerned, he's a guard."

"Were they able to describe him?"

"Tall, maybe six-one, six-two. Well-built. The one girl said he looked pretty buff. Like he works out. Maybe twenty-five to thirty, brown hair, brown eyes. Caucasian, but he looked like he had a good tan. No distinguishing marks."

"Any campus guards who fit that description?"

"I already interviewed the head of security. They have one or two guys who are almost six feet tall, no one he considers particularly buff. The guards here mostly sit around and look out the window, occasionally walk outside. He said they haven't even had anyone to chase all summer; there hasn't been a whole lot of activity on this campus since the spring semester ended."

"Have you been able to talk to the guard who was on duty last night?"

"Yeah. He says he heard one of those electronic alarms, like one of the doors had been opened. He checked the schematic of the building, says it looked like one of the basement doors. He went downstairs to check it, got to the door, saw it was slightly ajar. Went to close it, someone whacked him over the head, and he doesn't recall a thing after that."

"Where is he now?"

"He's at home with an ice pack on his head. Sergeant Mills there at the front desk can give you his name and address." Thorpe stood with his hands in his pants pockets. "Anything else?"

"Not at the moment, thank you, but I'd like a copy of the autopsy report on Gloria Weathers when it's available. You have my number. If you give me a call, I'll come pick it up."

"Will do." Thorpe nodded and started to walk away.

"Chief, your people have done a great job."

"Gee, thanks, Agent Shields. We live for the approval of the feds."

"I'm sorry, I didn't mean to imply—"

"Whatever." Thorpe turned his back. "Have a nice day, Agent Shields."

"Teach me to compliment the locals," Connor muttered to himself.

Once outside, he searched his pockets for the card Louise had given him and looked it over. Where to start, the archaeologists or the trustees?

He was thinking he'd start with the trustees when he saw Sabina Bokhari walking toward him. Daria had been right. The woman was not only uncommonly beautiful, but alluringly feminine. She was accompanied by a tall, thin, serious-looking man with dark hair and a well-trimmed beard.

"Agent Shields," she called to him. "How is Daria? Is she back at McGowan House?"

"She might be on her way by now," he told her, adopting her friendly tone. "She was still waiting to see the doctor when I left about an hour or so ago."

He turned his attention to her escort.

"We haven't met. I'm Connor Shields."

"So sorry. Where are my manners?" Sabina smiled pleasantly. "Stefano Korban, a colleague of mine here at Howe." She turned to the bearded man. "Connor is the FBI agent who is working with Dr. McGowan."

"Good to meet you." Korban's voice was surprising deep and rich, the kind Connor generally heard coming from more robust bodies.

"And you." Connor nodded.

"Stefano and I were just taking a walk. I can't get into the library to go to my office, and I just can't sit around my apartment any longer. I keep thinking about the terrible things that have been happening lately. Poor Mrs. Weathers"—Sabina shook her head—"and those other people who were killed . . . it's just tragic."

"Does the FBI have any suspects?" Korban asked. "Any idea who killed all those people?"

"The FBI isn't handling the murders," Connor told them. "The police departments where the killings took place are in charge of those investigations. The Bureau is really only investigating the art thefts."

"That's funny," Korban frowned. "At the press conference this morning the detective from Delaware said you were in charge of the whole thing, and everything was going through you."

"I'm afraid you misunderstood. I have agreed to serve as a liaison between the police departments and the FBI. There will be certain information that will be relevant to the murder investigations as well as to the theft of the artifacts."

"What is the status, Agent Shields?" Korban asked. "Of the thefts, I mean."

"Still under investigation," Connor said shortly. "But while we're on the subject of the investigations, I would like to ask you both a few questions. Would it be all right if I stopped at your apartments later?"

"Why not now?" Sabina asked. "We're all here."

"For one thing, I don't have time to talk to you both," Connor explained. "For another, I'd like to keep the party small."

"I see." Sabina smiled. "Are we suspects, then?"

"Sabina, don't be ridiculous," Korban admonished her.

"I just have a few questions I'd like to ask each of you."

"I'm actually on my way to the grocery store," Sabina told him. "As you know, I've been out of the country for two months. My cupboard is bare. However, if you'd care to stop over later, say around seven, I should be back from all my errands."

"Seven is fine. I'll see you then."

"Good. Stefano, I'll leave you here. My car is right behind the arts building. I'll catch up with you later."

"See you." Korban watched her walk away, then turned his attention to Connor. "I'm available right now. I was just on my way to the parking lot."

"That's where I'm headed. Okay, we'll talk on our way."

The two men fell into step.

"So you picked up Dr. Bokhari at the airport last night," Connor said.

"Yes. She flew into Philly from Cairo, got in around six. We stopped on the way home for dinner, small place out near Kennett."

"What time did you get back to campus?"

"Must have been around seven-thirty."

"How'd you end up at Dr. Burnette's office?"

"We saw her lights on when we drove past the administration building. Sabina wanted to stop in and let her know she was back. Also, she wanted an update on the thefts from the museum."

"So you stopped at the office . . ."

"The door was partly open, so Sabina stuck her head in to say hello. Dr. Burnette invited us in. A couple of the trustees were there, and they were talking about the artifacts that were stolen and the collectors that were murdered. Everyone was pretty shocked by the whole thing."

"What time did you leave the office?"

"It was after eight. I don't remember exactly. It was shortly after Dr. Burnette spoke with Dr. McGowan."

"Where did you go after you left Dr. Burnette's office?"

"I drove Sabina back to her apartment. I helped her get her luggage inside. She invited me in for a glass of wine. Sabina was very upset about the entire thing and wanted to talk. Not just the thefts, or the murders, but also about Dr. McGowan discovering that the thefts had taken place."

"Why do you suppose that was?"

"Because Sabina's the head of the archaeology department here. She was already upset that the university brought someone in over her to handle the reopening of the museum. When Dr. McGowan discovered the thefts, that made it even worse. Not to say that they are rivals, exactly, but they share the same area of expertise."

"The archaeology of the Middle East."

"Yes. Sabina's quite the scholar, you know."

"I think Daria—Dr. McGowan—might have mentioned that."

"Sabina's spent a lot of time studying over there," Korban said as they walked toward the parking lot.

"You think she was familiar with this city that Dr. McGowan's great-grandfather found?"

"Shandihar?" Korban stopped next to a green Jetta and took the key from his pocket. "Sure."

"How do you know for certain?"

"Because she mentioned once that she was reading up on all of Alistair McGowan's expeditions."

"Why would she do that?"

"Because she wanted to follow in his footsteps. She wanted to re-discover the city. She was going to find Shandihar again."

Korban unlocked the Jetta. "Was there anything else you wanted to know?"

"No," Connor told him. "I think that should do it for now."

SIXTEEN

Daria sat in the wicker chair, her feet propped up on the matching ottoman, a cool drink in her hand, and a pounding inside her head. For all Mia's efforts to make her as comfortable as possible, Daria just wanted to rest her head and cry. The former was doable. The latter would have to wait until she was alone. She'd never been particularly comfortable sharing her emotions.

"What else can I get you?" Mia asked.

"Nothing, thank you." Daria put the glass down on the table next to her. "And thanks again for bringing me home."

"Don't mention it. Now, how about another pillow, or . . . well, I guess a blanket isn't necessary, since it's about eighty degrees in here."

"Opening the windows and turning on the fan helped." Daria glanced up at the fan that was whirling over their heads. "I think the room will cool off if we give it a few more minutes."

"This is a really great room. If this were my house, I'd live out here." Mia sat in a rocking chair across from Daria. "I guess you spend a lot of time out here."

"I love it. It was built as a conservatory, and it's easy to imagine the room filled with leafy plants, and flowering things." Daria gazed around the room, imagining just that. "But I've hardly been in here at all. We've been so busy since I discovered the thefts from the museum, then Connor arrived and we started looking up the collectors, and the next thing you know, we discovered several of them were dead—murdered."

"For someone not used to that sort of pace, I can see where it would be distressing." Mia nodded. "But one thing I've learned over the years, it all passes, sooner or later. One case ends, the next one begins."

"How long have you been in the FBI?"

"I was in for nine years. I left the Bureau about a month ago." Mia began to fidget, picking at the paper label on her bottle of root beer.

"Were you just tired of it, or . . ." Daria wasn't sure how to continue, or if she should.

"Tired of it in the sense that I'd seen enough bad stuff to last a lifetime or two." Mia took a long drink from the bottle. "Or three. It just got to me after a while. All the suffering. All the terrible things people do to one another. I just had to step back from it for a time."

"Do you think you'll go back?"

"To the Bureau?" Mia shook her head. "No. But I will stay in law enforcement."

"In what capacity?"

"I'm applying for a job as a small-town cop," Mia said, grinning, "in a little town on Maryland's Eastern Shore."

"After years with the FBI, will that be too slow a pace for you?"

"Nah. I love the town, and I am so ready for that change. Besides, the chief of police is a hunk."

"Oh." Daria laughed. "I guess that's incentive."

"More than enough." Mia gathered the paper scraps and rose to take them and the empty bottle to the kitchen. "Can I bring you anything?"

"No, thanks, Mia. The sandwich was just enough."

"I'll bring the cookies back, just in case."

Mia stepped over Sweet Thing on her way out of the room. The dog had planted herself in the doorway like a furry sentinel, as if to say, *You'll have to go through me to get to Daria,* and Daria took some comfort knowing her canine companion was on guard duty. Of course, the fact that Mia was armed added to Daria's comfort level.

All at once, Sweet Thing rose, a deep growl beginning somewhere deep inside like thunder, her gaze fixed on the door.

"It's okay, girl, it's me," Connor called to the dog as he came through the kitchen. "Good girl."

He paused in the doorway to pet the dog and praise her. "Way to be on the case, Sweet Thing."

To Daria, he said, "How are you feeling? Head still throbbing?"

"Unfortunately, yes. Not as bad as yesterday, though."

"Did you take the medication the doctor gave you?"

"Not yet, but I will. I didn't want to fall asleep on Mia. She's been so nice."

"Yeah, she has her moments." Connor lifted Daria's legs by the crossed ankles and sat on the ottoman at her feet.

"I heard that." Mia came into the room, carrying a plate with a sandwich wrapped in butcher's paper and a plastic container. "We got you roast beef on rye and some potato salad. Pull that table closer, Con."

He did as he was told and Mia placed everything on the table for him.

"Can I get you a beer?"

"No, thanks, Mia. I have a meeting in about ten minutes on the other side of campus. I really appreciate you thinking of me when it came to food."

"We found a really great deli on our way back from the hospital. It's right down there in the middle of town, so we stopped for sandwiches. Neither Daria nor I felt like having a large meal tonight." Mia turned to Daria. "Would you like me to get your meds for you now? You must be ready to take something for the pain."

"I probably am," Daria admitted and started to get up. "But I can get it."

"You stay put. I don't mind." Mia started toward the door.

"Hey, this is a side of you I've never seen before. I like it. I've never seen you wait on anyone before."

"It's a whole new me," Mia told him as she left the room. "It's living the small-town life, what can I say?"

"She was just telling me she'd left the FBI," Daria said.

Connor nodded. "She needed to do that. She'd seen too much in too few years. It was time for her to move on, maybe find some peace in her life."

"Do you think she will?"

"I think she has. She's looking forward to starting a new job in the fall—maybe she's told you about that?"

When Daria nodded, he continued. "Got herself a new guy, a great guy. I think she's going to be okay."

"I hope so. I like her a lot."

"Yeah, she's all right."

Daria could tell by the way he said it that he thought his cousin was more than just all right.

He unwrapped the sandwich and began to eat.

"Anything new to tell me?" she asked.

Connor finished chewing, swallowed, and said, "I stopped at the library after I left the hospital and had a chat with the local chief of police."

Daria listened intently as Connor filled her in on how the killer had gotten the people in the library to leave.

"Wasn't there a real guard there?" Mia asked as she came back into the room with a small tray.

"Yes, but he'd gone into the basement to check on an open door and was bashed over the head," Connor told her.

"Was he killed?" she asked.

"No, just knocked out for a while, much like Daria. Though he had a few more stitches than she does," he replied.

"At least he's alive. How'd the door get opened?"

"That's one thing I can't find an easy explanation for. There's no way to jimmy it from outside. I have to think someone on the inside either left it open by accident—maybe went out by the back door and didn't close it all the way—or someone deliberately opened it for the killer."

"Which means an accomplice."

"There has to be more than one person working this thing. I'm seeing two, maybe three."

"Like some kind of ring." Mia bit the cuticle on one finger. "Have you given any thought to this being an organized theft operation? You know, stealing valuable artifacts to resell them to other collectors?"

"Why would they target these specific artifacts?" Daria asked.

"Because they're very rare—didn't you say the things in the museum basement are the only known artifacts from Shandihar?" Mia asked. "If you're going to steal to sell on the black market, why not steal the stuff that's going to bring you the greatest return for your effort?"

"It feels like more than a simple theft," Daria told her. "You have these ritualistic killings. Whoever is behind this knows the Shandiharan culture well enough to know how they punished people they felt had committed some sort of transgression. That greatly limits the pool of suspects."

"Could be a combination of both, though," Connor said thoughtfully. "Maybe someone with inside knowledge who's out to make a killing—no pun intended—on the black market. But at this point, I think we need to consider all possibilities."

Mia set the small metal tray on the table she'd earlier pulled over for Connor. "I hope you don't mind me going through the kitchen cupboards, but I thought if I could find a little tray, I could bring everything in at the same time."

"I don't mind at all. I'm grateful for your help."

"Here's a bottle of water for you"—she handed it to Connor—
"and here's one for you, Daria, along with those painkillers you've
been avoiding. I can tell by the expression on your face that you're not
very comfortable right now."

"I should probably take them now." Daria reached for the small
orange container Mia held out to her.

"In other news, I had a chat with Stefano Korban a little while
ago," Connor said.

"He's the archaeologist on the faculty here?" Daria popped the
pills into her mouth and swallowed them with some water.

"Right. Daria, what do you know about Sabina Bokhari?"

"I know she's very well regarded in the field. So much so that I was
surprised to find out she was on the faculty here at Howe."

"Why's that?" Mia asked.

"Because she could certainly be teaching at a much more presti-
gious university. She could pretty much write her own ticket anywhere,"
Daria explained. "I really don't understand why she's here, frankly."

"I'm guessing you didn't know about her interest in Shandihar?"
Connor asked.

"She did mention that she was familiar with the legends. She told
me there was a curse . . ."

"Did she also mention that one of her goals is to someday follow
in Alistair's footsteps?"

"I don't understand," Mia said. "What does that mean?"

"It means she wants to rediscover the city, according to Professor
Korban. Seems she's envisioning Shandihar's second coming, if you
will." Connor used the napkin Mia had given him and rolled up the
now empty paper in which his sandwich had been wrapped.

Daria looked dumbstruck.

"Yeah, that was pretty much my reaction, too," Connor told her.

"She never said anything about that to me. She was in my hospital room with me for hours, and never said a word about that. She just mentioned reading some book about the Sisters of Shandihar, which was apparently another name for the priestesses, and some vague curse associated with them and the *gallas*."

"The evil spirits who roamed the earth and did bad things for Ereshkigal," Connor added.

"Er . . . who?" Mia asked.

"The Shandiharan goddess of the Underworld." Daria explained the dark goddess and her cult of followers to Mia, who rolled her eyes.

"*Gallas* and goddesses and evil sisterhoods, oh my," Mia parodied. "You think any of these evil sisters or evil *gallas* are here at Howe University?"

"Maybe someone—or more than one—who believe they are," Connor told her. "Just as deadly, in the long run. Someone who believes they have a sacred mission is going to be just as dangerous as someone who really does."

"You mean, like someone who knows that some items were stolen from the storage room, and who wants to get them back?" Daria thought aloud. "But that someone would have to know that the items were missing in the first place."

Connor nodded slowly. "All along, we've assumed that no one knew anything was missing until Daria did her inventory. What if someone had already figured that out?" He stopped and thought for a moment. "Well, of course, if this theory is the right one, someone had to know. The Blumes and Mrs. Sevrenson were both killed several months ago. Months before Daria arrived at Howe."

"Then it follows that someone else would have to have known exactly what was in those crates," Daria said.

"Which means that someone had to have read Alistair's journals to have known exactly what he'd brought back," Connor said. "How much do you want to bet Dr. Bokhari is well acquainted with Alistair's journals?"

"How much do you suppose she knew about the artifacts? And did she know they were missing?" Mia asked.

"Just two of the questions I'll be asking her." Connor glanced at his watch. "I'm on my way over to her apartment now."

He turned to Daria. "I'll check in on you when I get back. Is there anything you need? Anything I can bring you?"

"No, thanks." She shook her head. "Mia's taking good care of me."

"Great." He patted her leg, then stood and turned to Mia. "I owe you one."

"My pleasure, sport." His cousin smiled.

"Mia, come with me and lock the front door after I leave."

"Good idea." To Daria, Mia said, "I'll be right back."

Daria watched Connor pause to pat the dog on the head before he and Mia left the room. Several seconds later, she heard the front door close, then listened as Mia's footsteps came closer.

"This is a really interesting case," Mia said as she stepped over Sweet Thing. "Almost interesting enough to make me want to re-up." She smiled at Daria. "Just kidding. It's interesting but I have no intention of going back."

She sat back on the rocker and picked up the plate of cookies. After inspection and selection, she offered the plate to Daria, who at first started to decline but then shrugged and leaned forward to take it from Mia's hands.

"What's bothering you?" Mia asked as she handed the plate over.

"Thinking about Sabina," Daria said softly. "I wasn't aware her interest in Shandihar ran so deep. I'd hate to think she's involved somehow. I can't understand why she didn't say more when we were in the hospital."

"Maybe she thought it wasn't the time or place to talk about work."

"Trust me, you put two archaeologists in a room, that's all they talk about. And we did. We talked about mutual friends, and a dig she was on with some people I've worked with." Daria frowned. "But she never mentioned that she wanted to search for Shandihar."

"What else is bothering you about her?" Mia asked.

"What makes you thing there's something else?"

"Just the look on your face."

The words Daria could have spoken stuck in her throat.

"It's Connor, isn't it?" Mia said it for her. "You think he's interested in her?"

"Well, she is pretty . . . well, gorgeous." Daria sighed.

"If all it took to get Connor's attention was a pretty face, he'd have been snatched up long ago." Mia nibbled on her cookie. "He's been chased by many, but he's never come close to being caught. At least, as far as anyone in the family knows."

"Strange. You'd think he'd . . . well, he's just such a warm person."

"Connor? Warm?" Mia laughed. "There are very few people who would describe him as warm, Daria. He's been a loner all his life, even more so since . . . well, since Dylan." A shadow crossed Mia's face.

"Who's Dylan?"

"His brother."

"The one who died?"

"He told you about that?" Mia asked.

"Not exactly. He just said he had a brother who died." Daria paused, then asked, "How did he die?"

"I think you ought to ask him that." Mia stood and began to clear the plates and empty water bottles. "It's not something I like to talk about."

She left the room, leaving Daria with another round of questions that were not likely to be answered anytime soon.

"Come in, Agent Shields." Sabina Bokhari stood in the doorway of her second-floor apartment in an old brick building at the edge of the Howe campus. "You're very prompt."

She wore the same kind of khaki shorts that Daria was in the habit of wearing, and a loose-fitting coral-colored knit top. Her long black hair was pulled back on one side and held with a clip. He was struck once again that she was, as Daria had noted, uncommonly beautiful.

"Do come in." She stepped aside and he entered the spacious living room.

"Interesting décor," he said as he looked around at the art-filled room. "Souvenirs from your last dig?"

She smiled. "I am not in the habit of tomb robbing or pilfering from the job site. I do, however, frequent the gift shops of museums all over the world. Please have a seat."

She gestured toward the sofa, but he chose the chair on the opposite wall.

"You wanted to ask me some questions." She took a seat on the sofa facing him.

"Let's start with Tuesday night. What time did you get back on campus?"

"I'm not sure, but I think around seven-thirty or so. Stefano picked me up at the airport and we stopped for dinner on the way home. We passed the administration building on the way to my apartment, and I noticed that Louise's office lights were still on. I asked Stefano to stop so I could see her. I wasn't aware she had people in the office, but when we arrived, she invited us to join her and the two trustees."

"Had you met them before?"

"Yes, of course. They've both been around forever. Nora Gannon's a legacy, if you follow."

"I don't."

"Her father and her grandfather were both Howe graduates. They both served on the board."

"And the other trustee?"

"Olivia Masters." Sabina nodded. "She's a Howe alum, and she lives right outside Howeville. She volunteered to be the new public re-lations person for the university, at least until this is resolved."

"So Louise invited you and Stefano to come in and be part of this impromptu meeting." So far, Sabina's story matched Stefano's per-fectly.

"Yes. She said she was just getting ready to call Daria to come over when we arrived."

"Was there anyone else?" he asked. "Anyone else she was going to call that you know of?"

"No." She shook her head slowly.

"You were away for the summer on a dig with some students. Was the dig sponsored by Howe?"

"Howe and three other universities."

"You were away for how long?"

"Eight weeks. It would have been twelve, but when I heard about what was happening here, I told Louise I'd come back early. There were other archaeologists on the site—I don't feel that my leaving was detrimental to the students."

"I was wondering about when you left . . . where were you again?"

"In Turkey."

"That's where Shandihar was, right?"

"We were in northeastern Turkey. Shandihar was located in the south of Turkey. Of course, it's been buried under sand since the earthquake early in the last century, so who knows exactly where it is."

"Rumor has it that you do."

She appeared to be taken off guard, but only for a moment.

"Oh, you've been talking to Stefano." She waved a hand dismis-sively. "Yes, I did tell him that I'd like to be the one to find the city again. Me and five hundred other people in the field."

"Five hundred other people are not head of the archaeology de-partment at the university where every known artifact from Shandihar is housed."

"For me to deny that I knew the McGowan collection was here would be an insult to your intelligence, and mine. Yes, of course I knew about it when I sent my résumé in to Louise several years ago."

"I wasn't aware that the whole Shandihar thing was widely known. I was under the impression that Alistair McGowan and his find were pretty much forgotten after his death. How did you hear about it?"

"In this country, yes, it isn't a story that's widely known, that's true. But I grew up in Turkey, Pakistan, Afghanistan—my father was a professor of ancient history and taught in several universities. So I'd hear things, you know, legends, stories, that sort of thing. I picked up a book in a bazaar in Turkey when I was about thirteen, and I read about this city that everyone had believed was made-up, but then it was found by a foreigner who took away with him everything he could move."

"I imagine that didn't sit well with the Turks," he said. "That this entire culture had been taken from them."

"The old people in the region said the earthquake buried the city again because the goddess was angry that her treasures had been stolen, that her temples had not been safeguarded." She smiled at him. "I was quite impressionable at thirteen, Agent Shields. I read about how Alistair McGowan found Shandihar by reading the ancient epic poems and studying all the legends, so I did the same. I read what he'd read, and I dreamed about finding the city again someday."

"So you know about Ereshkigal?"

"Of course. And I know how her priestesses punished sinners." She slashed at one wrist with the side of her hand.

"Why didn't you mention this to me when I met you in the hospital?"

"For one thing, I was afraid it would move me to the top of your suspect list."

"You think?" he replied sarcastically.

"Do you honestly think I killed those people? That I cut off their hands and cut out their tongues and stole their artifacts?"

"You seem to know a lot about it."

Sabina rolled her eyes. "Everyone who watched the press conference this morning knows that much. The detective from Delaware was quite graphic in his description of the manner in which those people were killed."

"He should not have done that." Connor grimaced.

"Not my fault, Agent Shields." Her voice held a snap he hadn't noticed earlier. "The detective described the couple as being athletic, and the man as rather large. Do you really think I'm capable of subduing two such people, then killing them both? In case you hadn't noticed, I'm five feet five inches tall and I weigh one hundred and fourteen pounds. I'm in good shape, but I'm no match for people such as the ones the detective described. And besides, I've been out of the country, as you know."

"You could have had accomplices." Connor shrugged. "I imagine it wouldn't be too difficult for you to get a guy— or two—to do things for you."

"And my motive would be . . . ?"

Connor shrugged. "Maybe you fancy yourself one of those *gallas* and you believe you're working for the goddess. Or maybe you read Alistair's journals and took a look at what was in the basement of the museum, figured out what was missing, and decided you'd get it all back and sell it on the black market." He was throwing out the theories he'd earlier tossed around with Mia and Daria.

"I think that's enough." Her dark eyes flashed. "Am I a suspect in this, Agent Shields?"

"Everyone at Howe is a suspect, Dr. Bokhari."

"Then you should probably leave." She stood, her earlier courtesy now gone.

"Were you upset when you found out that Daria had been asked to come in and oversee the restoration of the museum?"

"Of course I was upset." She crossed her arms over her chest. "I'm qualified to do the job. I am head of the department here, but they brought her in because her name was McGowan. So yes, I was upset, and frankly, I was embarrassed by the fact that I'd been overlooked for the position. And then, to make matters worse, she finds that important pieces from the collection are missing."

"Why does that make matters worse?"

"Because I like her. I respect her for who she is, but I also like her. I'd hate for her to think that I'm an idiot."

"Why would she think that?"

"Because I'm the head of the department and this happened on my watch."

"If you're referring to the theft of the artifacts, I can assure you that happened long before you came to Howe. The murders, on the other hand, they're definitely on your watch."

She stared at him.

"I think I'd like you to leave now." She opened the door for him.

"Does Louise know about your fascination with Shandihar?" he asked as he crossed the room.

"No." She smiled wryly as she ushered him into the hall. "Though I suspect she will before much longer."

"One more thing," he started to ask. "When did you first find out that artifacts had been stolen from the—"

She slammed the door in his face.

"Okay, then," he murmured. "Thanks for your time."

SEVENTEEN

He stood in the shadows and watched the house. Though tall, he was more boy than man, with long, gangly arms and legs, and just the barest bit of stubble on his face. He held his breath when the front door opened unexpectedly and the tall, dark-haired man with the dangerous eyes came down the steps and set off down the path that led farther into the campus.

Was anyone inside with the woman? He wasn't sure.

He wished he'd arrived sooner. He wished there were more eyes to watch all the places that needed watching.

He wished he was back home with his friends, playing soccer in the fields and huddling together on the hillside at night, sharing cigarettes and telling lies and listening to Western music on the radio.

Most of all, he wished he could be anywhere but here, hiding amid the thick growth of evergreens outside this house where the woman lived.

But he'd taken an oath, hadn't he? He'd stood between his father and his brother, there on the hillside overlooking the valley where it was said an earthquake had swallowed up an entire city.

He thought of his trips to Istanbul and to Cairo. On their way to America, they had stopped in that most wondrous of cities, London. How could the earth open up wide enough to swallow an entire city? How was it possible that the earth could eat whole buildings and leave nothing in their place?

But that's what his father had said between the loud racking coughs that had brought him back from wherever he'd been for much of the boys' life. For the past several years, after the sickness had taken hold of their father's lungs, it had been his brother who'd disappeared for months at a time, coming home for a few weeks here and there. Four weeks ago, his brother had returned, and had gone directly into their father's room, where they'd talked long into the night.

Then, on the night before his brother was to leave again, they'd taken him up into the hills where they told him they would teach him how to pray. There, where the sacred city had stood, they would all pray. The boy had looked down but saw nothing but rock and desert below.

The prayers had been most strange, had made no sense to him, and seemed to go on forever. When he opened an eye to peek—from boredom more than curiosity—his father and brother were both kneeling in the dirt, their arms outstretched toward the heavens, with tears on their faces.

That had been about the scariest thing he'd ever seen.

Scarier even than the words they were chanting and the oath they made him repeat. *I am* gallas, *and the priestess I obey. The faithful remember . . .*

He had no idea what the words really meant until he came to this place and the priestess told him what he must do. Now, *she* had been scary. Beyond scary.

After that, his nightmare really began.

Even now, his mouth filled with bile just thinking of it. At night he dreamed that the eyes of the dead followed him, and every morning he awoke with the scent of blood in his nostrils. And always, always, his hands felt the slick warm liquid that had poured over them . . .

"Why?" he'd pleaded with his brother. "Why?"

"Because the goddess demands it."

How long ago had it been—a week? less?—that he'd held the woman's head in his hands while his brother had carved out her tongue? And then the man, the woman's husband, whose eyes had gone wild with madness as he helplessly watched his wife's agony.

His hands had shaken but he'd done what he'd been told to do. He'd followed orders like a zombie, unable to really see, to feel, to think.

The man-boy hiding in the evergreens began to sweat. He tried to will the horrific images from his mind's eye, but they were always there now.

And there'd been the other one, the man who lived alone in the fine stone house, the man whose dog had chased him, had bitten his arm. He rubbed the place where the dog's teeth had sunken into his flesh, felt the scabs that had formed. All things considered, after what he'd helped his brother to do, he couldn't be angry with the dog.

The image of that man stayed with him, day and night.

His stomach turned, remembering.

How was it his brother could be so unaffected by what they had done?

"The goddess demands it, little brother. The priestess has told me so."

He loved his father and wished to honor him. He'd taken his father's place as a *gallas* as he'd been told he must do. But deep down inside, he wished he could run, wished he could just disappear and never see his brother or the priestess again.

But of course, no matter where he went, they would find him. The *gallas* always did.

EIGHTEEN

Connor paused to secure the dead bolt on the front door, then walked quietly into the sitting room next to the foyer to turn off the lamp that had been left lit for him. He smiled to himself. He'd lived alone for so many years, had spent so much time alone, that the thought that someone had left a light on for him warmed his heart. He made his way to the back of the house to check the doors and windows. All secure.

He turned when he heard Sweet Thing scratching at the door between the kitchen and the front hall, and he swung the door open for her.

"What's up, girl? Need a quick trip out?"

The dog went directly to the back door.

"I'm taking that as a yes."

Connor turned on the lights on the back porch, and for a moment, he hesitated, and considered putting Sweet Thing on her leash before deciding against it. The leash was in the kitchen on the counter, and the dog was scratching at the door. Besides, there wouldn't be much foot traffic out there tonight. He needn't worry about the dog chasing anyone.

He opened the door and Sweet Thing shot out. By the time Connor reached the bottom step, the dog had disappeared around the corner of the house.

"Hey, girl, where are you going?"

A loud growl came from around the side of the house. Seconds later, he heard Sweet Thing snarling, and then a high-pitched scream.

Connor followed the sound to the stand of evergreens outside the glassed-walled conservatory that ran along the side of the house. He called the dog's name, and the snarling stopped, but the dog refused to leave the base of the pine she was anxiously pawing. Connor looked up and saw a figure less than eight feet overhead.

"Come down now, slowly. And when you hit the ground, I want you facedown in the dirt."

The figure did not move.

"I'm going to say this one more time." He drew his gun. "And if you don't come down on your own, I'll shoot you down. Understand?"

"It bit me! The dog bit me!"

"If you don't start coming down from that tree, you're going to have more than a dog bite to worry about."

"Make the dog go away." The voice from the tree was smaller, younger than Connor had been expecting. "Make it go away, and then I'll come down."

Connor called the dog to him. This time, she obeyed and sat at his feet.

"Come down slowly, and step over here where I can see you."

"You have a gun."

"Yes."

"Are you going to shoot me?"

"Only if you don't come down and do as I say. Lie on the ground, facedown, hands behind your back."

The figure came down slowly, then backed away from the pine.

"Out here, away from the trees." Connor gestured with the gun. "Facedown on the grass."

"Connor, what the hell is going on out there?" Mia stood at the corner of the house. She took a few steps closer, then asked, "And why are you holding a gun on that kid?"

Chief Thorpe slammed the back door of the patrol car and turned to Connor. "You want to follow me down to the station? I'm assuming you're going to want to do most of the questioning."

"I do, thanks." Connor watched the car carrying the young boy pull away from the front of the house. "Think you could spare a man to keep an eye on the house here until I get back?"

"Sure." Thorpe turned and waved to a young patrol officer who was chatting with two others down near the parking lot. "O'Brien. I need you and your partner to watch the house until Agent Shields is finished with the suspect. Get Officer Silver up here with you."

"Yes, sir." The officer went off in search of his partner.

"I'm going to run inside and make sure the house is secured, but I should be right behind you, Chief," Connor told him.

"I'll see you at the station." Thorpe nodded and headed off for his vehicle.

Connor ran up the back steps of the house and into the kitchen where Daria and Mia were seated at the table, the dog between them like a large brown-and-white statue.

"You've got yourself a pretty damned good watchdog," he told Daria. "She knew that kid was out there, made a beeline for the trees the minute I opened the door."

"Who is he?" Daria frowned. "And why was he watching the house?"

"That's what I'm going to find out." He slipped his gun back into his holster. "There are two Howeville cops outside to keep an eye on you until I get back. I doubt there's going to be any more activity tonight, so I suggest you two go back to bed. Tomorrow's going to be a busy day."

"Why's that?" Daria asked.

"Because we have a meeting with Mr. Cavanaugh at his house, if you feel up to a drive."

"I'm up to it, yes, definitely." She nodded.

"Who's Mr. Cavanaugh?" Mia asked.

"An antiques dealer who might have sold one of the artifacts to one of the victims," he told her. To Daria, he said, "Go back to sleep. Get some rest."

She nodded again and the two women started out of the room.

"Come on, Sweet Thing," Daria called to the dog. "My hero . . . good girl!"

"Hey," Connor said as she was about to push open the swinging door. "Thanks for leaving the light on."

Daria smiled and met his eyes. "Anytime."

Connor took a seat at the table across from the boy and studied his face. Dark eyes, deeply set and filled with fear. Long thin nose, round face, wide mouth, tanned skin. Well, that wasn't unusual. It was, after all, August. The boy was tall and slim and of an indeterminable age, and according to Chief Thorpe hadn't opened his mouth since they arrived at the police station, where he was shown into this small room with the glass wall.

"What's your name, son?" Connor asked. No response.

"How old are you?"

Nothing.

"Want to tell me why you were hiding in the bushes outside Dr. McGowan's house?"

The boy's eyes seemed to narrow, but he did not speak. He sat with his arms flat on the table.

Connor held up the cell phone that had been taken from the boy's pants pocket.

"How about you tell me whose number this is programmed into your phone?" Connor pretended to study the number. "This the only number you ever call? Don't you have any other friends?"

It was like talking to a stone wall.

The kid scratched at his left forearm with his right hand. He acted as if he were the only person in the room.

"Have it your way, kid," Connor said as he got up from the table.

He met Thorpe in the hallway.

"I see you had about as much luck as we did," Thorpe told him.

"Someone trained him well. He's not offering a damned thing." Connor handed Thorpe the cell phone. "No luck, I'm guessing, tracing the number?"

"Prepaid to prepaid. There's no record of anything. We called the number several times. The first two times, a man answered, but nothing after that."

"He could have figured out that his little buddy here had been picked up."

"That's what I'm thinking."

They walked back into the room from which Thorpe had watched Connor and the boy. They both looked through the glass, but the boy sat still as a stone.

"You took his prints?" Connor asked.

"First thing we did."

"You run them against the prints you took from the library?"

"Not yet, but we will."

"Start with the prints you took from the basement door," Connor said, "then ask New Castle to run them against the prints taken from the Cross murder scene. Particularly the prints from the patio door."

Thorpe turned to stare at Connor.

"The boy has marks on his arm that look like a dog bite. The detective from Delaware told me the blood type from the back door of Cross's house did not match the victim's. When I opened the door of the house tonight, Sweet Thing took off like a rocket."

"Sweet Thing?" The chief raised his eyebrows.

"She's the dog we found at the Cross scene and brought back . . . that is, Dr. McGowan brought back, rather than have it taken to a shelter," Connor explained. "The dog smelled that kid the second I opened the door. She knew his scent. She's normally a really sweet dog, Chief, but she took off like a bat out of hell. She did get a nip in, but I'm guessing it's no big deal if he hasn't complained about it."

"He hasn't even mentioned it."

"There's no telling what she would have done to him if he hadn't gotten himself up that tree when he did."

"So you're thinking this kid was at the scene of the Cross murder?" Thorpe rubbed his chin. "You're thinking the dog bit him on the arm at Cross's?"

Connor nodded. "Let's start with the fingerprints, see if they match. I'd love to see if his blood matches the blood on Cross's door, but there's no way he's going to give us a sample."

"We can get his DNA off that cup he just drank from and test it against the DNA from the blood smear," the chief suggested.

"DNA takes too long. I can send it to the Bureau labs and beg a tech I know to rush it through, but we're still talking days. I'm not saying don't do it, I'm just saying that isn't going to give us what we need now." Connor stood and stared through the window at the boy. He turned back to the chief and said, "If we can put him at the murder scene, maybe we can get him to talk. Get him to tell us who he's working with."

"Whose number is programmed into that cell phone."

"Right."

"Too bad the dog can't talk," Thorpe said. "Tell us just what happened that night."

Connor turned and stared at Thorpe as if he'd said something brilliant. "I'm not so sure she can't . . ."

NINETEEN

"Where did they take him?" She stood in the dim light, anger radiating off her like heat.

"I'm assuming to the police station in Howeville," replied the man who sat on the chair near the fireplace. He was taller than her by almost a foot, and outweighed her by seventy pounds. He was terrified of her.

"If he talks . . ."

The man shook his head. "He will not talk. We have discussed this possibility many times. I'd bet my life on it."

"You already have." She turned away and paced in a circle.

"I've done everything you've asked of me. I've retrieved every one of the sacred artifacts you sent me after."

"All but one," she reminded him. "There's still that woman in Massachusetts. You let her get away."

"The FBI got there before we did."

"You should have moved faster. You gave them too much time."

Or you could have figured out sooner that you could locate some of the collectors by using the Internet, instead of stealing Daria McGowan's list. But of course, he dared not say that. The priestess was neither a tolerant nor a forgiving woman.

"I'll take care of her," he said.

"What's the point? The FBI has the necklace."

"But shouldn't she still be punished?" He was puzzled by her sudden lack of interest in the woman. Hadn't she still sinned by having a sacred object in her possession? "And what of Dr. McGowan? Shouldn't she be punished for what her great-grandfather did?"

"Let me think." She barely heard him, and dismissed him with the wave of her hand as she continued to pace.

She needed a plan. She needed to focus.

But most of all, she needed to insure that there was no way any of this could ever be traced back to her.

TWENTY

"Connor, what the hell are you doing?" Mia came into the kitchen carrying an empty coffee cup.

"Collecting evidence." He sat on the floor, a sheet of white computer paper in front of him on the old linoleum, Sweet Thing sitting as nicely as could be. Connor leaned closer, the scissors in his right hand, his left hand holding the dog's jaw upright.

"Connor? What are you . . . ?" Daria asked from the doorway.

"Come here and hold her head for me," he said without looking up.

Daria walked over and placed a hand on the dog's head.

"What are you doing, Connor?" she repeated.

"I need to cut some of the fur from around her mouth," he told her. "Would you please hold her head?"

Daria did as he asked, speaking softly to the dog, who really didn't appear to be too distressed.

"Does she have a mat?" Daria asked. "I didn't notice a mat."

"No, but what she does have is a different color in the fur around her mouth than on the rest of her body. See?" He pointed with his index finger. "The brown here is a little lighter."

"Funny, I didn't notice that before," she said.

"It wasn't there until late last night."

"I don't get it."

"It's dried blood. From where she nipped the prowler."

He concentrated on snipping the bits of fur where the brown was darkest.

"I know you have a point, but you've lost me."

"I think the blood from the handprint on Damien Cross's back door came from the kid we picked up here last night. I think when he and whoever he's working with killed Cross, he was attacked by Sweet Thing. She bit his arm. His arm would have bled down onto his hand. When he opened the back door to run out and get away from the dog, he left a print." Satisfied that he had all he needed, Connor carefully folded the paper and stuck it in his shirt pocket. "He also left blood in the dog's mouth last night."

Mia leaned closer to look. "It does look like dried blood."

"What made you even think of that?" Daria asked.

"While I was questioning the kid—or trying to, because he isn't speaking—I noticed the puncture marks on his arm. Looked like a dog bite to me. It wasn't hard to connect those dots."

"That's why she took off after him last night. She remembered." Daria patted the dog's head. "What a smart girl you are."

"A dog isn't likely to forget the scent of someone who killed her master." Mia nodded. "So you're going to match the blood from her fur to the blood on the door at the victim's house, to put him at the scene of the Cross murder."

"Yes. And then we're going to match the marks on his arm to Sweet Thing's bite. All nice and tidy." Connor stood up and put the scissors on the counter. He went to the cupboard and got a biscuit to reward the dog for her very good behavior.

"Won't you have to get a warrant for that?" Mia asked.

"We have two jurisdictions here. The murder we want to match the blood to is in Delaware. The kid, however, is here in PA, being held on trespassing and prowling charges. I think the warrant to match the bite marks is going to have to come from Coliani in New Castle. He's going to the DA this morning to see if he can get the warrant now, or if the kid has to be transferred to Delaware first. But red tape aside, I think we'll be able to get the kid to crack before we have to match the bite marks. We'll let him know we have his DNA from the cup he drank from, and we'll tell him that we matched it to blood we found at the scene. Now we have his blood from last night, and I'm certain it will match up to the blood on Damien Cross's back door. Is he going to want to take the fall for this? I doubt it." Connor gave Sweet Thing another treat. "I think at that point, we can get him to give up whoever is calling the shots."

"You don't think this kid did the killings by himself?" Mia asked.

"No way, unless he drugged them, and there was no indication of that in the autopsy reports. I see the kid as an accomplice, willing or un-willing. He isn't the one behind this, and that's the person we want." He turned to Daria. "Can you be ready to leave in fifteen minutes or so?"

"I thought we didn't have to be at Cavanaugh's until noon?"

"We don't, but we're going to have to stop at the New Castle County police station. I already left a message for Coliani. I want to turn the clippings from Sweet Thing over to him and I want to see if he knows of a vet in his area who can do the impression from the dog's mouth. It's his murder scene, his jurisdiction. He should be handling the evidence."

"How long will they keep her?" Daria knelt and put an arm around the dog's neck. Sweet Thing's pink tongue unfurled like a small flag and licked the side of Daria's face. "When will we be able to get her back?"

"I guess it will depend on when the vet has time to do the impres-sion. They might have to sedate her to do that."

"But she'll be okay, right?"

"I'm sure she'll be fine." Seeing that Daria still appeared uneasy, Connor added, "Hey, she's the star witness. They're going to take good care of her."

"All right. Give me five minutes to change, and I'll be ready to go."

"Listen, if you don't need me for the rest of the day, I think I'd like to head back to St. Dennis," Mia said after Daria left the room. "The weekends are so busy there, with all the tourists, and I promised Vanessa I'd help her out in her shop. The girl who usually works for her is on vacation."

"Vanessa?" Connor asked absently.

"Beck's sister. She owns a boutique there on the main street, and does a lot of business this time of the year. The weekends are especially busy."

"I think I can handle things from here." Connor took a glass from the cupboard and filled it at the sink. "How is Beck, by the way? That working out for you?"

"Couldn't be better, actually. I'm trying to take things slow, but you know how these things are." Mia smiled.

"Yeah, I guess I do."

Mia's smile widened. "I guess you're learning, anyway."

His cell phone rang just as he opened his mouth to reply.

"Answer your phone, Con." Mia laughed. "I'm going to go upstairs and pack."

"Shields. Yes, Detective, thanks for calling me back . . ."

"Maybe we should go with her to the vet," Daria said to Vince Coliani in the parking lot at the New Castle County police station. "She might get upset. Maybe she'll think we've abandoned her."

"She's going to be just fine," the detective assured her. "Dr. Price is great with dogs. We take our K9s to her."

"We can come back and pick her up later today if she's finished?" Daria asked.

"The vet didn't think she'd get around to the impression until pretty late in the day. She has two surgeries this afternoon," he told her. "But don't worry. We'll take good care of her, and you'll have her back by tomorrow, no later."

"Okay. Sweet Thing, you behave yourself." Daria gave the dog a parting hug and got into Connor's car. "We'll see you in the morning."

Connor handed the fur he'd cut from Sweet Thing's neck over to the detective. "Here's the dog hair I told you about. Get your lab guys to compare the blood on it to the blood on the door."

"Great. Hey, I owe you one," Coliani said.

"Get me a match and we'll both be happy," Connor said as he got into the car.

Daria looked out the window as Connor turned the car around.

"She'll be fine, Daria. I promise."

"I wasn't going to say anything."

"You've really become attached to her."

Daria nodded. "I really have. I hope I can keep her."

"Coliani said no one's even stepped forward to ask about the dog. Cross had one nephew; he made arrangements for the body to be transferred to a funeral parlor in Virginia when the medical examiner releases it, which will probably happen today. But there wasn't a word said about the dog."

"Maybe the detective can tell me who I have to talk to to adopt her."

"I'm thinking possession is good enough at this point. I doubt anyone's going to challenge you."

"Good. That would be good." Daria rested her head against the back of the seat. "Tell me again where Mr. Cavanaugh lives."

"Outside of West Chester. It's not far from here. He said to come up Route 202. Which according to that sign, is right here."

Connor followed the signs that led them onto a heavily commercial stretch of road that ran several miles through Delaware and into Pennsylvania.

"Did you ever get that package of material from your mother? The one with the PI reports about your brother?"

"What made you think of that?" she asked.

"I don't know." Connor waited for a moment, and when she didn't answer the question, he said, "Well, did you?"

"It came yesterday or the day before. Vita dropped it off right after Mia and I got home yesterday. The mailman evidently left it at the administration building."

"When were you going to give it to me?"

"When things slowed down a bit. I figured you have your hands full. I didn't want to bother you."

"It's no bother. Did you look through it?"

"I started to yesterday, but to tell you the truth, reading gave me a headache."

"How's your head now?"

"Much better. I took some of the pain meds after breakfast and the throbbing is pretty much gone."

"Good." He maneuvered the Porsche around a tractor trailer and settled back into the right lane. Traffic was heavy and the road wasn't particularly smooth, so he did what he could to keep Daria's head from bouncing around too much.

"Connor, can I ask you something?"

"Sure."

"What happened to your brother?"

"Dylan?" Connor slowed for the light. "He died."

"I know that. How did he die?"

"What brought this up?"

"Just something Mia said."

"What did she say?"

"That I'd have to ask you about him. As if she didn't want to talk about it."

"I imagine she didn't." Connor took a deep breath. "Dylan was murdered by Mia's brother, Brendan."

Daria's jaw dropped. She tried in vain for several seconds to close it. "But they were—"

"Yeah, cousins. Yes, they were." Connor's jaw tightened and she wished she could see his eyes behind those dark glasses. "You know how every family has a black sheep? Brendan was ours."

He pulled in front of a green pickup and gunned the engine. "The thing is, Brendan hadn't wanted to kill Dylan. That was a mistake. The person he'd wanted to kill—the person he thought he was shooting— was me."

"God, Connor." She tried not to gasp. "But why?"

"Long story short, I saw something he didn't want me to see. I was in Central America on a job, and ran into him while something very bad was going down. He told me he was on the case for the Bureau, that he was shutting down the local operation. I believed him. Later, he and his partner realized it was only a matter of time before I found out that there was no FBI operation. He set me up when I was supposed to be working a drug bust, but there was a change of plans, and Dylan worked that job in my place."

"What was the bad thing he was into?"

"Selling children on the black market."

"My God . . ."

Connor fell silent then. They drove for several miles without speaking.

Finally, Daria said, "Why do you feel responsible for your brother's death?"

It was a question he had heard before. He'd heard it more times than he'd like to think about, and had never bothered to reply. Not to his brother, Aidan, or his cousin Andrew, or to Mia. Nor to Annie, the woman Dylan had been engaged to when he died. He'd tried to blow off the others, but Annie was a psychologist and wouldn't permit him to bully her.

He was trying to decide if he wanted to bully Daria into shutting up when she reached over and grasped the hand that was resting on the gear shift.

Neither of them spoke until they arrived at Cavanaugh's.

"This is it here, I think," Connor said. "Number 438 Broad Run Road."

He turned into the drive and followed it up a slight incline until he reached the house, set well back from the road. It was gray stucco and stone, three stories high, and surrounded by tall trees.

Connor parked near the walk that ran next to the drive and before he could say anything, Daria was out of the car.

"It's beautiful here, isn't it? Did you notice that pretty stream when we pulled in?" She gazed around admiringly. "Like a painting."

He was about to respond when a short, balding, jovial-looking man in a yellow polo shirt and lime green pants came down the walk.

"Agent Shields, I'm guessing," he called out as he approached.

Connor removed his ID from his pocket and held it up for inspection as the man drew near.

"Mr. Cavanaugh?" Connor asked.

"Yes, yes, let me have a look at that." He appeared to study it before handing it back. "You're wondering if I know how to tell if it's real or not. Well, I can tell you that I do. I have a good friend in your Philadelphia office. Jack Gaffney, you know him?"

"I'm afraid not."

"Well, he works with the art-theft people. I met him many years ago when he was trying to track down some forged Wyeth watercolors. Damned scandal, that was." He turned to Daria. "You an agent, too?"

"No, sir. I'm an archaeologist," Daria told him.

"That so. Well, then come on in. You wanted to talk to me about Elena Sevrenson." He shook his head with obvious sadness. "Damned fine woman, Elena was. One of my favorite customers. Not just because she bought a lot, and didn't mind paying top dollar for what she wanted. No, sir. Elena had a real appreciation for the things she collected. Didn't buy a thing she didn't love, didn't matter how trendy or how unfashionable. She bought what she loved. Art and artifacts she respected. Her husband was the same way when he was alive. God rest their souls. I miss them both, and I don't mind saying it."

When he held the front door open for them, Daria saw the tears in his eyes. It was clear that Elena Sevrenson had indeed been more than a customer to him. She'd been his friend.

They stepped from the heat of the day into the air-conditioned comfort of the old house. Peter Cavanaugh led them through the front hall and the living room into his office, which was in an addition off the side of the house. An ancient Scottish terrier waddled along behind them.

"Don't mind Fergus," he told his guests. "We're just back from our annual vacation in Maine. It always takes the old boy a few days to get used to things again."

"You take him with you?" Daria asked.

"Of course I take him. You think I'd kennel my best friend?" Cavanaugh looked indignant. "He just needs to acclimate himself to the house again. I'm thinking he has a form of doggie Alzheimer's."

Before either of them could reply, Cavanaugh took a notebook from a desk drawer.

"You were asking about the griffins." He paged through the notebook. "It took me a while to find the sale, but I did."

He opened an eyeglass case that was sitting on the desktop and took out the glasses. He put them on and pored over the notebook carefully.

"I thought I marked that page . . . just give me a minute here . . ."

"Do you remember if you sold them to Mr. or to Mrs. Sevrenson?" Connor asked.

Cavanaugh peered at him from over the top of the glasses. "I said the dog has Alzheimer's, not that I did." He coughed. "Of course I know. I sold them to Mitch back in 1964. Forty-three years ago."

He looked out over his desk at nothing in particular and said, "Can you imagine, it was that long ago? Where the hell have the years gone?"

He thumbed through a few more pages, then said, "Ha. Here it is. Pair of gold griffins. They had arrows in their claws. Never saw anything like them, before or since. They were just spectacular. Mitch bought them for Elena, for their anniversary. They'd only been married a few years back then, but they both had an eye for art, that's for sure. Always bought the best."

"How did that sale come about?" Daria asked. "Did you have the griffins, and offer them to the Sevrenson's, or did he come to you, looking for something special?"

Cavanaugh smiled at Daria.

"You understand that, don't you? That relationship between dealer and collector." He nodded. "Mitch came by my shop several times, bought the occasional piece. Delightful man, knew his stuff. We'd been doing business for several years when he came in one day—in the spring, I seem to recall. Said they'd be having an anniversary in the fall and he wanted something very special, something very unique, to surprise Elena. I told him I'd see what I could find."

"Where did you find the griffins?" Connor asked.

"Dealer down your way, actually. Friend of a friend of a friend. Name was Dragonis. Henry Dragonis. When you said Howe University, that's the first thing I thought of, what a coincidence that was, that you were down there at Howe, and that he lived in Howeville."

"Dragonis lived in Howeville?" Connor asked.

"Yes. Seems to me he had some connection to the college there, but I don't recall what it was."

"Was he employed there?"

"I don't remember ever discussing that with him, Agent Shields, but it's in my mind that there was some connection."

"Did you know him before you bought the griffins from him?"

"No. I'd heard that he had some very unusual pieces, so I drove down there one afternoon to see what he had."

"The griffins were in his shop?" Daria leaned forward, enjoying the story.

"No, no. He asked me what I was looking for. I told him what Mitch had said, and that I hadn't been given a price limit. Well, he thought it over and told me to come back in a week and he'd have something for me. I went back a week later and there were the griffins. I knew they were just what Mitch was looking for. We negotiated a price and I left with them in a cardboard box."

"Did he tell you where he got them?" Connor asked.

"No, he wouldn't give that up," Cavanaugh said. "He just said he had a source, a collector who from time to time had something special to sell."

Cavanaugh turned to Daria. "Fifty years ago, provenance wasn't as big a deal as it is now. There were few laws on the books, none of them enforceable unless a piece was out-and-out stolen. For the most part, collectors back then didn't ask many questions. Up until 1970, there wasn't even much international interest in the subject."

"That was the year of the UNESCO convention that addressed the international trade of cultural property," Daria said.

"Correct. There was no ban on the sale of artifacts back then. So while it was nice to know how a piece came to be placed on the market, it wasn't against the law to not know, and collectors weren't that concerned where an item had been." Cavanaugh met her eyes without apology. "All that has changed, of course, but things were different then."

"Were you aware that the griffins were from Shandihar?"

"Yes, though I knew almost nothing about Shandihar. I knew it had been some ancient city in Turkey, but truthfully, I knew little more than that. When Dragonis showed me the griffins, he merely referred to them as Turkish. I believe Mitch may have educated himself a bit, sought out some books so that he could discuss the origins of the griffins with Elena, but I don't know that even he knew all that much."

"Did you purchase other pieces from this dealer?" Connor asked.

"Oh, yes, several pieces over the years, though nothing else from Shandihar. The Sevrensons were aware that what they had was extremely rare, but they weren't interested in starting a collection of objects from Shandihar. Mostly what I bought from Dragonis, as I recall, were earlier objects. Mesopotamian, I believe."

Daria exchanged a long look with Connor.

"Would that have been around the same time, Mr. Cavanaugh?"

"After the griffins, yes. I purchased items from him up until his death in 1998."

"Do you know if someone took over his business?"

"I don't believe anyone did. I never heard about it, if so."

"So his shop just closed?"

"He didn't have a shop. He did business out of his home."

"Do you remember the address?"

"No, I'm afraid I don't. I can look through some old files, see if I can come up with something, but . . ." He shrugged.

"We'd appreciate it." Connor stood. "We'd appreciate anything else you can recall, as well. Anything at all . . . a description of the house he lived in, the neighborhood, landmarks—anything that could help us track his family."

"Doesn't seem to me that he had much of a family." Cavanaugh closed his notebook. "Had a daughter, she was just a little thing. I think he raised her by himself. Seems there was something about the wife dying. And I think he may have mentioned a brother, but I don't think I ever met him. Sorry I can't be more helpful."

"You've been very helpful," Connor told him. "You've certainly given us a lot to think about."

· · · · ·

"So where do you go from here?" Daria asked when they'd arrived back in Howeville.

"First things first." He parked in the shade of a huge oak tree. "We find this Henry Dragonis."

"He's dead, remember."

"I mean we find out everything about him that we can."

"How do we do that?" Daria asked.

"When you're learning about an ancient culture, what's the first thing you do?"

"I look for written records."

"Same thing here. We look for written records." Connor took the phone from his pocket and dialed a number.

"Will . . . Connor. I've got a job for you. I need some information and I need it really fast. I need you to run a check on a man named Henry Dragonis. Howeville, PA. Everything you can find." He reported what little information he'd gotten from Cavanaugh. "And while you're at it, could you run a few more names? Start with Louise Burnette. Casper Fenn. Vita Landis. Nora Gannon. Olivia Masters. Sabina Bokhari. Stefano Korban."

"Can you think of anyone else?" he asked Daria.

"You mean any other names that have come up?"

He nodded. "People connected to the university over the years."

"I can't think of anyone else right now."

"Will, that's it for now. If there are others I'll call you back. Yeah, yeah, I know. The tab is running. Thanks, buddy." He closed the phone. "I want to question the kid again, before they transfer him. Come on, I'll walk you back to the house. Unless you want to come with me."

She opened the car door and got out. "Thanks, but I think I'm going to try to work a little this afternoon."

"Wait up. After last night, I want to go through the house before I leave." He got out from behind the wheel.

"Ordinarily I'd say that's not necessary, but with Mia gone and

Sweet Thing at the vet's, I won't protest." They had walked halfway to the house when she asked, "What do you think your friend at the FBI is going to find? What exactly are you looking for?"

"I'm not sure, but I'll know it when I see it. All my instincts tell me there's something there. Cavanaugh said that Dragonis had some connection to Howe. I can't help thinking there's some link to what's happening now." He paused at the end of the path. "Sabina mentioned that Nora Gannon's father and grandfather were both trustees here. And the other one, Olivia Masters, had some family tie to the school as well."

"And Louise? What makes you suspicious of her?"

"I'm not saying I am suspicious of her. I just don't know anything about her. Same goes for her assistant, and for Korban. And for all you know of Sabina Bokhari's reputation, what do you really know about her?"

"Not much," she admitted.

"We still know very little about the people closest to the situation, and we should. Hopefully, by this time tomorrow, we will know everything that matters."

"But there's a good chance nothing will turn up."

"Well, you know what they say, Daria. You throw enough stuff against the wall, sooner or later, something is going to stick . . ."

TWENTY-ONE

"You know, things will be a whole lot better for you if you talk now." Connor sat across from the boy, who still refused to speak to anyone. "Look, here's the thing. We know you were at Damien Cross's house when he was killed." He leaned closer. "How do we know?"

Conner reached over and pulled up the sleeve of the boy's shirt to expose the dog bite.

"Because the dog that bit you here is the same dog that bit you on the ankle the other night. You left your blood on the back door of Cross's house, and you left your blood on the dog's fur. That puts you right there, bud. And in the absence of any evidence that puts anyone there with you, the police are looking at you for Damien Cross's murder."

The boy went white, but still did not speak.

"So what you need to understand is this. You are going to be sent from here to Delaware, where Damien Cross was killed, and they're going to prosecute you—just you—for his murder."

He stared at the boy for a long time, but the boy never blinked.

"Thing is, I don't think you killed him. But you were there when it happened, and you know who did it. You probably even know where that statue of Ereshkigal is right now."

A look of surprise crossed the boy's face, the first change in his demeanor since Connor sat down.

"Oh, sure, we know about that. We know Cross was killed because he had the statue of the goddess. Same as the others, right? The Blumes and Mrs. Sevrenson. And that nice couple in Connecticut last week."

Connor kept his eyes on the boy's face. At the mention of the last victims, he appeared to flinch slightly.

"You tell us who was there with you, who did the actual killing, and the police will protect you. They'll guarantee that nothing will happen to you, and that—"

The boy's eyes smiled. The smile became a chuckle, and before long, the boy began to laugh.

Then he put his head down on the table and cried, but still, he would not speak.

"What do you make of that?" Chief Thorpe asked Connor when he finally left the boy and went into the hallway. "What do you suppose that was all about?"

"I have no idea." Connor shook his head. "How much longer are you keeping him?"

"They're getting the paperwork together right now to send him to New Castle." Thorpe stared through the window at the boy. "Christ, Shields, I got a grandson around that age."

"I guess no one's called to report a missing kid."

"Nah." Thorpe shook his head as he walked away. "That would be too easy."

· · · · ·

"What's that you've got there?" Daria unlocked the back door when Connor knocked. He came into the kitchen carrying a brown paper bag and a cardboard box.

"I stopped at the supermarket and picked up a few staples. Then I stopped at one of those Amish farm stands and picked up some things for dinner." He placed the box on the counter. "Tomatoes, peppers, onions, cucumbers, some fresh garlic."

"Sounds like the making of a good salad."

"Or a great gazpacho."

"There aren't any cookbooks here," she told him, "but we could probably get a recipe off the Internet."

"I don't need a cookbook. I make this all the time in the summer." He turned and dazzled her with a smile. "I told you, I'm a great cook. And I promised you a dinner while I was here."

He held up a loaf of bread wrapped in plastic.

"And whole wheat bread baked this morning by the nice Amish lady at the farm a couple of miles down the road." His hand disappeared into the box one last time. "Shoofly pie for dessert."

"Made by the same nice Amish lady, no doubt."

"Her sister-in-law, Sarah, does the pies." He put the pie in the refrigerator, then started to wash vegetables in the sink. "So, how'd you spend your afternoon?"

"I started thinking about this Henry Dragonis. He first sold to Cavanaugh in 1964. So it got me wondering who else he might have been selling to." She sat down at the table and sorted through a stack of papers. "I went back through the list of galleries and museums that we know either purchased Shandiharan artifacts outright or acquired them on loan from the owner. I was able to locate five that gave acquisition dates. All in the 1960s."

"Good work. I'll pass on that information to Polly. She can have the galleries trace the items back to the original sellers. I'm sure it will help her in her investigation," he said over the sound of running water.

"Well, that got me to thinking about Dragonis. Maybe he was

stealing from the museum himself, or working with someone who was."

Connor glanced over his shoulder at her. "Go on. I can tell by the look on your face that there's more."

She laughed. "More questions than answers, I'm afraid. I guess what I'm wondering is why now. If these artifacts were stolen forty or fifty years ago, why is someone trying to get them back now?"

"Good question. I guess we could answer that if we knew who was at the bottom of it."

"Or vice versa."

"Right." He turned the water off. "I guess there's no colander."

"I think maybe in that cabinet to your left, down at the bottom."

"Got it."

"Can I help you at all?" she asked.

"No. This is my show. How about a sharp knife and a cutting board?"

"Maybe there to the right."

He found a knife that would do, but no cutting board. He cleaned off the counter, then began to cut and chop on it.

"Did you learn anything from the boy at the police station?"

"Not a damned thing. Except maybe he's really afraid of double-crossing whoever's calling the shots." Connor told her about the boy crying. "The shame of it is that he's just a kid. At least I think he's a kid. He won't tell us how old he is. And while I know that kids kill every day, somehow I don't think this one did. But he won't say a damned word."

He chopped at the onions with a vengeance.

"Anyway, he's going to be handed over to New Castle, probably to-morrow. Maybe Coliani can get him to talk."

"Shouldn't he have a lawyer?"

"Thorpe offered to get him one, but he wouldn't even respond to that."

"Maybe he doesn't speak English."

"He spoke enough English the other night, when he wanted me to call off Sweet Thing." Connor found a large pot in one of the cabinets and tossed in the onions. "In other news, I stopped in to see Louise on my way back. She's going to get me a list of the trustees."

"Did you tell her you're having them all investigated? Including her?"

"She isn't stupid. She already figured that out." He took a bottle of olive oil out of the paper bag, opened it, and drizzled some in the bottom of the pot. He put the pot on top of the stove and turned the burner on low. "She did confirm what Dr. Bokhari told me about both Nora Gannon and Olivia Masters. Both have roots that go deep into Howe University soil. Legacy students in their day, both of them, and both had relatives who served as trustees at some point during the past century."

"So both of them could have known about the artifacts in the basement of the museum. At the very least, maybe one of their relatives did." Daria pondered the possibility. "Did you ask Louise about Henry Dragonis?"

"Yes, but she said the name didn't mean anything to her."

"So we really don't know any more tonight than we did this morning." She tapped the end of her pencil on the pile of notes she'd been going through. "And we're back to the why of it. Why now? Why is someone after the artifacts now?"

"The obvious answer is that someone is avenging the goddess, or whatever, but that just seems too easy," he told her. "Like that's what someone wants us to think. It all seems very pat."

"Maybe your friend Will can come up with something that will point you in the right direction."

"He will. I have faith in him." He finished chopping the tomatoes and peppers and started in on the cucumbers. "All we need to do is find the right string . . ."

"You give it a tug and the truth spills out?"

"That's how it usually works."

"You're very confident, aren't you."

"I'm good at what I do." He said quietly.

"You still haven't told me what that is, exactly."

When he didn't respond, Daria said, "I have all that information from my parents about Jack, if you want to take a look."

"Great. I'll just be a minute more."

Daria stared at his back for almost a minute before reaching into her briefcase for the investigators' reports. He'd said all he was going to say about himself earlier that day, and that was going to have to be enough.

"I miss Sweet Thing," Daria told him. They were sitting in the conservatory listening to the cicadas. Occasionally one slammed into a window screen and made her jump.

"I'll check with Coliani first thing in the morning to see when we can pick her up." He stifled a yawn with the back of his hand.

"You don't have to sit up with me while I read. I can see you're tired. Why not just go up to bed?"

He hesitated and she knew he didn't want to leave her downstairs alone, so she added, "I'm going up now anyway."

"In that case, I'll go, too. Go on up. I'll lock up the house."

"All right." She closed the notebook she'd been working in. She wanted to show him the sketches of the displays she'd worked on that afternoon, but they could wait until tomorrow. "Thanks again for making dinner. It was wonderful."

"You're welcome. It was fun. I hope I get to do it again before I leave Howe." He gathered the reports he'd been reading and returned them to the envelope in which they'd been mailed. Several sheets of paper floated to the floor. He looked up to find her staring at him.

"When do you think that will be?"

"I don't know." He shrugged and picked up the errant sheets. "I feel like we're close to putting it all together, you know? Like there are only one or two pieces missing, and once I get those, the case is going to fall into place."

"I see." She stood and walked to the door. "Well, thanks again."

She paused in the hall to pick up the sandals she'd left by the door before starting up the steps. She hadn't thought about him leaving, though she knew it was inevitable. His presence had dominated most of the time she'd spent at Howe, and she wasn't ready to say good-bye.

She heard him moving around downstairs, heard windows slam in the conservatory and in the kitchen. She knew his routine, and in her mind she followed him through the first floor as she undressed for bed. After he closed the windows, he'd check the locks on the back door. Then he'd move into the dining room, check those windows, then the two front rooms. Next he'd lock the front door and turn off the lamp, and then he'd come upstairs.

She heard his footfalls on the steps, and saw the overhead hall light go out and the small table lamp turn on. Before she had a chance to think about what she was doing, she called to him.

"Connor?"

"Yes?"

He stood right outside her doorway, silhouetted by the light. She walked into the hall and reached a hand up to touch his face.

"Kiss me," she whispered.

She thought at first he was going to decline, because for a moment he simply stood and looked at her. But then he leaned down and covered her mouth with his. She'd expected him to more or less start out slow and work his way into it, but he came at her full blast, taking her mouth and owning it.

He lifted her off her feet and held her to his chest, kissing her as she'd never been kissed before. But she'd known it would be like that. She'd known this moment was going to happen, and she'd known it would feel just like this, like a tidal wave that swept her down into its depths and spun her around and around until she was dizzy with it. Drunk with it. Drunk with him.

She felt her body respond to him, every cell, every fiber, and she had no thought of stemming the tide. Go with it, she told herself. Just . . . go with it.

"Stay with me," she whispered into his neck when their lips finally parted. "Please stay with me . . ."

He carried her into her room and eased her back onto the bed. She tugged at his belt as she fell back.

"Daria—"

"Don't," she told him. "Just . . . don't try to talk me out of this."

"I just want you to be sure that—"

"Shut up, Connor."

He laughed softly and joined her on the bed. His mouth sought hers, his tongue playing at the corners of her mouth. She parted her lips and teased his tongue with her own. He raised himself on one elbow and stroked her body with his free hand. She was barely aware of her legs wrapping around his hips to draw him closer and closer, or her fingers unbuttoning her top to free herself for him. When his mouth closed over her breast, her brain turned itself off and her body went on autopilot. The last thing she remembered was Connor whispering her name over and over and over. Everything after that was lost, drowned in an intensity of emotion and sensation that took her breath away and left her feeling stunned.

Afterward she lay against his chest, listening to his beating heart. She felt as if she could stay right there in that moment forever—until his phone started to ring.

Connor groaned and rolled over, and searched through his clothes on the floor for his phone.

"This had better be damned important," he growled at the caller.

He sat up straight.

"When?" He listened for another minute, then said, "Save it. I'm on my way."

He closed the phone and turned to Daria. "I hate to do this to you, but that was Chief Thorpe. The kid just tried to hang himself with his T-shirt."

"Oh my God. He's not . . . ?"

"No. The guard on duty stopped him, but they don't know if any serious damage has been done."

He took her by the hand.

"This isn't exactly the way I pictured this night ending, and I'm sorry."

"It's all right," she assured him. "I understand. I know you have to leave."

"*We* have to leave," he corrected her. "In the past week, you've been attacked, your head's been split open, and someone tried to break into the house. You're out of your mind if you think I'm going to leave you here alone for the rest of the night."

TWENTY-TWO

"What's going to happen to him now?" Daria stared through the window at the boy in the hospital bed. Tubes were everywhere, and a machine was monitoring his vital signs.

"We're not sure what to do with him," Chief Thorpe told her. "We don't even know how old he is, so we don't know whether to send him to juvie or to the county prison. If he's too old for juvie and we send him there and he does something to another inmate, we're liable for putting that other kid at risk. If we send him to the county and he's set upon by the big boys, we're liable for having put him at risk. We're damned if we do, and we're damned of we don't."

"Well, as of today, he'll have been in your custody for forty-eight hours. You're going to have to decide what to do with him," Connor noted, "once he comes around."

"I'm calling the DA's office, see what they recommend. Besides sending him to Delaware and letting them deal with it."

"Shouldn't he be given an attorney?" Daria asked.

"Well, that's sort of a problem, too, since we're changing jurisdictions." He leaned on the glass and watched the boy's chest rise and fall. "Though I guess that's up in the air right now. Maybe I'll just see if we can get the court to appoint someone to represent him for as long as he's here."

"Has he been charged?" Connor asked.

Thorpe frowned. "I was leaving that till the last minute, too, thinking maybe he'd crack and give us something more than trespassing." He rubbed the back of his neck. "Guess I should talk to the New Castle detective. See what he has in mind. I don't know what the law is in Delaware, when it comes to things like this. It's all I can do to keep up with Pennsylvania."

The chief shook his head. "Would make it a whole lot easier if we knew who he was. We don't even have a starting point."

"If you get any information from him—anything at all—let me know and I'll have our guy at the Bureau see what he can dig up," Connor said.

"Won't his fingerprints help?" Daria asked.

"Only if they're already in the system," Thorpe told her. He turned to Connor. "That reminds me. We matched the kid's prints to one set of prints from the library. They didn't match the ones on your window, though. You'll never guess which ones were a match."

"My money's on the basement door," Connor said.

"Good guess. How'd you figure it?"

"I don't see him for smashing the computer," Connor explained. "I don't believe he sent the e-mail messages to the collectors that were on the hit list, and I don't believe he killed Mrs. Weathers, so his prints wouldn't be on the railing in the stairwell going up to the second floor. That leaves the prints on the back door."

"Which tells us how the killer got into the library," the chief said. "He must have had a time prearranged to go downstairs and open the door. The alarm would go off, the real guard would come down to see what was going on, and the killer knocks him out. The kid leaves with the other students, no one's the wiser."

"Do you think the killer intended to kill Mrs. Weathers?" Daria wondered.

"I think she just got in his way," Connor told her. "She probably surprised him when she came down the stairs, and he took off after her."

"He didn't kill the guard, though. He only hit him over the head, right?" Daria asked.

"Right."

"Then why did he kill Mrs. Weathers and not the guard?"

"Good question," Connor nodded thoughtfully. "Maybe she saw his face when she came down the stairs. Maybe she recognized him. Maybe that's why he panicked and got careless, leaving his prints at the scene."

"Which means he could be someone connected with the school," Thorpe said. "Wouldn't it be nice if we could narrow the pool just a little?"

"Yesterday I gave a list of names to our computer whiz at the Bureau. We'll see if he came up with anything interesting." Connor turned back to the window and watched the boy for another minute. "I guess he didn't have any visitors while he was at the station."

"Not a one."

"Why would he have done this?" Daria asked. "Why would he have tried to kill himself?"

"Holding-cell suicides, or attempted suicides, aren't uncommon," Thorpe replied. "It could be that he realized he's really going to be doing some time as an accomplice to the Cross murder."

"Or he could be afraid he'll end up talking."

"What would make him more afraid of talking than dying?" Daria asked.

"Maybe someone who likes to cut off people's hands." Connor

said. "Maybe someone who threatened him big time if he ever talked about what happened."

"Maybe when he comes to, he'll be more inclined to talk," Thorpe suggested. "Maybe we can convince him that the gods spared him so that he could tell the truth."

"The goddess," Daria corrected him. "There were no gods in Shandihar. Just the one goddess."

"Who do you suppose told him about her?" Connor thought aloud.

A nurse came by and they backed away from the door to let her enter the room.

Connor turned to Thorpe. "Will you give me a call if anything changes here?"

"I'm going to be moving out myself," the chief told him. "I'll leave one of the officers here to keep an eye on things. But sure, I'll let you know if there's a change in his condition."

Connor and Daria walked to the elevator with the chief.

"Chief, are you from this area?" Connor asked as the doors closed.

"Born and raised," Thorpe said.

"You know of any antiques dealers around Howeville who've been in business for a long time?"

"Not offhand, but my mother might. Want me to ask her?"

"Please do."

"I'll give her a call later." He glanced at his watch; it wasn't yet 7 A.M. "No way she's up now. Last night was her night out. She goes up to that new casino in Chester once a week with her friends. She gets pretty pissy if you call her much before noon the morning after. But I'll be talking to her later, and I'll give you a call if she knows of anyone."

"I appreciate it." Connor nodded and stepped aside for Daria to exit the elevator when the doors slid open.

Thorpe stopped to talk to a uniformed officer in the lobby, and

Connor and Daria continued on into the parking lot outside the emergency room.

"I hope the boy is going to be all right," Daria said. "He looks so young."

"It's a damned shame he's the one who's taking the brunt of this. I wish there was some way we could get him to talk." He took Daria's hand as they walked to the car. "He's obviously protecting someone. Maybe more than one someone."

"Maybe your friend at the FBI will have some information for you today."

"Yeah, we need a break." He opened the car door for her. "How about if we stop somewhere on the way back to Howe and get some breakfast? I don't know about you, but I'm starving."

"I could definitely eat," she said. When he got in behind the wheel, she asked, "Have you heard anything from Polly? Has she been able to determine if any of the artifacts in the galleries have been stolen?"

"I talked to her yesterday. So far, none of the galleries or museums appear to have been targeted."

"So whoever it is, is only going after private collectors."

"Because it's easier to break into a private home than an institution." He thought it over for a minute. "But if you're trying to retrieve things that you believe are sacred, you're on a sort of holy mission, right?"

"I would think so, yes," she said, nodding.

"So if you're doing holy work, it shouldn't matter if the job is hard or easy, right? You just do it. You find a way to make it happen."

"I guess so, if you believe you're doing the work of the goddess. Especially this goddess, who is known to take no prisoners when she's pissed off."

"Who would be giving the orders on behalf of the goddess? The priestess, right?"

Daria nodded.

"So we have to figure out who the priestess is," Connor said thoughtfully. "Obviously, it has to be someone who's familiar with the culture. And someone who knew the artifacts were missing before you did."

"The first murders were months ago. Someone had to had read the journals or seen the photos—or both—before the first murder," Daria said.

He put on his turn signal and made a left into the parking lot of a small country restaurant that advertised breakfasts served until noon. "There can't be too many people who have access to both. We just need to figure out who they are. But for now . . . first things first. I'm thinking coffee. Eggs. Bacon. Toast with marmalade . . ."

"Sounds wonderful."

"Hey, it's the least I can do, after dragging you away from a warm bed in the middle of the night."

"It was the dragging away from a warm man that I objected to."

He paused with his hand on the door handle.

"I will make that up to you."

She smiled and opened the passenger door. "I'm counting on it."

TWENTY-THREE

They were almost finished breakfast when Will Fletcher called Connor's cell, but Connor had to go outside to take the call due to a bad connection.

He came back in a few minutes later and told Daria, "Nora Gannon checks out. There's nothing in her background that raises a red flag."

"One down. What about the others?"

"Will is still working on them. He'll get back to me as soon as he has something else." He looked at her empty plate. "Unless you're going to order seconds, let's go back to the house and take a look at those photos."

"Good idea. I have a meeting with Louise this morning. I'd like to be on time."

Twenty minutes later, they sat at the table in the kitchen at McGowan House, the stack of photographs between them.

"Still no golden griffins," she noted. "No large statue of the goddess. No golden necklace."

"Who had access to them? We keep coming back to the photos." He tapped his fingers on the tabletop.

"There's no way of knowing. Louise said that Vita found them in the basement of the administration building, but there's no way of knowing if someone found them before she did."

His phone rang before he could respond.

"Great. I'll drive over right now. Thanks a lot."

He hung up and told her, "Sweet Thing is ready to come home. Want to take a ride with me?"

"I would, except that I have that meeting with Louise and Olivia, the new public relations person, in five minutes. She wanted me to talk to her about Alistair and his expeditions, and what we want to accomplish by reopening the museum so she can start doing her thing. Louise and the trustees are afraid all the publicity about the murders is putting the school in a bad light, and they want to put the emphasis back on the museum."

"Accentuate the positive."

"So to speak." She checked her watch. "I need to get over there now."

He grabbed her by the wrist and pulled her close. He kissed her mouth, then the tip of her chin. "Sweet Thing and I will be waiting for you when you get back."

"How long do you think you'll be?"

"Hour and a half, two hours, tops. Do you want me to wait so you can go with me?"

"I'd rather have her picked up sooner than later. Poor baby. She's probably wondering what's going on." Daria grabbed her bag and slipped it over her shoulder. "I don't expect this meeting to run too long. I should be back here by the time you are."

"Great." He stood and gave her one more kiss. "I'll see you then."

. . . . .

Louise was standing at the end of the conference table when Vita showed Daria into the office. Olivia was seated at the table with a notebook in front of her.

"How are you, Olivia?" Daria extended her hand to the trustee. "Louise tells me you've agreed to take on the media on the university's behalf. You're a brave woman."

"I liken it to falling upon my sword for the greater good." The carefully coiffed blonde smiled.

"Let's hope it doesn't come to that." Daria inwardly grimaced at the image.

"Poor choice on my part." Olivia rolled her eyes. "I don't know what I was thinking."

Swell, Daria thought. A PR person who doesn't think before she opens her mouth.

"We thought we'd put out a press release before we planned a real press conference." Olivia paused. "You don't suppose there will be any more murders, do you? I'd really like to avoid inviting the media to the school and then have to explain another murder."

"There's no way of knowing what's going to happen."

"Well, then, I suppose we can't worry about it." Louise pointed to a chair. "Daria, I'd like you to fill Olivia in on everything you know about your great-grandfather, his expeditions, the museum . . . all of it. Olivia, I expect you to take copious notes."

Over the next hour, Daria shared everything she could think of, from the earliest stories she'd heard from her father to actually opening the crates in the museum basement and holding in her hands the very objects her ancestor had found.

"This is a wonderful story," Olivia told her. "I think you're definitely going to have to be at whatever media gathering we schedule. No one will be able to tell that story the way you just did. And I think I'd like you to look over the press release once it's written, maybe add a little something in your own words, if you don't mind."

"I'd be happy to."

"And I'm happy to see a positive light shining down on my home-town and my alma mater." Olivia tucked her notes into her purse. "Louise, if we're finished . . . ?"

"If you're satisfied that you have enough information, then I'd say we're done." Louise reached for the phone and pressed the intercom button. "Vita, could you step in here, please?"

"I'm more than satisfied. I'm going to run right home and work on this today."

"Here's my cell number." Daria wrote the number on a slip of paper and handed it to Olivia. "Call me if you think of anything else."

"Will do." Olivia smiled.

"By the way, Olivia," Daria said, "you grew up in Howeville?"

"Well, right outside of town, yes."

"Does the name Dragonis ring a bell?"

"No, I don't think so." Olivia frowned. "No, that doesn't ring a bell."

"Louise, did you need something?" Vita walked into the room.

"Yes. I have a meeting with the architect in about thirty minutes. Would you please make a photocopy of the original floor plans for him?"

"They're in your bottom drawer."

"Oh, right. Just take them, if you would. Thanks, Vita." Louise shook her head. "I do not know what I'd do without you."

"You'd never be able to find a thing and you'd never get anywhere on time." Vita winked as she started out of the room, the folder hold-ing the floor plans in her hand.

"Vita," Daria called to her. "Could I ask you a question?"

"Sure. As long as it has nothing to do with my weight or my age."

"Neither." Daria stepped around Olivia, who had been sitting next to her. "I was just wondering. The photos that you found, the ones that were taken at Shandihar. Were there any other packs of photos?"

"No." Vita shook her head. "I gave you everything I found."

"Could you tell me again where you found them?"

"In a box in one of the filing cabinets downstairs."

"Was the cabinet locked?" Daria asked.

"No. Those cabinets down there are so old, I don't think any of them even have locks."

"Did you show them to anyone else? Or mention them to anyone?"

"No. Once I realized what was in the envelopes, I brought them right up and handed them to Louise."

Louise looked up from her briefcase where she was packing what she thought she'd need for her meeting.

"Well, no, not exactly," she said. "Don't you remember, the envelopes were on your desk, and while you were at lunch, I accidentally knocked them off when I grabbed a file that was sitting on top and all the pictures fell on the floor . . ."

"I did forget about that." Vita laughed and rolled her eyes. "What a mess trying to put the files back together."

"Luckily for me, Sabina came in while I was trying to pick it all up," Louise continued. "These old knees don't bend the way they used to."

"Sabina saw the photographs?" Daria asked.

"She saw the ones she picked up off the floor, certainly. A whole set of them fell under Vita's desk, and Sabina was kind enough to retrieve them for me."

"Interesting that they turned up right after you started talking about the museum," Daria said.

"Well, actually, we started talking about the museum back in the fall," Olivia said. "Remember, Louise? It was right before Halloween, and I was telling you how we used to have Halloween parties in the courtyard when I was a student here. And I said what a shame that the university couldn't reopen it and maybe find a way to make some money from it." She turned to Daria. "I didn't know about the treasure in antiquities in the basement then. If I had, I would have pressed Louise to bring it up to the board right away."

"Well, yes, now that you mention it, I do remember." Louise smiled. "I think that might have been what planted the idea in my head. Sometime after that, I asked Vita to see what she could find in the archives about the museum. And that's right about the time I realized some of Alistair McGowan's journals were right there in my bookcase, and made the connection to the museum. So of course I read them, and about that time Sabina returned the ones she had borrowed . . ."

"I'll make these copies for you so that you can get on your way." Vita left the room.

"Louise, if there's nothing else . . ." Daria stood in the doorway processing the information. Sabina had seen the photos . . .

"No. I'll be in touch." She paused. "Though maybe if the architect has any questions about the display area . . ."

"Just give me a call." Daria nodded. "Nice to see you again, Olivia."

"Thanks again, Daria." Olivia waved from the conference table.

"See you, Vita," Daria called as she left the outer office.

"See you, Daria."

"I think there's a problem." The woman stepped into the empty hall, the phone close to her face.

"What's that?"

"Daria McGowan has been asking about the photographs."

"So?"

"She's wondering who might have had access to the photos before they were given to her." She hesitated. "As you know, that's a mighty small pool. I'm sure by now she's figured out that some of the photos are missing. It won't be long before she'll connect the dots."

He was silent.

"And one more thing." She took a deep breath. "She was asking about Harry Dragonis."

"So? So she finds out that he worked as a guard at Howe a long time ago. So what?"

"So how long do you think it will take the FBI to connect me to Dragonis?"

"Well, you want to hope they never do, Priestess." He thought for a moment, then added, "You know, I'm thinking maybe it's time for Daria to meet the goddess."

"Maybe so." She sighed, knowing it was true. She liked Daria, but knew only trouble would come from her asking too many of the right questions. It was only a matter of time before she shared what she knew with her FBI friend. If she hadn't already . . .

"About the boy."

"What about him?"

"What if he talks?"

"The boy isn't going to talk." She tried to keep from sounding exasperated. "And even if he does, what's he going to say? 'I'm a *gallas* in training and the priestess told me what to do?' "

"You're being awfully cavalier."

"Look, the boy doesn't know my name. He's seen me once, at night, in a dark basement. There's no way he can identify me. He has no idea who I am or where to find me."

"You're forgetting about the older brother," he reminded her.

She hesitated for a moment, and she knew he sensed her uncertainty.

"He knows you," he reminded her.

"Of course he does," she snapped. "But he's also a *gallas*. He'd never betray a high priestess of Ereshkigal."

The man's laugh was hollow and mocking, and her anger flared.

"You just don't get it, do you?" she said. "Unlike someone else I could name, he *believes* this. His father was a *gallas*, and his grandfather before him. Since his father died, the responsibility—his family's honor, for God's sake—has fallen to him. His destiny is to safeguard the priestess, to guard the sacred treasures—"

"Oh, please, I can't listen to any more of this crap." He sneered. "No one in this day and age really believes that stuff. It's all bullshit."

"To you, it's bullshit. To him, it's as much a part of his life as breathing. If you don't understand anything else about this whole deal, understand this." She tried to keep her temper in check. "He *believes*. He will cut out his own tongue before he'd give me up."

"I hope you're right."

"I know I am." But even as she said it, she wondered if she was placing too much trust in the wrong person.

"Your momma didn't know what she was starting when she fed you all that priestess crap." He was mocking her again, and she hated him for it.

"Don't be so disrespectful. My mother was a believer," she insisted.

"Sure she was. That's why she let your father steal all those items."

"She didn't know." She bit her lip.

"Right. She just figured he could afford that big house and a new car every couple of years on a security guard's salary."

"She didn't know," she repeated emphatically.

"Whatever. Look, keep the artifacts we've gotten back hidden, would you please? I have buyers lined up who are willing to pay top dollar. Everything's been spoken for except for two items. Let's not blow this now." He paused. "Where are they, by the way?"

"Under the floorboards in the carriage house," she told him, then immediately regretted it, though she couldn't have said why.

"Don't forget to give me a call if you need me."

"Will do."

"We have to take care of Daria McGowan."

She hung up on him and went to the window. It seemed that every conversation she'd had that morning had disturbed her.

Bastard. Talking about her mother like that. Her mother *was* a priestess. She *was*. She'd said so.

She rubbed her eyes. Her head hurt like crazy. It was the things he said.

He was seriously pissing her off.

Maybe it was time to move on without him. She could find someone else to sell the artifacts.

She really didn't need him now that most of the artifacts had been returned. The thought soothed her and the pain in her head started to ease. What she did need was a plan to eliminate not only Daria, but everything that was getting on her nerves.

Including him.

TWENTY-FOUR

"**D**aria."

Daria turned and waved when she saw Vita bustling across the lawn.

"I'm glad I caught you." Vita appeared slightly out of breath. "Dr. B. was trying to get in touch with you." She stopped and fanned herself with her right hand. "Good Lord, it's another scorcher, isn't it? It must be ninety in the shade."

"Close enough." Daria smiled. "It's eighty-eight on the back porch."

"Dr. B. wants you to meet her at the museum. She's with the architect and they want your input on something."

"Why didn't she call instead of making you run all the way over here?"

"She said she did, but you didn't pick up."

"I must have left my phone in the kitchen." Daria put down the bowl of water she was holding. "Come in while I get my things. I've made sketches of some of the displays for the new exhibit. I'm guessing that's what Louise wants me to show the architect."

"I'm sure that's it." Vita followed Daria up the steps and into the kitchen.

"Can I offer you some water, Vita? You look flush with the heat."

"I'd appreciate that, thank you."

Daria took a glass from one of the overhead cupboards. "I usually have bottles of spring water in the refrigerator but I'm afraid I'm all out."

"Tap water is fine, really."

Daria filled the glass at the sink and handed it to Vita, who drank gratefully. When she was finished, she said, "I don't think I've ever been in this house but once or twice in all the years I've been at Howe."

"How many years is that?"

"Most of my life, so it seems."

"You grew up in town? You went to school here?"

"I did." Vita nodded. "I didn't graduate, though. I got married when I was nineteen and dropped out."

"What was your major?"

"Ancient history."

"Oh, mine, too, the first year. Was there any particular period that you were drawn to?"

"Not really."

"Do you have a family, Vita? Children?"

"Unfortunately, no. My marriage didn't work out. Lasted less than a year, actually." She shrugged. "I never tried it again. Once bitten, twice shy, and all that."

"How long have you worked for Howe?"

"Oh, my goodness, let's see. It'll be twenty-two years come October." She stared into space for a moment. "I did think about coming back for my degree, but my mother was ill—had been for several years—and there just didn't seem to be time. I was busy caring for her.

That's really why my marriage fell apart—he thought I was spending too much time with her, but really, what could I do? She was my mother and she needed me—"

She realized she was talking too much, too fast. She stopped and took a deep breath. "Anyway, after she passed on, I got a job here at Howe and never left."

"I'm sure you've seen a lot of changes over the years."

"Yes, indeed. There's been a lot of water over that dam." Vita finished her drink and set the glass down on the counter.

"Was the museum ever open while you were here?"

"Just the dinosaur exhibit, when I was younger."

"I'd love to hear about it sometime." Daria hoisted her bag over her shoulder. "Let's go out through the front door, since we have to go in that direction anyway."

Daria locked the back door before leading Vita through the swinging door into the hall.

"This is a really beautiful place," Vita said admiringly, as she glanced from side to side. "I think I was here once for a reception of some sort. I remember the twin parlors on each side of the foyer."

"It is a beautifully designed house. I hope Iliana—my great-grandmother—was happy here. I'm sure it was hard for her, after her husband died, to stay here and raise her children alone."

"Do you ever feel her here?"

"No, I don't." Daria laughed a little. "Louise said there was some talk about her haunting the place, but you can't prove that by me. I wanted to find, I don't know, a sense of her, maybe . . . but I haven't. I'm sort of disappointed, to tell you the truth."

"The past does have its pull, doesn't it?" Vita stood in the center of the front hall. "You feel it, don't you?"

"I suppose I do. I guess that's why I went into archaeology to begin with. That and the fact that I was surrounded by it growing up."

"You really can't escape the past." Vita looked upward at the stairwell. "Inevitably, you're drawn into it."

"I suppose." Daria got her house key out of her bag. "Ready?"

"Yes," Vita replied. "I'm ready."

There was little chatter on the way across campus. Vita was pre-occupied, and out of breath by the time they arrived at the museum. There was one guard at the front door, a tall, well-built man of inde-terminate age, who stood stoically by as Daria and Vita made their way inside.

"I thought there was supposed to be more than one guard," Daria said as they stepped inside the cool of the building.

"Maybe the others are making rounds through the building, or they could be at lunch. Dr. B. said something about a reduced staff for an hour in the middle of the day. The university guards, like the one out there now, step in and cover for the bank's people."

Daria looked around the Great Room. Louise was nowhere in sight.

"I thought Louise was here with the architect," she said.

Daria walked down the unlit hall. "Louise? Are you down here? Louise . . . ?" She turned to Vita. "Where could they be?"

"They were here a while ago. Maybe they went downstairs," Vita suggested. "Maybe Dr. B. decided to show some of the artifacts to the architect."

"Maybe." Daria went to the stairwell and called, "Louise?"

"They might be in one of the back rooms. Come on, I'll walk down with you."

"Thanks, but you don't have to do that." Daria started down the steps. "I know my way."

"I'll just check to see if Dr. B. wants me for anything else."

Vita followed Daria down the steps.

"You'd think she'd turn the lights on if she came down here," Daria said when they came to the bottom of the stairs and gazed down the dark hallway.

"She's probably using a flashlight," Vita said as she walked along. "I think the insurance people said something about the wiring being a hazard, and keeping the electricity off until it was replaced."

"I suppose that's a possibility," Daria said. "Louise?" she called.

Vita opened the door to the room where the Jacobs collection was housed. The room was dark, but the room beyond, where Alistair's find was stored, was dimly lit.

"They must be in there." Vita pointed toward the light. "Go on in, Daria. I'm right behind you."

Daria stepped into the room and looked around. A man was leaning against one of the crates.

"Stefano," she said. "What are you doing here . . . ?"

TWENTY-FIVE

Connor could not remember the last time he felt this free or this good. He knew enough of life's twists and turns to know that things could change on a dime, but for right now, he couldn't think of anything better than being behind the wheel of a fast car on a winding country road, on his way to see his favorite girl, singing along with Jimi Hendrix's "Gyspy Eyes," a silly dog in the passenger seat next to him, hanging out the window catching a faceful of air.

He didn't hear the phone ringing until the song played out.

"Shields."

"Connor, it's Will Fletcher."

Connor turned off the music and slowed the car.

"You get a chance to run any more of those names I gave you?"

"Ran 'em all. I e-mailed everything to you this morning, but when I didn't hear back from you, I thought maybe I should give you a call."

"I haven't checked my computer yet today. What did you find?"

"Harry Dragonis." Will was not one to waste words. "Born Hakan Drago, February 22, 1937, Adana, Turkey. Family immigrated here in

1946. Worked as a security guard at Howe University from 1958 through 1988. Married a Turkish girl, Ayfer Demerkan, in 1955. One child, Vedat, born 1962. Wife died in 1984. Body was returned to Turkey for burial. Hakan—Harry—died in June of 1988. Don't know what happened to the daughter after that."

Connor drove slowly, thinking it through. "Look, thanks—"

"Wait, there was something else. Stefano Korban. Interestingly enough, he was also born in Adana, Turkey. Immigrated at age nineteen. Guess which year that would have been."

"Can't."

"July of '88.

"Right after Drago died?"

"Less than a month later."

"Think you can find out why?"

"I can find out anything if you give me enough time."

"Thanks. Let me know if you come up with anything else."

Connor hung up and thought it through.

Harry Dragonis the dealer had been a security guard at Howe and had selectively helped himself to some prime collectibles.

Way to cut out the middleman, Harry.

Stefano Korban arrived here shortly after Drago—Dragonis—died in 1998. What connected Drago to Korban?

Connor wasn't sure what it all meant, but he was damned sure it wasn't coincidental. It was all part of the same puzzle. Right now, he was still missing a few pieces, but he knew from experience that if he followed his instincts, they would lead him to the solution.

He dialed Daria's number and was disappointed when it went right to voice mail.

He placed the phone on the console and drove under the arch that marked the entrance to the university. When he reached the lot, he parked in his favorite spot under the oak tree. In the fall, when he came back to see Daria, he thought he'd have to park elsewhere so that acorns wouldn't ping off his precious Porsche. He snapped the leash onto Sweet Thing's collar and got out of the car. The dog leaped across the console and out the driver's side door. Connor slammed it, locked it, and jogged down the path leading to McGowan House.

When they got to the back door, he found it was locked. Sweet Thing barked several times, staring up at the door.

"Maybe she's out front. Come on, girl." Connor and the dog trotted around the side of the house to the front porch.

"I know you're happy to be home," Connor said. He knocked, then rang the doorbell, but there was no answer.

The dog jumped up at the door, barking and whining.

"I don't think she's in there, girl."

He dialed Louise's office, and was surprised when she, rather than her assistant, answered the phone.

"Louise, it's Connor. I was trying to catch up with Daria. She's not at the house, so I was wondering if your meeting was still going on."

"We finished well over an hour ago. As a matter of fact, I just got back from the bank. I had a meeting there with the architect. He dropped off his numbers for the proposed renovations at the museum." He could hear the shuffling of papers. "I have to say, things are looking very good."

"Great. I'm happy to hear that." Sweet Thing started pulling him to the edge of the porch steps and he tugged back on the leash. "Louise, if Daria shows up, would you ask her to give me a call? I'm at the house but I'm locked out."

"Sure. And as soon as Vita gets back from lunch, I'll ask her to run over with an extra key for you."

"Vita." He said the name aloud as if testing it. "Louise, what do you know about Vita's background?"

"I know she grew up around Howeville, and that she was married briefly when she was young. She's worked at the university for a long time. Why?"

"Do you know what her maiden name was?"

"I don't think I ever heard her mention it. She's been Landis for as long as I've known her."

"Thanks."

He hung up the phone, not liking the thoughts that were running through his mind.

Vita.

Vedat.

He tried Daria's phone again. Still no answer. The uneasy feeling grew. Where was Daria?

Logic told him she was likely to be in one of three places. She wasn't here at the house and she wasn't at Louise's office.

That left the museum.

"Come on, girl." Connor led the dog down the porch steps. "Let's find Daria."

"Where are the guards the bank sent over?" Vita asked Stefano.

"Dismissed," he said simply.

Daria looked from Stefano to Vita.

"What's going on, Vita? I thought Louise and the architect—"

"I'm sorry, Daria, I really, really am," Vita said softly. "I really do like you. Under other circumstances, I'd have liked to have gotten to know you better."

"Please, cousin." Stefano was becoming impatient. "We really don't have time for this."

"Vita, I don't understand what's going on here, but I think I want—" Daria started toward the door, but Stefano blocked her way.

"I'm sorry. I'm afraid we can't let you leave, Daria."

"It's too late, honey," Vita told her. "You just know too much."

"I don't understand," Daria repeated.

"It's only a matter of time before you do." Vita shook her head. She turned to Stefano. "Do it quickly."

"Uh-uh." He shook his head. "It has to be like the others."

"Why?" Vita frowned.

"Use your head, Vita. She's the great-granddaughter of the guy who dug it all up and brought it here. If we're going to pull this off, make it look like a religious ritual, she has to be killed just like the others were."

"Oh my God, *you* killed those people?" Daria gasped. "You killed all those people . . . ?"

The closer they came to the museum, the more agitated Sweet Thing became. When the front door opened and the guard stepped out, the dog began snarling and snapping, demonstrating a viciousness Connor never suspected her capable of.

"Stop it," Connor commanded. "Stop it, girl. Sit. Stay."

The well-trained dog did as she was told, though her posture made it clear it was with the greatest reluctance.

"I'm sorry, but no one's allowed in." The guard stood with his back against the door, his eyes never leaving the dog.

"I think this gets me in." Connor held up his FBI credentials. The guard reached for it, and Sweet Thing lunged.

"Sit!" Eyeing the guard curiously, Connor restrained the dog.

After returning the ID, the guard stared at Connor, as if trying to decide what to do.

"I have my orders," he finally said.

Connor held up his ID again. "I think this supersedes any orders you have from anyone else."

"I will escort you." The guard began to open the door. "However, the dog—"

"Comes with me."

"There are no animals permitted inside the museum." He glanced nervously at Sweet Thing, who, though seated, continued to growl from deep inside her chest.

Clearly there was something about the guard she did not like.

"Sit," Connor told the dog. "Sit, girl."

Connor dropped the lead and the guard stared at the dog as if expecting an attack. His hand was on the holster that hung from his belt.

What security guard employed by a university was armed?

The guard nodded and beckoned Connor inside. Connor followed, careful to leave the door ajar behind him.

Connor hadn't mentioned who or what he was looking for, or where he was headed, but the guard led him down the steps into the basement without hesitation. His suspicions aroused, Connor silently removed his Glock from its holster at the small of his back. All was quiet, all was dark as they entered the long hall leading to the storage areas. When the guard turned and motioned for Connor to go ahead of him, Connor shook his head slowly, and gestured with his gun hand. The guard stared at the weapon, then shrugged.

Guided by the light from the far doorway, the two men proceeded through the room where the Jacobs artifacts were stored. At the sound of voices from the next room, the guard slowed, then stopped just outside the lighted door.

"You killed all those people?" Daria's voice drifted out to the anteroom. "You made it look as if the *gallas* . . . ?"

Connor could see over the guard's shoulder into the room beyond, where Daria stood between Vita Landis and Stefano Korban, who held a handgun pointed directly at Daria.

"*Gallas?*" Stefano Korban's laugh was loud and brittle. "See, Vita, didn't I tell you that was the way to go? Even the esteemed Dr. McGowan fell for that crap."

"Don't be disrespectful," Vita said softly. "You are *gallas*, Stefano."

"Yeah, yeah, I know: As was my father, so am I. So are Tabib and the kid. Your father was, too, but that didn't stop him from helping himself to the goodies, did it, *Priestess?*"

Connor moved forward but the guard's arm shot out to stop him. The look on the man's face was pure rage. Under his breath, he was whispering in a language Connor couldn't quite make out.

"Priestess?" Daria looked to Vita for an explanation.

"I suppose I should explain." Vita sighed. "For the past two thousand years, there have been those who remained faithful to Ereshkigal and have kept watch over the place where the city once stood, believing that one day, the city would be reborn. As centuries passed, the numbers of the believers diminished until there were fewer and fewer to guard the city. Finally, Shandihar was rediscovered, but instead of being restored, the temples were stripped of the sacred objects; they were packed up and brought here. Those who still served the goddess followed, and have been keeping watch over the treasure for the past century, right here at Howe."

"Vita, for Christ's sake!" Stefano's patience had run out. "No one gives a shit about any of that."

"Shut up, Stefano," Vita snapped. "You're going to kill her. She might as well know why."

She turned back to Daria. "In every generation, there have been those who have served the goddess—the *gallas* and the priestesses. These roles can only be inherited. I inherited the title of priestess from my mother, as Stefano inherited the role of guardian from his father," Vita said softly. "And yes, my father was also a *gallas,* but all those priceless treasures were too great a temptation for him to resist. He was a weak man. He stole some of the artifacts and sold them."

"Vita, enough." Stefano rubbed his free hand over his face in frustration.

She ignored him.

"In the beginning, I only wanted to . . . *reappropriate* everything my father had taken, and return them to the crates they came in. That way, no one would ever know what he'd done. I never intended for anyone to get hurt."

"You are so full of shit," Stefano said, sneering. "Once you found out how much that stuff was worth on the black market, once you heard *millions,* all that talk of family *honor* went down the tubes." He turned to Daria. "The plan all along was to get those artifacts back and sell them to the highest bidder. It was a piece of cake to get those two losers to go after the artifacts and make it look like some act of ancient retribution."

Vita turned on him. "It was your idea to convince Tabib and his brother that they had a sacred obligation to avenge the goddess. You pounded that into their heads, you taught them how to kill."

"So much more interesting than simple thefts, don't you think?" He laughed. "And who would suspect a respected archaeologist and the president's assistant? Tabib and Anatole were *honored* to do whatever the priestess told them to do. Honored to protect your identity. After all, it was the will of the goddess . . . and these dumb jackasses were willing to do anything for their goddess."

Three rapid gunshots split the air.

Daria screamed and covered her ears as Stefano's head exploded and he fell face forward. Vita dropped where she stood. A blur of white flashed past the guard, jostling him before he could fire off another round. Before the shooter had a chance to recover his balance, Connor tackled him from behind and wrestled the gun from his hand.

"Daria! Are you all right?" Connor called.

"Yes. I'm not hit." She had taken cover crouched behind a crate. She hugged the dog gratefully. "Sweet Thing, you did good, girl."

"Who else is there?" Connor lifted the guard's head. "Who else is working with you?"

"Just those two." The guard spat in the direction of Stefano's lifeless body.

"The boy?"

"Anatole. My brother."

"Daria, do you think you can call 911?"

She nodded.

"Tell them we need Chief Thorpe over here and we need an ambulance immediately."

Daria stood on unsteady legs and reached for her bag. She tried to locate her phone but her fingers felt numb.

"Use mine." Connor took his phone from his pocket and slid it across the floor to her.

"Why do we need an ambulance?" Daria looked down at Vita, whose body was sprawled on the floor five feet away. "They're dead."

"Korban didn't survive that shot to the head, but I think he only winged Vita. She's still alive," he told her. "I want to make sure she stays that way. She has a lot to answer for."

TWENTY-SIX

"How is she?" Daria stood outside the museum, Sweet Thing's leash wrapped around her hand, and watched as Vita Landis was carried from the building on a stretcher. There was a lot of blood, but the older woman appeared to be alert.

"Looks like not much more than a flesh wound, for all the blood," Chief Thorpe replied. "The more important question is, how are you?"

"I'm fine, really. I wasn't injured. Just scared." Daria sat on one of the concrete benches in the courtyard.

"Think you'll feel up to answering some questions later?" he asked. "I'm going to be tied up for a while at the hospital, but I'd like to stop over later today to get your statement."

"I'll be home. Whenever it's convenient for you will be fine with me, Chief."

They watched the man they knew only as Tabib being placed in the back of a patrol car.

"What's going to happen to the boy in the hospital now?" Daria asked.

"If he comes out of the coma, he'll be tried as a juvenile. At least, any lawyer they get for him is going to push for that," Thorpe told her, "since his brother says the kid is only seventeen. But crimes like these . . . they may want to try him as an adult. Tabib there says he'll give us a full confession if we let him visit the kid, so after he's booked, that's where we'll take him."

"Ask him who his accomplice was for the Blume and Sevrenson murders," Connor said as he joined them. "According to the information the Bureau found, the boy, Anatole, has only been in the States for the past month, so he could have only participated in the last two attacks. There had to have been two killers at the Blume home."

"We'll see what he says about that, but I'll bet big money it was Korban." Thorpe turned back to Daria. "I get the reason why these two targeted the owners of the artifacts they wanted to steal. But why you?"

"Apparently I asked the wrong questions when I was in Dr. Burnette's office. When I asked about the photographs, Vita said she'd found them and taken them right to Louise, but Louise said she'd found them under some papers on Vita's desk. There were photos in the envelopes of just about every artifact that Alistair found and brought back to Howe. Except for the ones that had been stolen."

"So you figured that whoever had gone after the artifacts had taken the photographs so they'd know what to steal." Thorpe nodded.

"I had figured out that the killers had access to the photos, and I'm pretty sure Vita gave the photos to Tabib so he'd know what he was looking for. But at the time, I didn't know that Vita was involved. I thought that if the photos were just sitting on Vita's desk, someone else could have found them. I didn't put it together, especially since both Louise and Sabina had seen the photos, too."

"But Vita—being guilty—assumed that you figured out it was her," Connor said.

Daria nodded. "I guess when she heard me ask Louise if the name Dragonis was familiar, she figured I knew more than I did."

She looked up at Connor and asked, "How did you figure out what was going on?"

"When our guy at the Bureau told me that Dragonis had a daughter named Vedat, the name was just too similar. Then, when I couldn't find you and Louise didn't know where Vita was, I thought you had to be at the museum. When I got over there, the guard gave it away."

"How?"

"You know, there was a reason Cross named this dog Sweet Thing." Connor sat next to Daria on the bench and rubbed the dog behind the ears. "She's a very gentle, affectionate animal. But she totally snapped when she saw this guy at the museum door. She was snarling and growling, and it was pretty clear she wanted a piece of him."

"You think she would have attacked the guy?"

"There's no question in my mind. So there had to be a reason, right?"

"She remembered him from Cross's."

"That's what I was thinking. He wouldn't let the dog in the museum so I told her to sit while I went in. I left the door slightly ajar just in case she decided she needed to check up on things."

"She's usually so obedient." Daria frowned. "How did you know she'd follow?"

"I didn't tell her to *stay*."

"You're such a clever doggie," Daria said, and rubbed the dog's head.

"Hey, how about me?" Connor feigned indignation. "I'm a pretty clever guy."

"Yes, you are. You're my hero," she told him.

"Yeah, well, I did have a little help from Tabib. When he heard Stefano talking about how the whole thing had been a ruse to recover the artifacts so that he and Vita could sell them, he realized that he and his brother had been used. Of course, he didn't seem to have any scruples about killing in the name of the goddess, but killing for the sake of making someone else rich was apparently against his principles."

"You have to understand, he believed that what he'd done was honorable," Daria explained. "He'd been taught all his life that protecting his heritage—doing the bidding of the priestess—would be his life's work. He'd been brought up to believe he had a special role to play, just like his father, and his father's father. For him this was a privilege. A sacred duty."

"Korban, having been brought up the same way, would have understood this completely," Connor said, thinking it through. "So while he thought it was all bullshit, he knew exactly how to exploit it."

Daria nodded. "For Tabib and his brother, knowing that Vita was a priestess would have sealed the deal. They'd have done anything for her."

"He sure turned on her fast enough," Thorpe noted.

"Once Tabib understood what she'd done, he was obliged to kill her, or Ereshkigal would send other *gallas* after him," Daria told him. "She was a heretic. She'd committed a sacrilege."

"Well, she's still alive, so I guess he failed in this sacred duty of his." Thorpe seemed to think that over for a moment. "You think there are more of these *gallas* out there? Think they'll be coming for Tabib?"

"I find it hard to believe the entire Shandihar culture came down to just these four individuals after surviving for almost two thousand years, Chief," Daria told him. "Surely there are others. Whether or not they'll go after Tabib is anyone's guess."

"Swell," Thorpe murmured. "So as long as the university has all their statues and things here, we're going to have to be looking over our shoulders, worrying about some deluded guys who think it's their duty to cut out people's tongues? Or women who think they're priestesses sending out these so-called guardians to cut off people's hands?"

"The university has housed these artifacts for almost one hundred years, Chief. Up until Harry Dragonis put this all in motion by stealing some of them, there were no incidents of violence, right?"

"None that I heard about," he conceded, "and I'm guessing something like this, I would have known about it."

"These people—call them *gallas* or guardians—are only interested in preserving and safeguarding their culture," she told him. "I'm not concerned about more murders."

"Even though you're going to be handling their sacred objects? And even though your great-grandfather was the one who stole their stuff away in the first place?" he asked.

"I think that as long as I show respect for the culture—and of course as long as I don't try to steal anything—I won't have anything to worry about. Besides," she added, "only a priestess could give such an order."

"How do you know Vita won't do exactly that?" Thorpe frowned. "Not that they're not welcome to Tabib."

"I don't think Vita will be the one giving the orders," Daria said simply. "I think the mantle's going to have to be passed."

"Well, you change your mind, you let me know," Thorpe said as he turned to walk away. "I'll have someone watching you day and night."

"That's my job," Connor told her.

"What about your real job?" she asked. "There isn't going to be a whole lot for the FBI to do around here, once this is all cleaned up."

"I'm thinking I could take the occasional stateside job," he told her. "This running all over the world, sleeping on rocky hillsides, is starting to lose its appeal."

"It has been kind of nice to sleep in the same bed—a real bed, that is—for more than two or three nights in a row." She smiled. "Throw in a real roof overhead, and I could get used to it."

"Well, you'll be here for the next year or so, right?"

"That's the deal."

"Maybe I could visit. A lot."

"I could get used to having you around. A lot."

She looked past him to the drive where the EMTs were getting ready to lift Vita's gurney and load it into the ambulance. He followed her stare.

They watched Vita hold up her hand, gesturing for the attendants to stop, just as Sabina Bokhari reached the gurney. She leaned over the wounded woman, who raised a hand and touched the young professor on the forehead. Sabina took Vita's hand for an instant, then stood and backed away. The EMTs continued transferring the patient to the ambulance, and closed the doors. As the vehicle pulled away, Sabina stepped back onto the grass, her arms folded across her chest.

"Are you thinking what I'm thinking?" Connor asked.

"Probably." Daria nodded. "This should be interesting. I've never worked with a priestess before."

"What do you mean?"

"I was planning to ask Louise if Sabina could work with me on the museum. There's just too much for one person to do, and there's no one else who knows as much about Shandihar as Sabina."

"Apparently, she knows even more than you figured."

"Which will work to our advantage. I was looking at the cylinders in the crates again the other night. It's going to be impossible for me to both translate them and design the displays. There just isn't enough time. Sabina would be perfect."

"I don't know, Daria. Maybe the chief is right. Aren't you even a little nervous about working with her?"

"Not a bit. She's no threat to me. Besides, Sabina is not Vita."

"Aren't you just a little bit concerned that someone is going to want to punish you for what Alistair did? After all, he was never properly punished."

"I'm not so sure about that," Daria told him. "There was something in one of Iliana's diaries that makes me wonder how he really died. I don't know if that story about a lung infection was true. That's something I'm going to have to investigate when I have the time."

"You might start up talk of the curse again."

"Someone's bound to bring it up sooner or later, anyway." She shrugged. "If nothing else, it'll make good press."

Connor's phone rang and he took the call. Daria stood and tugged on Sweet Thing's leash, and started walking back to McGowan House. In spite of everything, Howe had started to grow on her. She liked the campus, and wondered what it would look like in the fall, when all the trees turned color.

It had been many years since she'd experienced a true autumn. She thought back to the years when they lived in Princeton. Their house had been on a side street off Nassau, in a neighborhood of houses that all had yards and garages and front porches. The back of their property had been lined with maple and oak trees, and in October, the four McGowan kids fought over the family's two rakes, to see who would have the privilege of making the leaf piles. Jack had been the best raker, though Sam was older and stronger. He'd keep raking until the pile was chest high, and then they'd all jump in. When the boys had finished playing and gone on to other things, she and Iona would lie on their backs and look for angels in the clouds. The squirrels would race around the sides of the trees chattering at each other. Black squirrels, she recalled. She'd never seen them anywhere else but in Princeton.

She couldn't remember the last time she'd thought about that house and those years and the black squirrels.

"Penny for your thoughts." Connor caught up to her on the path.

"I was just thinking about a house we used to live in." She smiled as he fell in step with her. "It made me think about Jack."

"What a coincidence. I was just talking to my friend in South America." He took her hand.

"About Jack?"

"Yes. I told him that if your family approves, I'd send him copies of the investigators' reports."

"Of course we'll approve. Then what?"

"Then we wait and see what he comes up with."

"Do you really think there's hope? After all this time?"

"It's fifty-fifty, right? The odds are just as good that he's alive as not. So why not go for it? Why not hold on to that chance?"

"All right, yes. Let's do that." She squeezed his hand.

"I'm going to be leaving sooner than I'd planned," he told her as they walked back to the house. "I'll be meeting with Coliani later today to fill him in, and then I'll be meeting with Polly at the office early tomorrow. She's going to pretty much take over from here. You'll be hearing from her as soon as she can get her paperwork together. She identified a number of artifacts that are in institutions, and she's going to work with the university's lawyers to negotiate the return of as much as possible."

"Finally, some good news. Louise will be thrilled."

They reached the front steps of the house.

"Connor, how long do you have to be away?" she asked.

"I'm not sure."

"Will you come back?"

He reached up and tucked a strand of her hair behind her ear. "I will always come back to you," he said simply.

The moon was still full when Daria heard Connor slip out of bed.

"Are you leaving already?" She covered a yawn with an open hand.

"As soon as I get my stuff together."

"I'll get up."

"You don't have to do that. Go back to sleep."

"I'll come down and make you some coffee." She swung her legs over the side of the bed.

"Daria, you haven't made coffee the entire time I've been here."

"It's a substitute for breakfast."

"You haven't made breakfast, either." He hastened to add, "Not that I expected you to."

"I know. That's the point." She stood and stretched. "My mother is the most undomesticated woman on the face of the earth. She can't cook worth beans, and I can't remember her ever making an entire meal from scratch."

"Who made dinner?"

"Most of the time, the housekeeper did. But the point is, she never let us leave the house in the morning without doing something for us. Even if it was pouring cold cereal in a bowl and splashing some milk on it. Iona went through a stage where she ate nothing in the morning except bananas. Every morning, my mother peeled her banana. That was just her way of sending us off."

"You make the coffee." He leaned over and kissed the side of her mouth. "I'll make the eggs."

"Deal." She started toward the bathroom.

"I'm going to run Sweet Thing outside for a bit. I'll meet you in the kitchen."

Ten minutes later, Daria came downstairs to an empty kitchen. She went to the back door and looked out, and in the illumination of the streetlight at the end of the path, she could see Connor strolling along, his hands in his pockets, the dog by his side. There was a slight mist on the ground and a halo around the light at the top of the pole. She wished she had a camera so that she could capture that moment and save it, the beautiful man and the dog, walking through the mist before dawn. Walking back to her.

I will always come back to you.

Most of the moments she'd saved through the years had been of things. Of places she'd been, work she'd accomplished. Ruins and the secrets she uncovered beneath them. She'd spent her entire life examining the bits and pieces of other lives, lives that had been spent centuries ago, but she had rarely examined her own. She'd always felt the pull of the past more strongly than the present, and almost never gave thought to the future.

Maybe it was time for that to change.

She heard Connor coming up the back steps. She went to the door and opened it, and let the future in.

ABOUT THE AUTHOR

MARIAH STEWART is the bestselling author of numerous novels and several novellas. She is a RITA finalist for romantic suspense and is the recipient of the Award of Excellence for contemporary romance, a RIO (Reviewers International Organization) Award honoring excellence in women's fiction, and a Reviewers' Choice Award from *Romantic Times* magazine. A native of Highstown, New Jersey, she is a three-time recipient of the Golden Leaf Award and a Lifetime Achievement Award from the New Jersey Romance Writers, of whose Hall of Fame she is an honoree. Stewart is a member of the Valley Forge Romance Writers, the New Jersey Romance Writers, and the Romance Writers of America. She lives with her husband, two daughters, and two rambunctious golden retrievers amid the rolling hills of Chester County, Pennsylvania.

ABOUT THE TYPE

This book was set in Minion, a 1990 Adobe Originals typeface by Robert Slimbach. Minion is inspired by classical, old style typefaces of the late Renaissance, a period of elegant, beautiful, and highly readable type designs. Created primarily for text setting, Minion combines the aesthetic and functional qualities that make text type highly readable with the versatility of digital technology.